# UNNATURAL JUSTICE

*Also by Quintin Jardine*

# UNNATURAL JUSTICE

Quintin Jardine

headline

First published in 2003
by HEADLINE BOOK PUBLISHING

10 9 8 7 6 5 4 3 2 1

Cataloguing in Publication Data is available from the British Library

ISBN 0 7472 6886 X (hardback)
ISBN 0 7553 0941 3 (trade paperback)

Typeset in Times by Avon DataSet Ltd,
Bidford-on-Avon, Warwickshire

Printed and bound in Great Britain by
Mackays of Chatham plc, Chatham, Kent

HEADLINE BOOK PUBLISHING
A division of Hodder Headline
338 Euston Road
London NW1 3BH

www.headline.co.uk
www.hodderheadline.com

This one's for Dominic and Kirsti . . . and their Mum, of course.

DO I have your attention?

Good.

Are you prepared to hear me out, without making any judgements until my story is finished?

Even better.

Do you have everything you need? Tea? Coffee? Or perhaps something stronger? (Before I'm finished you may wish for it.)

You're ready? Fine, then come close, for this story of mine isn't something I'd want anyone overhearing.

The world is populated by spirits, you know, and some of them aren't very nice at all. The fact is, they can be downright evil . . .

# 1

'Nobody's perfect. Still, I've always thought of myself as a nice guy at heart.'

He was smiling when he said it, that same old all-gathering smile of his; all teeth and glisten at first glance, but look really close and you may see the maw of the beast. His eyes had that shine beyond twinkle; they dazzled like the sun, a journalist once wrote, but she'd have been nearer the mark if she'd said they were as bright as the flames of hell, yet as hard as the stone that builds a city.

I looked at him and felt nothing, no emotion. Or did I? Was I simply masking my loathing? After all, that reviewer in the *New York Times* did say I had become a consummate actor. How was it put again? (As if I didn't know.) '*Plucked from the relative obscurity of an announcer slot in a wrestling circus, Oz Blackstone's instinctive but consummate touch somehow manages to steal the movie out from under his more illustrious co-stars – and sometime in-laws – Miles Grayson and Dawn Phillips. Skinner's Festival is Blackstone's breakout, his one-way ticket to the A list.*'

And anyway, what's nice got to do with it, as Tina Turner almost sang? Isn't it said to carry with it the certainty of finishing last?

There was a time, around ten years ago, maybe, when I was a nice guy . . . or so I thought I overhead someone say at a party back in Fife. (Looking back on it, I'm pretty sure she was actually talking about my Dad.)

I wasn't, though, not really. Truth be told, if I consider objectively the way Osbert Blackstone behaved towards most of the people who cared for him, he didn't come even close to niceness. If I was forced

3

to come up with an excuse for my attitude, I suppose I'd say that I reacted badly to my mother's shockingly early death. I took it out on my lifelong girlfriend Jan more cruelly than on anyone else. Just when everyone assumed we'd be heading for the altar, I gave her the 'let's always be loving friends' routine . . . at which I was to become a master . . . and set off on a determined campaign to shag my way through as much of Edinburgh's available female population as I could.

Eventually, though, the Prince of Darkness put me in my place. A door opened, and Primavera Phillips stepped into my life. A simple entrance, but she might as well have been a bolt of lightning hitting me between the eyes.

I thought she was wonderful. For the first few months after we met, when our thing was all hot and steamy, I just wanted to eat her. (Now I wish I had. Life's full of irony, eh.) I didn't question my attraction then, or try to analyse it . . . even though inside, I knew that I still loved Jan, who was in a new relationship of her own by that time. I reckon I understand now, though, what it was that blinded me to everything but Prim for that period.

Cupid, that fat flying archer and model for a few million tattoos, gets much of the credit for bringing people together, but, in my humble view, almost all of it is misplaced. The real villain of the peace is the boy Narcissus.

Remember him from your classical studies, that idiotic Greek lad who fell in love with his own reflection? Well, I reckon that's what most of us do: we are attracted essentially to ourselves. We tend to fall for people who are in our own image, physically, emotionally, and in several other ways ending in 'y'. If there were more real blondes around, in my opinion the only gentlemen who would prefer them would be naturally fair-haired themselves. As it is, however good the dye job, instinctively, we can see the roots. (I'm not being sexist here, honest. Given modern man's hair fashions, my theory cuts both ways.)

Primavera is tasty, no doubt about that. She's an even better looker than her actress sister, she has a body that's as finely tuned as a Ferrari, and she has big, rarely blinking eyes, which, when they take on a bedroom look, are always backed up by action. In the instant that we met, I saw her as open, direct and lustful . . . just like me.

4

What followed was inevitable, and I'd be lying if I said that I didn't enjoy it.

But she has other qualities too; they live on her dangerous side. Behind that sensual façade, she is ambitious, scheming and manipulative. The concept of self-denial is unknown to her; her desires, carnal and material, exist only to be fulfilled, and almost invariably, they are. She isn't a bad person; I've never thought that. It's just that she has certain weaknesses and the insight to know, most of the time, that she lacks the moral fibre to overcome them.

In other words, in that respect, she's just like me.

Before we finally split, one thing that Prim and I did give each other, though, in addition to a large measure of grief, was luck. We both enjoyed comfortable family backgrounds, but separately neither of us was on track for the glamorous life, or to amass material wealth. But since our paths crossed, well, it's all just gone crazy. The luck of the devil, they say. In our cases, that is undoubtedly, and maybe even literally, true. Our first few months together saw us involved in separate escapades in Scotland, Switzerland and Spain, from which we emerged with our lives . . . just . . . and with a very significant sum of money.

I was edging into my thirties before I took a partial tumble to myself, and before Jan tempted fate too far by taking me back. Her love, and my first awakening to the real Primavera (although sometimes I wonder whether such a person actually exists), finally drew us back together.

Looking back, it's interesting to me that during that brief blessed period, my luck didn't change: at first. If anything it got even better, magnified by the sheer happiness of our life together. I used to wake in the morning, look at Jan's face on the pillow next to me, often smiling at whatever dream she was having, and think, 'This is all too good to be true.'

I was right; we didn't know it, thank God, but our lease on bliss was very short. When I lost her and our unborn child, killed in our kitchen by a lethal washing machine, I lost something else too. It took another Janet to help me find some of it again, but that was in the future; in the immediate thereafter I was lost, angry inside, and looking for someone to take it out on. I found him to an extent, but it wasn't enough. There was nothing for me to do, it seemed, but to go back to Prim . . . actually I should have done anything but that, but what the hell.

We took up more or less where we'd left off, only this time we were more overtly ambitious, and avaricious. Our luck went on; we amassed money, and in my case a public profile, without even seeming to try. My wrestling announcer job, into which I'd stumbled, led on to bigger things, and eventually encouraged Miles Grayson, Prim's actor brother-in-law, to cast me in a movie project. Naturally, I was a success, and more bookings followed; I found to my surprise that I really am an instinctive actor.

In material terms and in career terms I couldn't do anything but win. I decided that Prim was the lucky charm from which it all flowed, so we embarked on marriage. And that was as good as it got.

Because you see, I never loved Prim, any more than she ever loved me. Fairly early in our relationship we had got into the habit of deceiving each other; she was probably better at it than I was. When I eventually found out how many lovers she'd had, I was astonished . . . she'd had even more than me! But honestly, I can't say I was ever angry. The fact was, in emotional terms, I was as dead as my first wife. I gathered wealth, I used people, I had brief flings on movie projects and on wrestling trips that were forgotten about next day, but none of it excited me. None of it could extinguish the cold flame of bitterness that Jan's passing had lit in me.

It took Susie Gantry to make me see what I was.

One might suspect that I was drawn to her in the same way I was attracted to Primavera, but one would be wide of the mark. Susie and I started out with a single thing in common, and that was it. She had lost a partner too, in sudden shocking violence, and for a while there was the same anger within each of us. But that's as far as it went. Now, with the anger dissipated, in most respects we're chalk and cheese. I still keep my feelings locked up, while Susie's as volatile as they come. For all that I'm successful in what I do now, I'd never been into business, until recently. She is, and how; she runs her family construction group and she's won two out of the last four 'Scottish Business-woman of the Year' awards. I'm tall, dark and enigmatic (back to that *New York Times* review), she's compact, red-haired, open and fresh-faced. Most of all, she is one of life's givers, whereas I fall, with no room for argument, into the taker category.

She took me, sure, I'll admit that . . . on what was supposed to be my honeymoon, even . . . but she was still carrying her own anger then, plus she had no reason to love Prim, so I'll allow her that one.

What happened between us wasn't like a lightning strike, as it had been with Prim. We lit a slow-burning fuse when we got it together out in Spain, but what Susie did at the same time was to open my eyes to myself. She made me look in the mirror and see the real Oz, not the happy-go-lucky harmless oaf that I thought I was. I'd been pretending to be him for so long that I'd come to believe it myself. She's the most honest person I've ever known, apart from Jan, and she made me look honestly at myself. When I did, I didn't like what I saw.

For a while, the way I handled the new Oz was by simply dropping the pretence; I released him. I started behaving not as I thought I should, but as I really wanted to inside. A situation developed out in Spain. It was dangerous, as much so in real life as any make-believe I've ever filmed, but I dealt with it so that the good people came through while the bad guy didn't do nearly so well.

Afterwards, I went back to work on my second movie project, and for a while, although with no genuine enthusiasm, on my marriage. There was a complication there, though. Susie was pregnant, and planning to keep the baby. That was fine by me, but I wasn't sure how to handle Prim. I was totally out of love with her by then . . . especially after finding her with a Spanish guy in a Barcelona hotel . . . but I had a career to think about. Miles Grayson, the main man in my developing movie career, was still her brother-in-law, and I wasn't prepared to piss him off, not at that stage anyway. As it turned out, Primavera saved me from any trouble by running off to Mexico with a wanker of a B-list actor. As a consolation, Miles gave me a part in a detective movie he was filming in Edinburgh.

The contract was signed when Susie had the baby and the world found out who her father was, so he couldn't have done anything to me, but as it turned out he had no such thoughts. I was bankable in the UK and that came first with him; besides, he'd seen through Prim by then and decided he was on my side come what may.

And then there was Janet. Happily, she looks like her mother now, but in the moment she was born she looked just like they all do, wee and pink and wrinkled and gooey. She wasn't the only one who cried like a baby in that delivery room; I put on a virtuoso performance, but for the first time in a couple of years, I wasn't acting. A lot of stuff flowed out of me with my tears, a lot of the anger that was still inside me. All at once I thought I knew what I wanted. When I dried my eyes I was left with one question: was I brave enough to go for it?

I took it to the Oracle in Anstruther. My Dad, Macintosh Blackstone, Mac the Dentist, in my eyes the greatest man I'd ever met . . . and at that stage in my travels I'd met three Presidents, four Prime Ministers and seven princes . . . talked to me and made me believe that he hadn't bred a coward. He showed me also that maybe the ruthlessness within me hadn't always existed, that maybe it had indeed been put there by two unfair, untimely deaths, and that if it had, maybe it could be excised.

So I went to my family; to wee Janet and her mother. I asked Susie if she fancied marrying a movie star. She looked at me as if I was daft, and then she asked me if I thought she was. She laughed out loud, like a ring of bells. 'Marry you? With your track record? You slept with another woman on your honeymoon, remember,' she exclaimed. I can still hear her, still see the look in her eyes.

Then she said, 'Yes.' (If I'd told her I'd actually slept with two 'other women' on my honeymoon, I don't know how it would have gone, but I'm neither that brave nor that stupid.)

We did the deed quietly. We thought about Skibo Castle, but decided that would attract attention, since the press stake out the local registrar for famous names on the public notification board. Instead we settled for the Roxburgh Hotel . . . not the one in Edinburgh, the one near Kelso . . . after I had finished work on my fourth movie, set in theory in north California, but filmed in reality in Vancouver, British Columbia. (If it was good enough for Mulder and Scully, it's good enough for me.)

That was two years ago. Afterwards, barely a day went by without my pinching myself to make sure I was awake. I'd never imagined being really happy again, and yet I was. I no longer thought about might-have-beens. I found that I was able to forgive most of the rest of the world for Jan's death, and for my mother's. I barely thought about Primavera any more. All I had time for was Susie and Janet, and in the right proportions too, if you get my drift. What I'm saying is that I realised that Susie wasn't just Janet's mother. She had found her own mansion in my heart, one that was alone unto itself, and not reliant on anyone else. I love her, no strings attached: I just love her.

We got on with our lives without either of us asking any sacrifice of the other. Susie continued to run the Gantry Group, and I continued to make my movies, not because we needed the money, but because those were our jobs. She employed people, and so did I, indirectly. I put bums on seats in cinemas, I sold newspapers, I even advertised a very classy range of Scottish designer knitwear.

Then there was Roscoe Brown, my Hollywood agent, who was living up to his reputation as the smartest new guy on the Strip, and earning every dollar of his cut with the work he was lining up for me. The only limits I gave him were a gap of at least a month between projects . . . many actors would give their back teeth (never their front ones, obviously) for so short a break between engagements . . . and first class air travel back to Scotland wherever in the world I was and whenever the shooting schedule allowed.

When the Vancouver project, a period piece about early settlers, was over, *Skinner's Rules*, the Edinburgh cop-flick I'd made for Miles Grayson, was ready for release. It was a smash, world-wide, so big that after two days on release Miles took up his option on the follow-up, *Skinner's Festival*, and re-signed all the original cast. He didn't blink at all when Roscoe asked for above-title billing for me alongside him and Dawn Phillips, and he agreed to his financial pitch on the spot. I knew why; my character, Chief Inspector Andy Martin, is one of the key figures in the story. The role merited top billing.

We shot it in September . . . the city would have been just too crowded in August, when the real Edinburgh Festival was on. For me it was great; it meant that I could commute from Glasgow on a virtually daily basis for the six weeks of shooting, bonus quality time with Susie and Janet. From the start I knew how good it was going to be, and how good I was going to be too. It was my seventh movie . . . after Vancouver I had done one in the South of Italy (in which I had an almost nude scene with an actress whom ten years before I'd fancied like crazy; an odd and slightly scary experience) and another in Hollywood . . . and there was no hesitancy left in me. I knew what I was doing, I no longer felt out of place on set, and I had an acting coach to rub off my rough edges.

Even before it was released I knew I had made it in my own right as a performer, finally and irreversibly. I knew how good I'd been, especially in Andy's huge emotional scene at the end. I was pretty sure that the old, cold, angry Oz wouldn't have been able to do that.

I'd like to say that there wasn't a trace of him left, but, in my new spirit of honesty, I can't. In a few months he would make a return appearance, angrier, more ruthless and a lot more calculating. But I'll get to that in due course.

# 2

For that time, though, life continued as what passed for Susie and me as normal. I went back to work shooting *Skinner's Festival*, Miles Grayson in the lead, Dawn typecast as his wife, Scott Steele as the old chief constable, randy Rhona Waitrose as Miles's screen daughter, Alexis, and Liam Matthews, my wrestler buddy, following up his debut in the first *Skinner* movie, as one of the detective team.

There were a couple of additions, though: the story called for two villains, who turn out at the end to be brother and sister. My character, Andy, was to fall for the girl, while the other would get off with Alexis/Rhona, all with disastrous consequences. Miles cast a genuine brother and sister team in these parts, José and Roxanne Benali. Roxanne was pretty tempting, I have to admit. We had a couple of scenes where there was a lot of skin involved, and she didn't hold anything back in either of them. That made it difficult, because it meant that I could not allow myself to appear any less enthusiastic than her. In the end I just imagined that she was Susie, and gave her my best simulated shot, thanking my stars that it was a closed set, with only Miles and essential crew around. (A couple of years earlier and . . . given Roxanne's 'commitment to her part', as she put it, and under the duvet her interest in mine . . . it might not have been simulated.)

We shot the thing, start to finish, in a total of ten weeks. Most of the schedule was in Edinburgh, but we had a couple of trips south to a big sound stage for disaster scenes which could not have been filmed in their actual locations . . . it would have meant blowing them up.

Normally, once we were finished I would have looked forward to my usual lazy month between projects, but Susie had my dance-card well filled. Right at the top of our list of things to do was moving house.

We liked where we lived in Glasgow, our city centre apartment in an award-winning conversion, but now that I was becoming a bit famous, it was less and less practical. Our neighbours were nice people, and they never once complained about the punters hanging around the place, or the photographers who never seemed to be too far away. After a while, though, we decided that we couldn't inflict the inconvenience on them any longer. So we looked around Scotland and found a country house set in a small estate within sight of Loch Lomond, with plenty of room for us, for Janet, for any more Janets who might come along, for Ethel Reid, our nanny, and with a small lodge house to accommodate Jay Yuille, our chauffeur.

Actually, Jay was a bit more than a chauffeur, although driving Susie to the office and me to the airport was in his job description. He was our minder, an ex-soldier recruited by my eventually trusted friend Ricky Ross, whose consultancy handles nearly all the security work for Miles Grayson's UK movie projects. As my star began to get bigger, Miles had taken pains to impress upon me that famous people with children can't be too careful. He and Dawn employed a children's nurse for Brucie; she was ex-LAPD, and she took it ill out when they came to the UK and she couldn't pack her .38 S&W special. Our guy Jay had fought in Afghanistan and was formidable enough without firearms.

The house move went off with barely a hitch . . . not that we were moving much. Susie had hired an interior designer who had charged us a fee, then compounded the cost by furnishing almost all of the place from scratch. The only things we took with us were Janet's familiar things from the nursery and our big partners' desk, where we used to sit and work while looking down on the City of Glasgow, its traffic flowing beneath us. We found a spot for that in our new home, setting up our shared office in one of the big conservatories built on either side of the house, each having a panoramic view of the loch below. The other one enclosed a heated swimming pool, but its door was always locked; our Janet was into everything and in no time at all she would be big enough to reach the handle. Even though she's a water-baby, she wasn't to be trusted on her own.

12

The old apartment was sold, after a little soul-searching. We had considered keeping it as a *pied-à-terre*, but decided eventually to give the neighbours a complete break by moving it on. Barney Farmer, the Gantry Group lawyer, put it on the market at an exorbitant figure and had an unconditional offer next day. The buyer, he said, was a company, not an individual; slightly strange in Scotland, but in fact, so was the seller, and for the money that was offered Susie and I weren't bothered. The deal was signed off and we waved it a fond goodbye.

Life was idyllic again; there wasn't a cloud in the sky, and even my career was conspiring to keep it that way. We enjoyed Christmas with the family at home: my nephews, Jonny and his brother Colin, dry-nosed for once, and showing signs of becoming sensible, took to the new place, and especially to the pool.

I had to marvel at the change in Jonathan. To me it seemed to have happened overnight, but actually it had taken place when I was away on one of my projects. When I got home I'd called Ellie to catch up. Everyone was out, so the answer machine cut in. 'Hello,' I heard myself say. 'You've reached the Sinclair residence. I'm afraid we can't take your call just now, but if you leave a message we'll call you back.' I left a message, but I was seriously puzzled. I couldn't remember ever recording an answer message for my sister. I knew that my Dad hadn't done it. He and I sound almost identical on the phone, but not quite.

She laughed when I asked her about it. 'Time moves on, young brother,' she said.

I let my mouth fall open. 'You don't mean . . .'

'I do. That was our Jonny.'

I'd been curiously disturbed by that. Since Ellen and her husband split up, the boys have seen very little of their father, an irredeemable workaholic. My Dad's always been close, but he's their grandfather, and that's different. In search of a father substitute, Jonathan in particular has always drifted to me. I felt that I'd missed an important part of his life, and I was sorry.

After our family Christmas we brought in the New Year in Florida, taking Janet to Disney World; Susie had decided that she had gone long enough without sunshine. Once the festivities were over, I had to endure the hardship of a three-month film shoot in the Caribbean, and

13

on the horizon after that, Roscoe Brown's finest achievement to date, my first top billing part.

I was to play the title role in *Mathew's Tale*, a drama set in pre-Victorian Scotland, and directed by the eminent Frenchman Paul Girone, about the adventures of a Napoleonic War veteran who returns home to discover that he has been given up for dead and that his intended has married someone else. I was to co-star, my name headlining, with Louise Golding, an American hot ticket, and with the formidable Ewan Capperauld, who had been cast originally as Deputy Chief Constable Bob Skinner in my first Miles Grayson cop movie, only for personal problems to force his late withdrawal. I was glad that Ewan had decided to come out of his self-imposed exile. For all that he could be a bit of a lovey, I had found myself liking the guy.

Scott Steele was in it too, of course. These days you can't cast a movie in Scotland without finding a part for old Scott. He gets pissed off when reviewers call him 'the Finlay Currie of his generation', but it's easy to see what they mean. If they still made movies with Moses in the cast, he'd be the guy parting the Red Sea every time.

The added bonus about this project, apart from the incredible money that Roscoe had screwed out of the producers, was the location. Much of it was being shot in Scotland, in a scenic Fife village, in Edinburgh's Old and New Towns, and in a countryside setting not far from our house in Loch Lomond.

It couldn't have been better, it really couldn't. It was just too bad that, in the immortal words of a Polish guy of my acquaintance, it all went to rat-shit.

# 3

The Caribbean thing, a remake of *Island in the Sun*, was pretty good, and so, they all said, was I. Weekend trips back to Scotland weren't practical, but I had written a couple of visits for Susie and Janet into my contract, so the homesickness wasn't too bad.

It was wrapped on time. We had a Bacardi party to celebrate, then I headed back to Scotland at the beginning of an unusually pleasant spring.

Almost the first thing Susie and I did on my return was to take Janet up to Anstruther for a couple of days, to visit my Dad and Mary, my stepmother. On Saturday afternoon, with no patients to be seen, it was decided that the ladies would visit Ellen and Colin in St Andrews, to allow us guys . . . Jonny is a good enough golfer now to hold his end up with us . . . an afternoon on the links at Elie.

I've played some of the finest and most famous courses in the world . . . Pebble Beach, Valderrama, Wentworth, Kiawah Island, where alligators count as a hazard . . . yet I've never enjoyed any of them more than Elie on a nice day. The Old Course at St Andrews may be the most famous in Fife, but it's not the most distinctive. It doesn't have an old submarine periscope sticking through the roof of the starter's hut.

It's true, I swear, and since it was installed thousands of players have thanked the retired sea dog who gifted it to the club. Since the landing area for the first drive can't be seen from the tee, and has a tight out-of-bounds on the right, the opening hole was a confusing and dangerous place in the old days. It was before my time, but my Dad assured me that on the club-house roof there were mirrors through which the starter had to do his best to judge whether the fairway was clear.

However, once this obstacle has been overcome, players are released on to a pleasant undulating course that wends its way from the town out to its most westward beach and back again. In the wind it's a swine, but on a balmy spring day it's one of life's great pleasures.

And yet as we made our way towards the turn, I could sense that there was an invisible cloud hanging over us, or over Mac the Dentist at least. Actually, I had sensed it the night before over dinner, when he had been quieter than usual. When he missed successive putts from under eight feet on the fifth, sixth and seventh greens, I knew for sure there was something on his mind.

'Out with it,' I demanded as we set off up the eighth. 'What's up?' Jonny had pushed his drive to the right and was striding off after it. In step with the arrival of his baritone, he'd grown a hell of a lot over the winter; although he was still a few weeks shy of fourteen years old, he was as tall as his Granddad and catching up on me fast.

'Nothing's up.'

'Dad,' I told him, 'the rest of your golf may be shite, but you are the best putter in Fife. You haven't missed three on the trot like that in my lifetime.'

He looked at the ground as he walked and shrugged. 'Ach, it's my eyes,' he muttered. 'They've been playing me up.'

'Bollocks,' I retorted. 'You spotted my second shot on the fourth when I'd lost sight of it. When we were driving through here you recognised that patient of yours in Pittenweem from three hundred yards away. What's the score?'

'You're four up!'

'Not that score. Cut the crap, Dad. Telling me porkies only serves to confirm it.'

He stopped and sighed. 'Okay, there is. But let's not talk about it here, not with the boy around. Afterwards. Now come on, before we hold the course up.' He trudged off after his drive, which he had carved way out to the left; I had laid up with an iron off the tee, the only one of the three of us to find the fairway.

His mood seemed to improve after that. His concentration on the greens did, that's certain. He rolled in a few of his usual miracles and by the time we reached the seventeenth tee, he was only one down. He

16

tugged his drive down the left and out of bounds, though, and that was curtains.

Since Jonny, playing off a handicap that would have to be revised, and quickly, had won our separate three-way points competition by that time, we agreed that we'd skip the eighteenth. Another of the pleasures of Elie is the pub near the fourth and final tees, placed strategically to lure those whose games have ended early, or on occasion those who lack the bottle to battle outwards into horizontal rain and gale-force winds.

We parked our clubs at the door . . . no worries: it's that sort of place . . . and wandered in. If we had taken Jonny in with us, the licensee probably wouldn't have minded, given the size of him, but I told him that while he might be tall enough to go into a pub, he wasn't old enough. He's an amenable lad, so he didn't argue.

The lounge section was empty, and so we chose a table in the corner. I bought Jonny a pint of orange and lemonade, a bag of crisps and a filled roll, and took them outside, where I found him sat on the wheel of my Dad's caddy-car, watching a match going up the fourth. Then I fetched a couple of pints of Eighty and four more rolls . . . it was still a while to dinner . . . and brought them across on a tray. I laid the plate on the table, put a pint in front of my Dad, returned the tray, sat down and growled, 'Right.'

'It's nothing I can't handle, son,' said Mac the Dentist, abruptly.

'If it's making you play like that, you're not fucking handling it. Now out with it.'

He gave another sigh, a huge one this time, and sagged back into his chair. He picked up his pint and looked at it. 'I'm driving,' he said. 'I shouldn't be drinking this.'

'We'll get a taxi. Now out with it.'

'There's no putting you off, is there? What if I just refuse to talk about it?'

'Don't bother thinking about that; it's not an option. Come on.'

He took a drink and a decision. 'Okay, if you insist. I'm being blackmailed.'

I felt myself stiffen in my chair. 'You're what?' It began as a roar, but I choked it down before the licensee took too much interest. 'What do you mean?'

17

He leaned his head back against the pub window, and stared up at the ceiling. 'The husband of a female patient came to see me,' he began, his voice loud enough for me to hear, but not to carry across to the landlord. 'This was three days ago, on Wednesday, my afternoon off; I'd treated his wife the day before.' He paused and took another drink, and when he was finished, so was his pint. I went to the bar, bought him another and brought it back. Anger was welling up inside me, but I kept it in check.

'Thanks, son.' His tongue was loosening. 'I did an extraction under sedation,' he explained. 'It's unusual these days, especially in adults; most people just go for locals. But not this woman. She said she had a phobia, and that the only way she could do it was if I put her under. So I did, yanked her tooth, made sure that she had come round okay, and that was that. I told her to sit in the waiting room for a couple of minutes, but she said she was fine and went straight out the door.' He paused to ingest some more ale.

'Next day, her weasel of a husband came to see me, and said that his wife had made a complaint against me. She'd claimed that when she started to come round from the anaesthetic, she realised that her knickers were down by her knees, her skirt was up round her waist and that I was feeling her up.'

'So why didn't she scream?'

'My question exactly. The husband said that at first it was like a dream to her, that I must have realised she was coming round early and straightened her up. Only she realised very quickly that she hadn't been dreaming. As his story went on, she got out fast, went home and asked her husband to take a look at her. He said that he did, and saw, as he put it, "Clear signs of sexual interference." Bastard! Bastards!'

'So why didn't he go straight to the police? While the knickers in question were still moist, so to speak.'

'He said he wanted to spare you the indignity, you being a public figure and all that. He said he was sure I'd want to as well.'

'By how much did he reckon you'd want to spare me?'

'Fifty grand's worth.'

'Indeed,' I heard myself say, my voice grating. 'And if not?'

'The police and the tabloids.'

My anger had turned into rage, but not the kind that shows on the outside; this was like a great cold ball inside me, growing all the time. Then the obvious occurred to me.

'Wait a minute. You must have had a doctor there to give the anaesthetic. Surely he'll kick all this into touch.'

'Oh, I did; technically I wasn't anaesthetising the woman, only sedating her as I said, but I had Arthur Matthews in to do it. But that's the trouble. He can't back me up. He gave her the nitrous oxide all right, but the patient was no sooner under when his mobile went. A kid had been knocked down in the street, and he was the only doctor handy. He could see that everything was all right with the woman and he knows me well enough, so we agreed that he should get along there pronto. I never thought for a minute that I might be setting myself up, but I bloody well should have. I'm an idiot, son, and I know it.'

'You're not an idiot, Dad,' I told him, quietly. 'You're a very nice man who knows nothing of the dark side of human nature. So what do you plan to do? Go to the police yourself?'

He shook his head, firmly. 'Doing that would get you and Susie all over the bloody tabloids just as quickly, and inevitably mud would stick to me. I can't have that, for Mary's sake, or your sister's, or the boys'.'

'You're not thinking of paying them, are you?'

'If it comes to it.'

I could feel my eyes pulling at the corners as they narrowed. 'What's his name? This wee blackmailer, what's his name?'

'Neiporte.' He spelled it out. 'Walter Neiporte. He sounded American. The wife's name's Andrea; I'd say she was English. She said she works as a secretary in a hotel up behind Kingsbarns, and I believe that he's a lab technician at St Andrews University. They haven't been on my list for very long. This was only the third time the woman had been to the surgery. He's never been.'

'Address?'

'They live in Pittenweem. Do you remember me slowing and looking at someone on the way through here? If you do, that was her.'

I had had only a brief glimpse, from a distance, but I could remember her, and also the fact that my Dad had noticed her: tall, dark-haired, maybe thirtyish, although it had been hard to tell from so far away.

'How did your discussion finish?'

'With me grabbing him by the scruff of the neck and running him through the door. But then he phoned me that night. He said that he wasn't kidding, and that if I hadn't agreed to pay him off by next Monday at the latest, then he'd do what he'd threatened.'

'Mmm.' I looked down at my pint. My Dad was almost through his second, but mine was untouched. I shoved it across to him. 'You drink that. I'll drive back.' I picked up a filled roll . . . tuna mayonnaise . . . and walked over to the bar. There was a pay-phone in the far corner, with a telephone directory beside it, a year out of date and dog-eared from heavy use, but still in one piece. I picked it up and scrolled through it to the letter 'n'. The Neiporte clan is not thick on the ground in the East Neuk of Fife, but there was one, forename Walter, listed as residing at Grizelda Cottage, Main Street, Pittenweem. I knew exactly where it was; the name had fascinated me when I was a kid: it made me think of witches and stuff. In those days I thought they were fun, but now I knew different.

The third pint was gone when I got back to the table. I picked up the last roll and motioned my Dad towards the door, returning the empties as we left. (Bartenders like that small courtesy; it makes them more likely to fill your glass right up to the top next time.)

We collected Jonny, walked back up the winding path to the club car park, dumped the clubs in the boot of the old Jag, changed our shoes, then I drove back to Enster. Back at the house, I stayed in the car as Mac the Dentist climbed out, not showing a trace of unsteadiness.

'Where are you going?' he asked.

'We need Pampers for Janet. I'd better get some, just in case we forget tomorrow.' If my Dad had thought about it he would have remembered that his granddaughter was two years old, and toilet trained.

As soon as I turned out of the drive, my rage released itself. It flowed through me and there was nothing I could do about it. I felt ferocious, in a way I had only known once before in my life, when I found out the truth about Jan's death. This was almost as bad. This man, these people, were threatening my father's good name, and they were using his only weakness . . . me . . . as a lever.

I parked a fair distance from Grizelda Cottage, round the corner, past the legendary Pittenweem fish and chip shop, and walked the rest. Just as I turned into the main street, I saw the woman again, leaving the house and walking away in the opposite direction; going for the fish suppers, maybe. Closer to, I could see that she looked pretty tasty. By the time I reached the gate, all the old Oz was back, cold and calculating and in control. It did occur to me that there might be kids in the house, but if there were I'd give them a tenner and send them after their mother.

I rang the doorbell; as I waited I glanced around the front garden. It was untidy, but there were absolutely no signs of youngsters, no toys, bikes, footballs or anything like that.

The door opened and a man looked out at me. 'Yes?' he said in a slight drawl.

'Walter?' I asked politely.

He nodded, and I saw the light of recognition in his eyes, just about half a second before I hit him and they glazed over. I caught him in the middle of the forehead, a good spot if your hands are hard enough. I pulled it a bit, so I didn't knock him out, just stunned him. I shoved him into his hallway, then closed the door after myself as he tripped over his feet and fell backwards.

'Whose idea was it?' I asked as he scrambled back up. For a moment he thought about squaring up to me; maybe there was something about my smile that put him off that idea. 'Whose idea?' I repeated. 'Yours alone, or both of you.'

'I dunno what you're talking about.'

I started another right-hander; he swayed back from it and as he did I sank my left fist well into his flabby gut. He groaned and sat down again, hard.

This time I jerked him to his feet, easily, to let him see how strong I was. 'Don't piss me about,' I said evenly. 'You and your wife threatened my father, you arsehole. You tried to extort money from him. But what you've got is me instead. Somehow or other, you thought that nice old Mac was a soft touch. Maybe you thought that guys like me will do anything to keep our names out of the paper. If that's so, you were wrong twice. My Dad isn't a mug, not at all. As for me, there is nothing I will not do to protect him.' I had him by the lapels, his back against a door.

'I could simply beat the shit out of you. That would be no problem. But it wouldn't be enough. So I want you to listen to me, very carefully. I have a lot of money, and with it I have a lot of power. Being a Yank, you can probably understand that concept. So what I'm telling you is that if either you or your wife ever go near my father again, and if you go anywhere near the police or the press with this wicked story of yours, something very bad will happen to you. I'm not just talking about a good thumping here, you have to understand. I'm talking much worse than that; concrete Timberlands, that sort of stuff.'

The way his eyes widened, I knew right away that he was a believer. I smiled at him again. 'You know something? I'm offended that you only asked him for fifty grand. If he'd paid it and I'd found out about it afterwards, that wouldn't have been nearly enough to protect you from me.'

I let him go. 'Don't ever forget,' I told him, knowing that he wouldn't.

As I left the cottage, Andrea Neiporte was approaching the gate. She was carrying a parcel wrapped in shiny brown paper. Her mouth dropped open as I nodded to her on the way past. 'Enjoy those,' I said to her, 'while you can still chew.'

As I walked into my Dad's house he was waiting for me in the living room. I could hear Mary and Susie, Jonny and Janet, in the kitchen. 'What did you do?' he asked. 'You didn't pay him, did you?' He had worked out about the Pampers all right.

'I gave him what he was asking for, Dad, that's all. Now forget it, unless he bothers you again.'

He looked at me as if I was someone he didn't know quite so well. 'And what will you do if he does?'

I laughed out loud. 'What do you think I'll do? I'll have him killed.'

# 4

It was all bluff and bluster, of course . . . at least I assumed my Dad thought it was . . . but it seemed to work. The threatened call on the following Monday didn't happen, and he and I were able to breathe easier. I didn't forget about the Neiportes, of course; I began to think about what I would do if they did resurface, but mostly it was at the back of my mind.

At the forefront was the world premiere of *Skinner's Festival*, which Miles had decreed would be in the relatively new multiplex on Picardy Place, in Edinburgh, on a Monday evening a couple of weeks into my gap between filming.

Susie was really pumped up for it; she had never been on my arm at one of these gala events. She was so determined to look good that she put in extra hours in the gym and the pool, just to tone herself up.

There was no way she could hide wee Mac, though. He was the product of my pre-Christmas break and a small but noticeable bump was already in evidence. (Actually, it was too early for a scan that would have told us for sure, not that we really wanted to know, but given that I was younger brother to a sister, we just assumed that he was going to be a boy.)

Wee Janet sensed something was up. As soon as she saw us dolled up, she knew for sure, and demanded to be taken with us. In fact she screamed bloody murder. If she had only said, 'Pwease, Daddy,' I might have relented and taken her with us, but she overdid it and Susie put her foot down. So she was promised another trip to the Magic Kingdom before the year was out . . . that's what Susie calls being firm . . . and we headed off for Embru in our new BMW 7 series, with Jay at the wheel.

I was surprised by the size of the crowds outside the cinema, contained behind barriers on either side of the entrance. Miles was there first, waiting in the doorway to welcome us and the other cast members. I'd been in live situations often enough before, in my days as a wrestling announcer, but I was astonished by the cheering, the screaming even, as I stepped out of the car, holding my hand out to help Susie exit gracefully, without showing too much leg . . . or any knicker, as she put it. '*Listen to that*,' I whispered to myself, as the sound washed over me. '*There was a time when you walked around this city, and nobody knew you.*'

Then I looked over my shoulder, saw Liam Matthews emerging from a limo behind us, and my ego was deflated: he's a real babe magnet, is Liam.

Jay came round the car to join us as we stepped on to the red carpet. I had my left arm around Susie's shoulder as I waved to the crowd on the left, then turned to the right where the photographers were banked up. We paused there for a minute or so; Liam and Erin, his girlfriend, joined us, and we gave the snappers a ground shot, then Susie and I moved off towards Miles and Dawn at the door.

It was pure chance that I saw it when I did, a flash of yellow, out of the corner of my eye. I reacted instinctively, turning Susie away and putting my body between her and whatever it was. I sensed movement behind me as Jay dived to cover us, then I felt the splash of liquid hitting my shoulders and a sticky sensation on the back of my head. Then Jay had his arms around us both and was rushing us towards the door, past Miles and Dawn, both of them astonished, anger beginning to flare in his eyes.

'What the fuck was that?' I demanded as soon as we were safe inside. I put my hand up to feel the back of my head, but our minder stopped me.

'Don't touch it,' he said, 'it's only paint, but you don't want to get it all over you.'

'Only!' I barked. Osbert Blackstone is not known for losing his cool, but there are exceptions.

'Try shit,' Jay murmured, 'or acid, or phosphorous. I've had all of those chucked at me in the army.' I looked away from the door and at him for the first time. At once I saw that he had taken most of it. The

24

side of his face and the back of his suit were plastered with the thick yellow substance. I looked down at Susie. I was relieved to see that she was untouched, but she was not a happy lady.

'What the hell was that about?' she exploded. 'Don't tell me that was yet another of your old girlfriends making a statement.'

I shook my head. The only one who might have fallen into that category was Alison Goodchild, but she and I had squared accounts a couple of years back. But old girlfriends' new boyfriends, now that was another matter.

Miles and Dawn appeared by our side, with Liam and Erin. 'Are you okay?' asked my ex-brother-in-law, anxiously.

I nodded, beginning to rein in my anger. 'Fuck me, man,' I exclaimed, 'wouldn't we have had enough coverage, without pulling a stunt like that?'

For half a second his eyes narrowed, then he laughed. 'Yeah,' he said, in that Aussie-meets-LA drawl of his, 'you're okay. What about you, Susie?'

'I'm fine,' she snapped, 'which is more than you'll be able to say for the bastard who threw that stuff when I get hold of him! Have the police caught him?'

It was Liam who answered. 'Not a chance. That lot couldn't catch the clap. Whoever did it vanished into the crowd. I spoke to a couple of people behind the barrier, and to a couple of the security guys, but none of them saw anything but yellow paint.'

'Bloody hell, Jay,' exclaimed a voice from the side. 'You look like a no parking zone.' For all his levity, Ricky Ross looked anxious. 'I'm sorry about that, Mr Grayson,' he said . . . for an ex-detective superintendent, Ricky's good at being deferential to the clients. He had a right to be sorry, too, as security chief for the event.

Miles shrugged. 'Don't worry about it. There's not much you can do about something like that; it's happened before now at my events. Last time it was in Melbourne; a couple of pop stars had their fur coats sprayed with creosote.'

'Maybe not,' the security consultant muttered, 'but my guys are trained to react a sight faster than they did. We don't even have a description of the assailant. I'll catch up with it, though. The police will inspect all the telly footage and still shots that were taken. With luck, they'll put a face to the paint-chucker and take it from there.'

'I want to see it,' I said. 'When the police look at the tapes and the photos, I want to be there.'

Ricky looked at me. If he thought about telling me to forget it, he didn't bother; he knew me better than that. 'I'll see what I can do. They might play ball.'

'Of course they will. If it's someone with a grudge against me, I'm liable to know them, am I not?'

'True,' he conceded, 'but that's for later. Right now we'd better get that stuff off you and Jay before it dries, and get you a new jacket befitting your status . . . sir.'

# 5

As someone almost certainly did not say, 'Apart from that, Mrs Kennedy, how did you enjoy your visit to Dallas?'

Apart from having a can of yellow paint chucked at her, Susie thought the premiere was great. She and I had never been out as a showbiz couple before, and once she recovered her composure and her temper . . . with the help of a couple of Jack Daniels and Coke in the hospitality suite . . . she settled into the role like the true star she is. She'd never shown any sign before of liking the limelight . . . she found her Businesswoman of the Year awards more embarrassing than anything else . . . but when we picked up early editions of the *Daily Record* and the *Daily Mail* on the way home, and found ourselves on the front pages, it topped off her night. The fact that I was plastered in paint, and being hustled inside by security, didn't depress her at all. In fact, it made her laugh.

I read through the reports in both papers. The incident was reported, but not overmuch, because there wasn't much to tell, and I had ordered the publicists to laugh it off by saying that quite a few of my old Edinburgh friends had been my fellow-members of the Idiot Tendency when we had all been lads together, and that I was looking forward to renewing acquaintance with one in particular, when I traced him. I wasn't kidding; I had a mental shortlist of who the chucker might have been, and I was intending to find out. Having stuff tossed at me, and my pregnant wife, was no longer my idea of a laddish prank.

Susie, on the other hand, was so chuffed by the coverage that, first thing next morning, she called Mary, my stepmother, Ellie, my sister, and Joe Donn, her dark secret, to make sure they bought copies. The girls were suitably impressed . . . or made appropriate noises, at least . . . but Joe didn't answer his phone. 'Must have gone to get them already,' Susie muttered.

I was working at home that day, having fixed a session with my dialogue tutor to take a first look at the script of *Mathew's Tale*. I was working out in the gym that's part of the pool conservatory when Susie left for her office, on the South Side of Glasgow, across the Erskine Bridge . . . yes, some people really do use the damn thing. She had a board meeting that day and I was a director, but the agenda was routine and so she had said she would write my apology into the minutes. Joe wasn't so lucky, though; he was needed to make up the quorum. I hoped he hadn't forgotten; he was an even keener golfer than my Dad, and it took a lot to keep him off the course on a fine day.

My fine day was screwed almost as soon as I'd showered and dressed after my exercise programme. I was having breakfast with Janet and Ethel in our big kitchen, and looking forward to a game with my daughter in our enormous new garden. (Our games usually involve a ball. The way I see it, women's football is going to be a big thing in years to come . . . it's there already in the US . . . and there's no harm in giving wee Janet as many career options as I can.) Our new numbers were ex-directory . . . of course . . . so when the phone rang, my instant assumption was that Susie had forgotten something and was calling from the office, or the car if she was stuck in traffic. No such luck; it was Ricky Ross.

'What are you doing this morning?' he asked, with no preliminary banter, which isn't like him.

I told him.

'Can you scrub it? Postpone it? The police want to see you.'

'Uh?'

'About last night, man. About the paint-chucking. I've leaned on young Ron Morrow at Gayfield, told him it was a fucking disgrace that it happened on his patch and that Miles Grayson will be asking questions of the chief if nobody's apprehended. So now the boy's taking it very seriously. He's come up with a couple of images on video and still shots and he wants you to look at them.'

I blinked as I took it in. Truth be told, Susie and I were riding on such a high over the success of the event, and over our daughter's delight, young as she was, at seeing her Mum and Dad on the front page of the newspapers, that I at least had got over the incident that preceded it. We certainly hadn't discussed it since Miles had kitted Jay and me out in new jackets and since my hair had dried.

'Well?' Ricky demanded. 'You were the guy that wanted to see the tapes, remember. I've pulled the strings for you, so how's about it?'

'Yes, sure,' I said. 'I can put off my dialogue coach till tomorrow. When do you want me in Edinburgh?'

There was a laugh on the other end of the line. 'You still don't realise it, do you, Oz. You're a VIP now. They want to come to see you.'

Once upon a time, before he met up with me, Ricky Ross had a high-flying police career, a detective superintendent on his way to one of those uniforms with silver braid all over the place, and to the knighthood that goes with it. After it crash-landed he was inclined to blame me for a while, but in truth, if he had kept his fly zipped up, he'd still have had his prospects and maybe his marriage. Those days were behind us, though, and he'd become a pal; he may not be a bosom buddy, but we got on all right. The truth of the matter is that neither loss bothered him all that much. As a security consultant he makes much more money than he ever could have in the police force, even as chief constable, and as for Mrs Ross, he confessed to me that she had actually thrown him out before he began the ill-judged liaison that landed him on the carpet.

Over time he had ridden out the disgrace of his forced resignation. The old chief had gone, replaced by a younger model who had risen through the ranks under Ricky's patronage, and who had not forgotten it. He was *persona grata* in Lothian and Borders Police once again, and so I was not in the least surprised that when Detective Sergeant Ron Morrow rolled up our driveway, he was in the passenger seat of Ricky's car, a hairy new S-type Jaguar.

I had met Morrow before, on a few occasions in Edinburgh, most of them formal. He was a good guy, and Ricky rated him, which, given the climate of the time and the fact that Ricky and the new chief constable were regular golf partners, meant that young Ronnie was probably going places.

He shook my hand as I opened the door for him . . . we never use Ethel as a maid: as if she'd let us. He was toting what I thought at first

29

was a briefcase but realised was a laptop computer. Ricky was carrying something too, a toy for wee Janet, who'd come toddling out of her playroom behind the stairs to inspect the new arrivals. It's funny how people who don't have kids often dote over other people's. I was like that with my nephews, at least until Ellie and her husband split up; after that I felt the need to display a bit of male authority on occasion, at least with Colin, who was one of those kids with nuclear-capable mischief in him.

While Ricky made a fuss of Janet, under the amused eye of Ethel, I took Morrow through to our office conservatory. He didn't say anything as he looked around, but I knew exactly what he was thinking. He was casting his mind back to our first meeting, in the police station down in Leith, and he was asking himself, '*How the hell did this guy wind up here?*' Just as well he didn't ask me: I couldn't have given him a sensible answer.

I nodded towards the laptop, which was still in his hand. 'What's that for?' I asked him.

He held it up, as if I'd never seen one of the things before. I have one which travels everywhere with me; it's my interface to the real world. 'I've had all the video footage from the television and the security cameras copied on to a DVD-Rom disk; the still shots have been scanned in as well. I brought this so you could view them.'

'We won't need it.' I pointed to the partners' desk that we had brought from Glasgow. It really is big. Susie and I each have computers, state of the art high-speed jobs, each with its own dedicated phone line, and with wide-screen LCD monitors that sit back to back. I know of at least one married couple who conduct a significant amount of their communication by e-mail, but we haven't reached that stage yet. Mind you, for a laugh, we once held a video conference across the desk, using our web-cams, seeing ourselves on screen and hearing our voices repeat through the speakers what we had said a few seconds before.

When I'm away, I use that facility as often as I can, from my laptop, or from internet cafés or hotels, or just from whatever's available, for the sheer pleasure of seeing Susie's face and hearing her voice. I had tried to get my Dad to set himself up with the same facility, but he had always resolutely claimed computer illiteracy. All his appointment books and practice records are kept as they've always been, manually.

I switched my PC on and waited for it to boot up: it didn't take long. 'Let's see your disk,' I said as we waited. Morrow handed it over, in its clear plastic case, just as Ricky Ross joined us.

'I told you he'd have all this gear, Ron. He's a boy for his toys, is our Oz.'

'This is no toy, sunshine,' I told him. I sat down at my keyboard, opened an internet search engine and keyed in three words: 'Richard Ross Security.' Inside five seconds a list of websites flashed up on screen, the first in a list of several hundred thousand. Ricky's consultancy firm was at the top of the list. Next, I keyed in my own name; there were just over thirty thousand hits, my own website, set up in the US by Roscoe Brown, at the top of the list.

'Happily,' I said, 'you can also watch movies on it. Let's look at some of mine.'

I took Morrow's disk from its container, reached down and slipped it into the drive of my computer tower, in the footwell of the desk. A window opened up, showing a list of files and a folder called 'stills'. I clicked on it and a second list appeared, files with the suffix 'jpeg'. I hit the first one on the list and it opened, a photograph filling half of the screen.

This was not a reaction shot. Whoever the photographer was, he had hit his motor drive and been lucky; the paint was in mid-air, heading for Jay and me, as I put myself in Susie's way, and my minder put himself in mine. I looked at the crowd; there was a glimpse of an outstretched arm emerging from a throng of people, some of whose mouths were beginning to drop open as they realised what was happening.

'That one's no use,' said Ronnie. 'This is the only really clear one.' He reached over, took my mouse and clicked on an icon half-way down the list; a new image formed on screen in an instant. This time a face could be seen behind the outstretched arm, but the photograph seemed to have been blown up so much that it was grainy and unrecognisable.

I peered at it, but it told me only one thing. 'It's a woman, isn't it?'

'Correct,' Detective Sergeant Morrow concurred. 'Any ideas?'

I looked back at him, over my shoulder. 'You must be joking. That could be my sister and I still wouldn't recognise her from that. Can't we look at it from a shorter perspective?'

'That's the best we can do with it. It was taken on a telephoto lens.' He moved the mouse again. 'Let's look at the video clips.'

We had to wait for a few more seconds for the Windows Media Player software to open and load up. 'This is BBC,' Ronnie murmured, as the clip began to run. A ribbon at the foot of the screen within my screen told me that it was twenty seconds' worth. I looked and there we were, Susie and Oz, she sparkling in her designer dress, he smiling and waving to the crowd. We moved sedately along the red carpet, Jay Yuille a pace behind, and then it happened. I saw myself react as the paint was chucked, turning instinctively to cover Susie. I saw Jay do his job by putting himself in the way of the threat. I had the feeling that if it had been a bullet, or flying acid, he would have done exactly the same thing.

I was so busy looking at myself that I didn't pay any attention to the crowd. So I stopped the clip, reset it, and started again. This time I did as I was supposed to; this time I was staring intently at the people lined behind the barrier as the paint began to fly. As it did, I clicked on the pause sign and froze the image. The camera angle gave me a good view of the spectators, I looked at their faces one by one, but saw only shock begin to register in their expressions as they began to realise what was happening. Then I saw the arm again, outstretched as it had been in the still shot. I looked for the face behind it, but it was hidden from my sight by those in front. I hit the play button again and let the clip run on to its conclusion. The arm had been withdrawing. It disappeared into the throng, there was movement and then the clip ended.

I went to the ribbon and scrolled back, letting it run again, but looking at the timer and stopping it once more, a couple of seconds earlier this time. The view was different: this time the paint was still in the can. The chucker had it held to her shoulder like a shot putter about to release. She was leaning forward and her face was in shot; it was indistinct, but I could see her. I went into the Media Player menu and found zoom, then blew the image up to double size. That still wasn't definitive, so I went to full screen and rolled the clip again, starting from scratch and pausing at the exact moment I wanted. This time the shot was as big as I could make it, but that was big enough. I could see the face clearly in the crowd, eyes wide and angry as she steadied herself to throw. On the keyboard, I hit Control and 'P' simultaneously. The high-speed, high-definition colour printer that Susie and I share made its usual preliminary clicks and hums on its table by the side of the desk, then buzzed as it set to work. Inside half a minute, a photo-quality version of the image on screen was complete.

I picked it up from the tray and handed it to Morrow. 'There you are,' I said. 'That's as good as you're going to get.'

'And?' he exclaimed, impatiently.

'And I can't identify her. Sorry.'

The young sergeant's face fell. 'Bugger,' he muttered.

'Life is real and life is earnest, Ronnie,' I told him. 'It's very rare that we get a ride for free.'

'I know,' he conceded, with a nod to my homespun philosophy. 'I was just hoping this would be one of those times. Looks like we'll have to do it the hard way after all.'

'What for?' I asked.

'What do you mean?' Ricky Ross shot back, sharply.

'You know what I mean. Unless Ron here gets very lucky and gets a print match off the tin . . .' Morrow shook his head, dolefully '. . . or that face turns out to be well known to the police . . .' The detective looked at the printout and shook his head once again, '. . . tracing her is going to be bloody difficult, and costly in terms of manpower and everything else. Is it worth it?'

My friend gave me a strange look. 'Are you telling me this was a stunt?' he asked.

'Of course I'm bloody not! If it was, then I didn't know about it. Do you fancy asking Miles if he set it up just to make sure that we got on the front pages of the tabloids?' Ricky didn't need to answer that one. 'No. So all that I'm saying is this. If you decide to drop it, Ronnie, Susie and I will understand.'

The young DS shrugged his shoulders. 'Fair enough. I'll tell my boss that when I report back. It may well go that way.'

I ejected his disk from the computer and handed it back to him. In doing so I glanced at my watch; it was just after midday. 'Would you guys like some lunch before you head back?' I asked. 'It's no bother. It's my turn to make it today. Lucky for you, for one thing they did not teach Jay in the army was how to cook.'

Ricky grinned. 'Next time I'll fix you up with someone from the Catering Corps. Thanks for the offer, Oz, but I said I'd get the boy here back for two o'clock. I'm impressed, though. You still actually do your own cooking?'

'Sure we do. We food-shop on-line at Tesco, but we fix it up ourselves. It gives us the illusion that we're still real people.'

'You've never been a real person, Blackstone,' he countered, affably. 'Since I met you, you've been my worst fucking nightmare.'

I glowered at him, then looked over his shoulder. The door was open and Janet had come bouncing into the room. 'Oops, sorry,' he murmured.

'Thanks,' I said. 'I'd appreciate it if she didn't pick up the one word she hasn't learned yet.' As Morrow picked up his laptop, I scooped my daughter up in my arms and walked our visitors to the door.

'Have you got a date for *Mathew's Tale* yet?' asked Ricky, as we walked down the steps in front of the house.

'Three weeks or so, I think. I'm expecting the producer to go firm any day now. Why?'

'Because we're doing the security.'

I wasn't surprised to learn that. He seemed to pick up most of the freelance minding work in Edinburgh. 'See you around then,' I told him as he unlocked his Jag with a remote.

'Goodbye Sergeant,' I called out as Morrow settled into the front passenger seat. 'Sorry I couldn't help you.'

Actually I wasn't sorry at all. Imagine the can of worms I'd have opened if I'd told him that the paint-chucker was Andrea Neiporte.

# 6

I had plenty to think about as I stuffed some wholemeal pitta breads with pastrami and coleslaw. What to do about Mrs Neiporte? I thought about confiding in Ricky and asking him to sort the problem for me, but came down against that very quickly. There was still a lot of the copper in him, and I reckoned that he'd be more than likely to go down the official route. That was something I still did not want, for my Dad's sake.

Instead, I decided to tell Jay about it, or at least tell him as much as he needed to know, namely that my Dad had a nutty patient who had tried to put the black on him, and that my attempt to deal with it apparently hadn't worked. It was only right that I do that; after all, his job was to protect my family, so if I knew of a threat, he had to know too. I intended to brief him, give him the photograph . . . which I'd kept . . . and leave it to him. I had no idea how he'd go about dealing with the problem, but he was very much my man.

Whatever he did, I was sure it would be effective, and it would be discreet. When I'd interviewed him for the job, I'd noticed that there were sections of his CV . . . like most of the army bits . . . that were only described in broad terms. I didn't ask him about them, because I didn't want to make him have to lie to me. So I called a guy I know called Mark Kravitz who's involved in pretty dark and sensitive areas, and asked him instead. After Mark's report back, I had no qualms about hiring him. 'Disincentivising' is a bit of a buzz word these days, after that *Spooks* series on telly. It seemed that he had been pretty good at it.

When the pittas were ready . . . Ethel was responsible for feeding Janet, and herself . . . I called him in his cottage and told him to come up. Jay had a nice set-up and he knew it; the gatehouse, a Freelander to run around in, and a salary that was better than he'd have been on with any security firm. Of course he didn't just sit on his arse all day, waiting for the bad guys to turn up. He had installed geophones . . . movement sensors . . . around the perimeter of the estate, and he was careful to make sure that they were always working. Property maintenance was in his job description too, but mostly on a management basis. He might do the odd small job himself, but mostly he'd hire trades-people, and he supervised old Willie, the full-time gardener we'd inherited when we'd bought the place.

I was waiting for him in the kitchen as he let himself in through the back door. I'd fetched a couple of isotonic drinks from the fridge, and was taking the top off one when the phone rang.

'Oz.' It was Susie, and from the way she said my name I knew that something was up. Normally there's a laugh in her voice when she speaks to me, or to wee Janet. When it isn't there, it usually means that one of us is in trouble.

My third . . . and final . . . wife knows me better than anyone else in the world, probably better than even Jan did, for all that we grew up together, and certainly better than Primavera . . . she and I barely knew each other as real people at all, or at least until it was too late.

Susie's never seen me as I thought I was, or at least as I wanted people to see me. Even when we were just friends, she's always been able to see inside, to the bare bones, and to read bits of my mind that even I didn't really know were there. And I suppose it's always been true the other way round as well. As well as being different types, we're opposites as personalities, you see. Susie's always had this tough front . . . no surprises; it came from growing up as Jack Gantry's daughter . . . yet I've always been able to see the vulnerable wee girl inside. Me? For years I made such an effort to be user-friendly, I even fooled myself for a while, but as I've said, not her. She loves me, though, in spite of it, even if she was afraid to say so for a while. And I love her. One of the Sunday colour supplements described us as 'Scotland's golden couple'. Can you imagine that?

'Sorry,' I replied.

'What do you mean?' Susie snapped, not sounding at all golden.

'Whatever I've done, I didn't mean it.'

'Och, don't be daft.' Her tone changed, but the laugh was still missing; what I heard was that vulnerable wee girl.

'Come and get me, Oz,' she said. 'As fast as you can.'

'What's up?'

'I'll tell you later. Just get to the office.'

'Will I bring Jay?'

'No, leave him with Janet. Just you.'

'Susie, is this about last night? About that paint thing?'

'No. Nothing to do with it. Now get the finger out.'

I hung up the kitchen phone and looked at Jay. 'Sorry mate,' I told him. 'I've just had an order I can't refuse. Meantime . . .' I handed him the photo I had printed out from my computer. 'Last night's paint-chucker.'

'You know her?'

'Yeah. I'll tell you later. For now, the only thing that matters is that she doesn't get anywhere near Susie or Janet. Understood?'

I wasn't quite sure what I'd just told him to do, but he nodded anyway. 'Police?' he asked.

'Under no circumstances.'

I grabbed my pitta and my Gatorade and headed for the three-car garage that had probably once been a several-horse stable. The advertising says that the BMW 7 series is a new way to drive, but my attitude's just the same. I just point it and go like shit. There isn't usually a lot of traffic out our way, and there's never any traffic on the Erskine Bridge, so I was across the Clyde in no time at all, bombing along the M8, past the airport and towards Susie's South Side office, with one eye out for day-glo motors with blue lights on top.

Happily there were none to hold me back; I took the M77 turn-off, headed west, and pulled up at the office in Thornliebank in what must have been a record time from the house. For all that, Susie had an impatient look on her face as she stood at the door, fidgeting from one foot to the other.

I'll swear that as she slid her trim little body, with its bump, in beside me, she was about to ask me what had kept me, but I forestalled her by telling her to take a deep breath, calm down and explain to me why she'd made me do the David Coulthard bit. I mean, shit, I'm a valuable property these days, to be tearing around like that.

'We have to go to Joe's,' she replied.

'Joe Donn's?'

'Yes. Come on, get moving.' There was a strange, slightly desperate tone in her voice.

I set the car in motion . . . you don't put these things in gear, you programme them . . . and headed off. 'Tell me, love,' I said, gently. The engine's so quiet you can almost whisper over it.

'He didn't turn up for the board meeting,' she said. 'I couldn't start without him, so I called him to ask where the hell he was, but I only got the answering machine. I tried his mobile, but that was switched off. After that I called his golf club, thinking that he'd got the dates mixed up and was playing a medal or something. But the secretary said that he hadn't been there since Saturday.'

We were at Eastwood Toll by this time; Joe's house was in Motherwell, so I headed through Clarkston for East Kilbride, rather than risk getting snarled up in Glasgow.

'Finally,' Susie continued, 'I did the only thing I could think of. I phoned the woman next door and asked her to check on him.' I knew what was coming by this time. 'Twenty minutes later I had a call from the police.' She covered her face with her hands, pushing her fingers into her eyes as if she could keep back the tears that way. You can't; I know, because I've tried that myself. 'They said he was dead, Oz. Joe's dead. My . . .'

She lost the battle. Her shoulders shook as she started to sob. I pulled the car into a lay-by and hugged her. 'I'm sorry, love,' I murmured into her ear. 'I'm so sorry.'

It's a hard old world in business, and I can't think of too many chief executive officers who'd be as crushed as Susie by the death of a non-executive director. But she had an excuse. You see, Joe Donn was Susie's dad.

When Susie's mother fell for . . . no, I'll use an old-fashioned word, because I'm sure it was literally true . . . when she was seduced by the charisma of Jack Gantry, builder, developer, entrepreneur, power player and future Lord Provost of Glasgow, she was actually married to someone else. Yes, Joe Donn. Their break-up was civilised. In fact it was so lacking in acrimony that Joe gave Margaret a going-away present: Susie.

It turned out that for all his outward potency, Jack Gantry only shot blanks, although he didn't know that at the time. The divorce was through by the time Susie was born, and Jack's name went on her birth certificate. She was raised as his daughter and no one was any the wiser for several years without Susie siblings, until a full-scale medical showed that the Lord Provost's sperm count was lower than East Fife's away goals tally. Even then, the trio kept the facts to themselves, and Susie didn't find out until after her mum was dead and Jack was off in the laughing academy, pronounced crazy as a loon. Gone but not forgotten, though. The gold chain of office has had a couple of wearers since him, but to this day if anyone in Glasgow says, 'The Lord Provost', ten to one on it's Jack Gantry who comes to mind.

Susie and Joe were never close, until he went away. He had been finance director of the Gantry Group when she took over its day-to-day management from Jack, and she had grown up with him as a sort of unofficial uncle, but that didn't save his bacon. He had been absolutely duff as an accountant . . . ideal for the Lord Provost, since it allowed him to get away with all sorts of illegal activity . . . and Susie had fired him at the first opportunity, then had done it again after Jack had tried to reinstate him. But once she discovered the truth, she had him back, not with any hands-on financial responsibilities, but as a non-executive director, someone she could trust alongside her. The Gantry Group runs very smoothly, but Susie liked the extra insurance of having Joe and me alongside her. With a five-person board, the others being Gerry Meek, the new finance director, and Gillian Harvey, the bank's appointee, it gave her a built-in majority should she ever need it.

I let her cry it out by the side of the road from Busby to East Kilbride, and when she was ready, we set off on our way once again. It didn't take long until we reached Motherwell, a town that grew up at the close of the nineteenth century on the backs of the coal and steel industries, then ended the twentieth having to reinvent itself after the former had been worked out and the latter destroyed by a Tory Cabinet four hundred miles away. I never saw the strip and plate mills in their heyday, but from the way Joe described them they must have been a sight to behold, if not to live near.

Naturally, being a well-heeled bloke, his house was as far away from that part of town as you could get. It was in Crawford Street, no more than two or three minutes from the M74 exit, a chunky red-brick detached villa with more than a hint of art deco about it. An ambulance and two cars, one of them a police patrol vehicle, were stationed outside when we got there. The green-suited paramedics were sitting in their cab, talking to two police officers, a man and a woman, who stood on the pavement.

I parked short of them, just down the gentle slope, and took Susie's hand as she climbed out. The older of the two coppers, a sergeant, saw us and turned towards us, quietly crushing a cigarette under a large foot. 'Are you Miss Gantry?' he began.

'Only at work,' she replied, curtly. 'Everywhere else I'm Mrs Blackstone. This is my husband.'

The sergeant barely gave me a glance. Clearly the chap was neither a film fan nor a tabloid reader. 'Fine, but you reported Mr Donn missing?'

'No,' I interrupted. 'When he failed to turn up for a meeting and couldn't be contacted, my wife called his neighbour and asked if she would check on him. The next thing she heard was from you guys, that he was dead.'

'Aye,' the uniform replied. 'It was me that phoned. I'm Sergeant Kennedy.'

'So why did you want us here so fast?' I asked him.

'We needed your wife to identify him, since Mrs Cameron, the neighbour, was in no state to do it. We gather that Mr Donn had no living relatives, so we got back to you.'

'As a matter of fact, he has a sister-in-law, but they haven't spoken in years. But why the rush?'

'We just wanted it done quickly, so we could move him.'

'What do you mean move him? We'll take care of him. We're Joe's family.' It came to me that there was something wrong with the picture; Kennedy's attitude was wrong in some way. 'Look,' I demanded, 'what's happened here? Where is Joe, and how did he die? Was it a heart attack?'

The sergeant shook his head. 'No, it was not. Look, you were acquainted with the deceased and you're prepared to identify him, yes?'

'Yes, on both counts. Joe and I are colleagues; I've known him for years. Let's do it.' I turned and reached out to open the garden gate, but Kennedy put a hand on my arm.

'No, sir,' he said. 'Not that way; he's through here.' It seemed to dawn on him that being customer-friendly was in his remit. 'While we do this, maybe PC Money here can look after your wife, make her a cup of tea, like.'

'I want to come with you,' Susie protested.

I put my hands on her shoulders. 'It doesn't need us both,' I told her. 'Now please, humour me, and humour wee Mac in there. Do as he suggests and go with the constable. And ask her to make one for me while she's at it.'

For once in her life, Susie allowed herself to be persuaded.

As PC Money, whose first name, it emerged, was Cassandra, offering an extra reason to call her Cash for short, led her up the path to the front door, I followed the sergeant to the side of the house and up the driveway. At once I knew where Joe was. The garage had double doors; they were open and his Jaguar was inside. He was always a Jag man. It was like a badge of office to him. There was a rear door, leading to the back garden. It was open too, and the afternoon breeze was blowing through, but I could still smell the fumes.

'Mrs Cameron rang the doorbell after your wife called her,' Kennedy said as we approached. 'She was waiting on the doorstep when she heard the motor. It was just ticking over, very quiet. You had to be that close to hear it. She had the good sense not to try to open the garage herself; she went rushing back to her own house and called the station. Cash and I got here a couple of minutes after the shout, but it was too late, well too late. The doctor reckons he's been dead for several hours.' He stopped. 'It's quite a tight fit in there. Could you go in and take a look?'

From the doorway, I could see the figure in the driver's seat. I edged my way up the side of the Jag and looked through the open window. No surprises. It was Joe all right, and he was dead all right. His face was a funny pink colour. In fact he looked like a guy who's had a couple of bevvies and is sleeping it off. Except I knew that even if he had been a big drinker, which he wasn't, he would never have

41

done anything so stupid as to go to sleep in his car, in a closed garage, with the engine running.

I backed out the way I had come. 'That's Joe all right,' I told the copper. 'Is the doctor still here?'

He nodded. 'She was in the back garden writing up some notes last I saw her.' At that moment a short, busty woman in a tweed suit, maybe aged in her mid-forties, came through the back door of the garage and made her way to us.

'Dr Halliday,' she announced, briskly.

'Oz Blackstone,' I replied, shaking her hand. She blinked and looked closer at my face; this lady did go to the movies.

'Pleased to meet you. Identification complete?'

'Yeah, that's poor old Joe. The sergeant says he's been dead for some time. Is that right?'

'Yes, it is; probably since last night in fact, although the temperature in here with the engine running and everything makes it difficult to be precise. The pathologist should be able to confirm it, though. How did you come to know Mr Donn, Mr Blackstone?' she asked.

'Through business, but there's a family connection too. Joe was once married to my wife's late mother.' The whole truth wasn't relevant, so I kept that to myself. 'What do you think happened?' I continued instead.

'It's a bit obvious what happened, sir,' said Kennedy. 'Suicide by carbon monoxide poisoning.'

'It's not bloody obvious to me. Joe Donn was no more suicidal than you are, Sergeant; maybe less so, for all I know. If you report that to the Fiscal, I'll challenge it. This has to have been an accident.'

'It's difficult to see how you could accidentally gas yourself like that,' Doctor Halliday murmured, sympathetically.

'Joe was always tinkering with his car. Look at the way it's gleaming in there; anything less than perfection was no good to him. He could have heard something wrong with the engine and been checking it. Maybe it was dark, maybe he forgot the doors were closed, or he was overcome far quicker than he could have realised.'

'And maybe life got too much for him,' the sergeant said, 'so he just got behind the wheel, turned on the engine and said goodbye.'

'Was there a note?'

'We haven't looked yet, sir.'

'When you find one I'll start to believe you, but not before. You know what Joe was supposed to be doing tomorrow night? He was in the final of the Lanark Golf Club match-play championship. Joe's been a member for forty years and he's been scratch or damn near it for most of that time, yet he's never won the championship.'

'Maybe he's got the yips since the semi,' Kennedy retorted.

'Not funny.'

The sergeant winced. 'Maybe no', sir. I'm sorry. Still, I don't see this as anything other than a suicide, and that's what I'll be reporting.'

'Don't bet on it.'

His eyes narrowed. 'What do you mean by that, sir?' he said, with the beginning of a threat in his voice.

'I mean that I've got friends.' I took out my mobile. 'I make one phone call and there will be CID here to start a proper investigation. That will not look good for you, so do yourself a favour and call the cavalry yourself.'

Kennedy snorted. 'You think you can call out Strathclyde CID, do you, Mr Blackstone? You're a policeman, are you?'

'As a matter of fact I was, about ten years ago. Not that I hung around long, mind; I didn't like being shouted at by people who thought that having three stripes on their arm made them better than me in some way. I still have contacts, though. As a further matter of fact I was at a Chamber of Commerce dinner a week ago where I was sat next to your chief constable: he asked me to autograph his menu for his wife.' I looked at the sergeant. 'No bullshit,' I said, quietly.

A glimmer of recognition came into his eyes; whether it was of me, or of the inevitable, I wasn't sure. 'If you insist, then,' he muttered, then turned his back on me, walked a few steps away and spoke softly into his radio.

# 7

The CID came all right. They took photos of Joe in the car, and fingerprinted everything in sight, including the doctor and me, in case we had been careless. (They didn't take prints from Sergeant Kennedy and PC Cash Money; all police officers are fingerprinted for elimination purposes, although their records are kept separately from the Bad People.) They supervised the rolling of the Jag from the garage and the removal of Joe's body, then they searched the car.

I watched them from a distance as they did it, and Susie joined me after they had taken Joe off to the mortuary in Glasgow. Crawford Street isn't a place where crowds will gather naturally, but a few people had stopped to spectate. There would have been a lot more if the High School along the road had been in session, but it was closed for the Easter holidays.

The sudden, suspicious death of Joe Donn warranted two detective constables and two technicians. I thought they'd want to take statements from us, but they didn't. I began to wish that I had made that call . . . it would have been to Ricky Ross, whose Masonic arm reached everywhere. They searched the house too. I assumed that they were looking for a suicide note, and it gave me a degree of satisfaction when Kennedy came over to me and admitted that they hadn't found any trace of one.

'Did they check his computer?' I asked. I knew that he had one, since I'd sent him some photos of Janet once, by e-mail.

'I don't know,' he replied. 'But I'll make sure they do, don't you worry.'

There wasn't much to do after that but go home. Gerry Meek had been in the office, waiting for the board meeting, when the call had come from the police, so Susie phoned him from the car to let him

44

know what had happened. Gillian Harvey was out of town, on a visit to a bank client in Sheffield: Susie left a message with her secretary, asking her to call whenever she could.

There was no one else to inform, really, other than Joe's sister-in-law, Mira. I did that when we got back to the house, although with just a bit of trepidation. She had seen some tragedy in her life since our brief meeting, and I couldn't be sure that she didn't blame me for some of it. She was okay, though, sorry to hear about Joe's death, if not exactly grief-stricken. I promised I'd let her know about funeral arrangements, and we left it at that.

I guess that word got around the Motherwell nick after the CID officers reported back to their bosses, and they saw the names on the report. I had a call early that evening from a detective superintendent, who introduced himself as Tom Fallon, Divisional Commander. He didn't have anything startling to tell me; he called to let Susie and me know that the brass was in the know and that the brass was taking it seriously. However he went on to say that there were no signs that Joe's death was suspicious. His people hadn't gone firm on their report to the Procurator Fiscal, but he had steered them towards a finding of accident, subject to the post mortem report, rather than suicide. He assured me that they had 'expedited' the autopsy, and that in fact the old boy was being carved up even as he spoke.

The results came through next morning, after Susie had gone to work. That was one of the hardest things she ever did. She had had a strange relationship with Joe, one that had been turbulent in business terms, but when everything else was stripped away, he was her father, and his death hit her like a hammer. Okay, she had spent most of her life thinking of Jack Gantry as her dad, but blood is blood.

The trouble was, no one knew but me . . . well there was one other who did, but we hadn't seen Prim in a while, and didn't even know where she was . . . and Susie and Joe had decided that they would keep their true relationship secret. So that morning, she put on her tough face, hid the depth of her sorrow and carried on with business as usual.

As he had promised, Detective Superintendent Fallon called again, in the middle of my postponed session with Neil Quinnan, my dialogue coach. 'It'll be accidental death, Mr Blackstone,' he told me: no preamble, straight to the point. 'The PM showed a high blood alcohol level, more than three times over the permitted limit. I'll go with the assumption that he had a wee bit too much to drink, went out to tinker with his car . . . as you told the officers at the scene he liked to do . . . and just got careless. Maybe he switched the engine on to listen to the sound, and just fell asleep. Given that there was no suicide note, and given the other circumstances . . . he had no business worries, he was doing well in the golf championship . . . that's by far the likeliest explanation for the tragedy. I've got no doubt that the Fiscal will accept that.'

The guy was leaning over backwards to be helpful; I could see that. 'Thanks, Mr Fallon. I'm grateful for that, and so will my wife be, when I tell her.'

'My regards to your wife,' he said. 'I was stationed in A Division, in Glasgow, in the Lord Provost's time. I met her quite a few times at functions in the City Chambers, when she was accompanying her father.' I could almost hear him shake his head at the other end of the line. 'It was awful the way that turned out. Quite unbelievable at the time, and as far as I'm concerned it still is.'

My laugh had no humour in it. 'Maybe so, Superintendent, but it didn't stop it all being true.'

'Aye, that's a fact as well. Still, I'm glad it's turned out all right in the end for Miss Gantry and you. She deserves it, after what she's been through. First with her father, then my late and unlamented colleague Inspector Dylan. I really do hate it, you know, when an officer goes to the other side. I take it personally, and most of my colleagues do as well. Fortunately it doesn't happen all that often, and I've certainly never known one who went as bad as he did.'

I tutted my agreement, wondering how he'd react if he knew that Mike Dylan wasn't nearly as late as everyone thought.

'About Mr Donn, sir,' he continued. 'We're in a position to release the body, but I'm not sure who's going to claim it. I believe you told Sergeant Kennedy that there's a sister-in-law.'

'I did, but my wife and I will look after things. I'll instruct an undertaker and he'll be in contact with you.'

By the time Susie got home from the office, the arrangements were well underway. Joe's remains had been moved from the mortuary to a funeral parlour in Motherwell, and plans were in hand for a cremation at a place called Daldowie, in Lanarkshire, five days later, on the following Tuesday.

She kissed me when I told her, then we took Janet for a walk round the garden. We said nothing to her about Papa Joe, of course. Apart from being pointless, it's neither right nor fair to try to tell a two-year-old about death.

# 8

There were other things to be done, of course. The formality of registration had to be completed: I did that next morning in Motherwell, armed with Dr Halliday's death certificate, which I had collected from the friendly detective superintendent, and a cremation certificate signed by two other doctors. Fallon turned out to be a tall, thin man, with an even thinner moustache. I had told Susie about him, but she had no recollection of him from her City Chambers days. 'There were all sorts of people fawning about the Lord Provost back then,' she'd muttered, grimly. 'He'd just have been another face in the crowd.'

On the spur of the moment, I asked the policeman if he had ever encountered Ricky Ross; he responded with a nod, and what I took to be a very knowing wink. 'Oh aye,' he said. 'The famous fallen star. I hear he's rising again. As a matter of fact I was thinking of asking him if he had any openings. I can retire from this lot any time I like now.'

I promised that I would put in a word for him and headed off for the Registrar's Office, and after that for Joe's lawyer. I knew nothing of that side of his life, but I had looked through his papers, in his house, before going to the police station, and found a few letters addressed to a guy named Ewan Maltbie, of a firm called Rusk, Mansell and McGregor, of whom none now figured on the practice letterhead, or, I guessed, among the human race.

I found him in a grey sandstone building near Motherwell Cross. It was a lawyer's office as I had remembered them in my youth. Where Greg McPhillips' place in Glasgow is bright, airy and glassy, screaming 'Top Ranking Corporate Clients' at you as loudly as it can, this was dull, dusty and modestly furnished, the way a solicitor's chambers are supposed to be. Ewan Maltbie matched his surroundings almost perfectly; he had a superior, all-knowing look about him, he was modestly dressed and there was a presence of dandruff on his shoulders like the first light snowfall of a Fife winter.

There was nothing dull about him, though. His eyes were as sharp as little pins and they bored into me across the desk; he never seemed to blink. He didn't smile either, nor do anything else to make me feel welcome. As I looked at him, across the deeds and documents piled high on his desk, he reminded me of my first bank manager.

Maltbie had heard about Joe's death the night before; although there was nothing in the press, word had spread through the Motherwell grapevine like a flash fire through a pine forest. (I saw one of them once in Spain, from a safe distance; the flames swept through the fallen needles on the dry ground at about the same speed as a man could run.) He knew as much as I did; maybe Fallon had told him on the quiet, or maybe it had come from Dr Halliday.

'What exactly is your relationship to my client, Mr Blackstone?' he asked me finally.

'Don't you know?' I countered.

The wee eyes grew even sharper. 'Maybe I can't answer that.'

'Why couldn't you?'

'Maybe my client told me something once, but it was in confidence. Let's say he did, but that there was no proof of what he was saying, none at all. And he certainly didn't say that he'd told anyone else. For all I know, sir, you're on a fishing trip; if you are I'm not going to be caught.' His chest puffed out as he finished, as if he was telling me that he was a big man in this town. I was reminded of a character in a script that Roscoe had sent to me a few months earlier: we'd turned it down.

I gave him what was meant to be my 'Isn't this tedious' expression. 'I grew up in a fishing village,' I told him. 'If I was trying to catch you, I would. Now let's stop the sparring. I'll answer your question, then you can answer a couple of mine. Joe Donn was a main board director of my wife's company, the Gantry Group. I'm a director too, so he and I were colleagues at that level. We also had a more personal connection. Joe was my father-in-law.' Still Maltbie didn't blink. 'Your lack of reaction tells me,' I continued, 'that was the thing he may or may not have mentioned to you in confidence.'

49

'Let's say it was,' the lawyer murmured. 'But there remains the question of proof. I concede that Mr Donn did tell me some time ago that he believed that he, and not Lord Provost Gantry, was the father of his former wife's child. However he told me also that her birth certificate says the opposite.'

'It still does,' I conceded. 'But you're not quite up to speed on the issue. After Joe told Susie what he believed to be the truth, they agreed between them that they would confirm it by having DNA comparisons made.' I took an envelope from my document case and handed it to him, across the mountain of documents. 'That's the report; my solicitor assures me that it's all the proof a court would need. You can take a copy if you wish, to be retained on Joe's file, although not to be passed to anyone else without my wife's written permission.'

Maltbie slid out the A4 sheets and read through them, carefully. When he was finished, he nodded. 'I concur with your solicitor's opinion,' he said. 'I'm sorry Joe didn't choose to confide in me that he had done this.'

'What would it have changed?'

'My reaction to your visit, for one thing. It obviates my concern that Joe's body has been released to you.'

'Which reminds me,' I interrupted. 'Did Joe leave any specific instructions with you regarding his funeral?'

Maltbie shook his head. 'No, none at all.'

'That's fine, then.' I told him about our provisional arrangements.

He grunted agreement. 'Tell the undertaker to send me the bill. I'll meet it from the estate.'

'That won't be necessary,' I replied. 'My wife wants to bury her father herself.'

'I understand,' said Maltbie . . . whether he did or not. 'About Joe's death,' he went on, sounding hesitant for the first time. 'Do you have any view?'

'What do you mean?'

'Ah, I don't know, really. The police are calling it an accident. You were there, I gather. You don't think it might have been . . .'

'Suicide?' I retorted. 'Listen, I'm the main reason they're calling it an accident. No way was Joe suicidal. The verdict is that he had a bit

50

too much to drink, went into the garage to play with his car, and fell asleep with the engine running. It's cast iron.'

'No, I didn't mean suicide.'

I looked at Maltbie in a new light; the man had an imagination after all. I couldn't help laughing. 'You're kidding me, aren't you? Did Joe have an enemy in the world, that you know of?'

'No,' he conceded.

'You're not suggesting that his opponent in the Lanark championship final might have got a bit extreme, are you?'

The lawyer glared at me. 'Hardly. Joe was due to play my nephew.'

'In that case, forget it.'

'I suppose so. It's just that Joe wasn't much of a drinking man.'

'He wasn't dry either. They found a bottle of Amarone empty in the kitchen, and its contents in his stomach, at the autopsy. That's powerful stuff, if you're not used to it. A bottle would send me to sleep, I reckon, and I can shift a bit more than Joe.'

Maltbie shrugged his shoulders; the gesture caused a small flurry of dandruff. 'I suppose so,' he conceded, with a heavy hint of disappointment in his voice.

'I suppose also,' he went on, abruptly, 'that you'll want to know about the will.'

Actually, I didn't; indeed the thought had never occurred to me. I had only gone along to see the man to discuss the funeral. 'Joe left a will?'

'Of course. And there you certainly do have a locus, Mr Blackstone.'

'Eh? Joe hasn't left anything to Susie and me, has he?'

'As a matter of fact he has. He's left you his golf clubs . . . two sets, one Taylormade, about two years old, and the other a mix of Callaway ERC woods and Big Bertha irons. He acquired them at the start of the season; he asserted to me that they helped him play the best golf of his life. They don't come guaranteed, I'm afraid.'

I smiled. I'd given Joe the Callaways as a Christmas present, but I didn't tell that to Maltbie. He thought I was responding to his attempted joke and grinned back. 'On the other hand, Mrs Blackstone's legacy certainly does,' he said. 'You may be aware that Mr Donn was a keen collector of crystal.' I was indeed aware. On the few occasions

51

I'd been to Joe's place I'd seen it and admired it. 'All of it goes to your wife.'

I felt a twinge of something in my stomach; I felt oddly grateful to Joe, and I think I realised at that point just how much Susie and I would miss him. He may have been a bloody awful accountant, but he was a nice bloke, a friend to Susie as well as, in truth more than, a dad, and most important of all he'd been invariably on her side. Without his presence, and without his vote when needed, I had a feeling that our board meetings wouldn't be as smooth as they had been in the past.

'The rest of the movable estate, that is to say the furniture, paintings etc., goes to charity,' the solicitor continued, 'or the proceeds of its sale will. There are two small bequests of five thousand pounds each, to South Dalziel Parish Church, and to Lanark Golf Club.' He took a deep breath: I could tell that the meaty part was coming up. 'With one exception, the balance of the estate, that is the proceeds from the sale of the house in Crawford Street and of his car, plus the cash of which he died possessed, will, after payment of inheritance tax and professional fees, be placed in trust for your daughter, and for any further children you and Mrs Blackstone may have. You and your wife will be the trustees; winding up of the trust will be at your discretion, once the last beneficiary has reached the age of eighteen.'

I whistled, then found myself smiling again. Trust Joe to provide for the grandchildren; he had always thought that I lived in Fairyland . . . he wasn't a million miles wrong . . . and I guessed that in his heart of hearts he had worried that Susie might not be able to run the business without him. If I was right it was pretty rich, since Joe had been partly responsible for the Group winding up at the door of the knacker's yard, from which she had saved it, but in the circumstances, I was prepared to forgive him.

All of a sudden an alarm bell rang in my head. 'What about Joe's shares in the Gantry Group?' I asked. This was not a daft question. Joe owned just under seven per cent of the business, a chunk which, at current value, was worth around two million quid.

The structure of the group was complicated. Effectively, Susie owned a controlling interest in the business, but it wasn't straightforward. Her shares were locked up, like the kids' money from Joe would be, in a trust, of which she was the sole beneficiary. Before he went off his trolley, or at least before anyone noticed that he was off his trolley, Jack Gantry had signed over control to her, irrevocably. The legals had been done by a very high-powered firm of corporate specialists in Edinburgh, and her position was completely secure. I knew this because I'd asked Greg McPhillips to give me a second opinion on the way it was set up. He'd referred it to a top QC, who'd pronounced it iron-clad.

It may have been, but it tied her in too; she couldn't sell, even if she wanted to, other than in the event of an outright takeover of the group that was unanimously agreed by the shareholders. In essence, that meant that Joe had to vote for it.

When Jack Gantry had owned and run the group, he had held ninety per cent of the shares himself. The other ten per cent had been gifted to Joe Donn, years earlier, on the basis that they could only be sold with Jack's permission. That veto over the sale had passed to Susie through the trust.

Many things had changed since Jack had gone to the funny farm. For one there was the question of successor. The trust specified that in the event of Susie's death, its benefits and control would pass to her next of kin . . . other than Jack. At the time it was drawn up and signed, this had meant her hated aunt, the Lord Provost's sister, to whom she never spoke. But with Janet's birth, things had changed. The trust gave me no rights of succession; what it did was to specify that on Susie's death, her holding would pass to her children. In other words, my daughter and unborn son were heirs to a very considerable fortune . . . two, if you count mine.

The other significant change was in the structure of the company itself. Quite naturally, an enormous scandal had followed the unmasking of the Lord Provost as a murderer, drug baron and overall major league criminal. It had reached a crescendo when he was packed off to the State Hospital at Carstairs, without limit of time, into the care of the Secretary of State for Scotland, and later the First Minister.

In the aftermath, the bankers and assorted creditors who had collectively invested millions in the sprawling enterprise that was the Gantry Group had, not unnaturally, collectively shit themselves. When

Jack had installed Susie as chief executive, they had all gone along with it, because none of them had believed that she was actually running the show. In truth, she hadn't been, not entirely. The Lord Provost had always kept an eye on things, and offered 'advice' whenever she did something he didn't agree with. When she fired Joe as finance director, he bided his time, but when an opportunity to reinstate him came up, he had taken it.

With the great Jack gone, it was touch and go for a while; there was talk that the bankers might make Susie take a figurehead role, and force the appointment of their nominee as chief executive, but her extraordinary powers of persuasion won her a trial period. They found she could be tough too. They tried to insist on appointing new directors to the board to give them a voting majority, but she refused point blank. In the end they settled for Gillian Harvey as their sole representative.

From gathering round her like feeding dogs, it took very little time before they were eating out of Susie's hand. She took a series of strategic decisions, and put them into practice swiftly and, where necessary, ruthlessly. She identified potential weaknesses in the group Jack had built, and eliminated them. The Healthcare Division, a series of labour-intensive nursing homes through which the Lord Provost and his nasty nephew had obtained prescription drugs for sale on the streets, was the first to go. It was sold to another group, once she had cleaned up the operation by firing all the managers for failing to detect Jack's racket, or as she suspected in some cases, for turning a blind eye to it.

That, and a few shrewd sales of industrial properties, changed the cash position of the group; within a year of Jack Gantry's downfall, Susie had gone from being at the mercy of the bankers to being their mistress. She renegotiated the terms of their relationship, won herself a rolling borrowing facility that meant she didn't have to trot along to her bank manager's office to have every decision okayed, and put in place a five-year development strategy, based on sound research into future market trends, rather than on sheer guesswork, as most of her predecessor's projects had been. This is not to say that the Lord Provost was an idiot, but for sure his success was based as much on luck . . . and political power . . . as on judgement.

Her salvation of the Gantry Group won her the first of her Scottish Businesswoman of the Year awards. Her second came after she had floated the company on the Stock Exchange. After her early treatment by the bank's corporate department, Susie hadn't been entirely happy to have them funding all her future projects. So, after discussing things with Joe and Gerry Meek, she had decided to raise extra capital by going for a stock market listing. The lawyers conferred, and confirmed that this was something she could do under the terms of the trust. Her holding would simply be converted into shares in the new public company that would be created, and she would continue to control the business. Only one third of the company would be offered to the market.

It went through without a hitch. The group was valued at sixty million pounds, and the twenty million shares on offer were snapped up. As soon as trading opened their value rose by a third; with very limited trading they had stayed at that level until the downturn in the market took them back down to par. We didn't panic when that happened, though; it still left Susie worth a right few quid.

'Well?' I repeated to Mr Maltbie. 'What about Joe's shareholding?'

The solicitor pursed his lips. 'That's an interesting one,' he said. 'I'm sure it will revert to your offspring in due course, but it can't yet, I'm afraid. You see, technically it isn't part of the estate.'

I frowned and then I got it. 'Let me guess. They're held by a trust too.'

'Got it in one,' the solicitor murmured. 'Inheritance tax shelter. I'm surprised you didn't know that already.'

It's not easy to kick yourself effectively while you're sitting down, but I managed it nonetheless. A director of a company might be expected to be reasonably familiar with its shareholder register, and that would have told me right away. Worse, I was on the damn thing myself. Since Susie and I had been together, I had been building up a small shareholding in the company; a show of solidarity as much as anything else.

'Who set it up?' If ever there was a rhetorical question, that was it. Joe wasn't the sort of accountant who'd have thought that sort of arrangement up for himself. He was a common sense guy, but once the beans got above the five-figure mark he had always

55

struggled to count them. Plus, he'd never lived like a millionaire, or referred to himself as one, nor I reckoned even thought of himself in that way. No, considering the origin of the holding, there was only one answer.

'Lord Provost Gantry did,' Maltbie confirmed. 'Joe benefited from the dividend income from the shares, but he had no effective right of disposal. In addition to the chairman's right to veto any proposed sale, there is a pre-emption clause which gives Mr Gantry first refusal.'

'And with Joe's death . . .?'

'With his death, the shares revert back to Mr Gantry.'

'What, you mean they go into Susie's trust holding?'

'No, I do not. They revert directly to him.'

'But he's in the slammer,' I protested. 'He's in a maximum security mental hospital.'

'That doesn't stop him owning property.'

'It doesn't stop him owning a significant shareholding in a public company?'

'No, it doesn't.' Maltbie raised his right index finger, pointing at the dull, discoloured ceiling of his office. 'But it does stop him exercising some of the rights and privileges of a shareholder. He's entitled to participate in dividends, but he can't vote himself.'

I had never thought of Jack Gantry as a legal entity; in truth I had stopped thinking of him as a human being a long time ago. As far as Susie and I were concerned he was dead; that was how we coped best with our memories. His name was never mentioned in our house; there were no photographs of him, not even in Susie's childhood albums. She had destroyed them all, as she had thrown out every memento of the time when she had held the courtesy title of Lady Provost, and had accompanied him to official functions.

'So what happens to those rights and privileges? Are they just in limbo?'

'No, that's not the case. The Criminal Procedure and the Mental Health Acts make provision for someone to be appointed to take such decisions on behalf of a detained patient. As in England, he'll be regarded as a ward of court, more or less.'

'And in the case of a barker like Jack, who would this person be? The First Minister?'

'No, that wouldn't be usual. It would normally be a lawyer or accountant. On the other hand it is possible for a person's local authority to be appointed as his guardian, if there's nobody else.'

I gasped, then bellowed with laughter. 'What? You mean that the mighty Jack Gantry's gone from exercising complete power over Glasgow City Council to being completely in its power?'

The solicitor allowed himself a thin smile. 'You find irony in that?'

'I think it's fucking hilarious actually. Jack used to scare the shit out of all the officials in the City Chambers, and most of the councillors. I'll bet some of them would enjoy getting even.'

'They wouldn't quite have that sort of licence. The Mental Welfare Commission would be down on them like a ton of bricks. But . . .' He paused, and the extended finger was replaced by the palm of his hand held up like a traffic cop. '. . . as I understand the circumstances of Mr Gantry's case, he would be a State patient, and as such his hospital consultants would be responsible for him. I'm no expert in these areas, but where a patient has substantial resources it would be almost certain that the court would appoint a professional person to act on his behalf.

'Whatever the circumstances, the shares will not become inactive in voting terms.'

I wasn't laughing any more. Whoever was feeding Jack his gruel, I still didn't fancy having to tell Susie that one dad had replaced another as a major shareholder of the Gantry Group.

# 9

I needn't have worried. Susie had known all along what would happen to Joe's shareholding in the event of his death. I'd thought I'd been clever in tracking Mr Maltbie to his lair, but unlike me, my wife is a very good and conscientious director of a public company, and she had a metaphorical finger on the pulse of every one of its members.

'Can you do anything about it?' I asked her that evening, after I had given her a run-down on my day, as we sat beside the pool enjoying a nice chilled bottle of Sancerre.

'No. Not a damn thing.'

'You're not bothered?'

'Of course I'm bloody bothered! I don't want to be connected with him in any way. I wish with all my heart that it was him in that box in the undertaker's and not Joe. But sadly it isn't. He's still drawing breath and, no doubt, ordering his guards about each and every day, as if he was still the big cheese. Happily, that's one thing he'll never be able to do to me again. I may have to have him back as a shareholder, but his influence will never reach into my office, or into our boardroom.'

'How would you feel if I contacted his trustees in lunacy, or whatever the hell they're called, and offered to buy the shares? Just so you can be rid of him for good.'

Susie smiled at me. 'Curator bonis,' she said.

'What's that? An ice-cream or something?'

'A Curator bonis is a person appointed by the court to look after the affairs of someone who's mentally handicapped. You're a love, Oz, but I couldn't let you do that. Have you any idea what Joe's shares are worth?'

'About four million. Do you know what I'm going to earn this year, given the deals that Roscoe's done for me?'

She reached across and squeezed my hand. 'You're a love, you really are. Listen, I know you've been buying shares on the quiet, but that's too big a chunk.'

I shrugged. 'At the current price it would be a good investment. I might just do it anyway. The way I understand it, now the shares have reverted back to Jack, you don't have a veto over their sale.'

'That's true, I don't. But there are other reasons why you shouldn't do it. For a start, you need a willing seller to do a deal. I don't know who the Curator bonis is . . . although I'm bound to find out when Joe's estate is processed and the transfer is notified to the company's registrar . . . but given the value of the property he's looking after, he's probably a big-firm accountant or a heavy duty corporate lawyer. Whatever, he isn't going to be a mug, and if he's doing his job properly, he'll view those shares as a good long-term investment. If he sells them at all, it'll be at a premium. You'll have to pay over the odds, and if you do that . . .' She took a sip of her wine and gave me a knowing look. When Susie's business brain moves into overdrive, I struggle to keep up with her, but I always do my best.

'You and I are husband and wife; effectively what's mine is yours and vice versa. I own sixty per cent of the business as it is, through the trust; if you do this deal it'll take our family holding to damn near seventy per cent. On top of that, if you buy at the price Jack's Curator's likely to settle for, word will get around. What if the other share-holders, who are mainly institutional, get wind and come to us wanting the same price for theirs. We'd be in a pickle.'

'Couldn't the group buy them in?'

She snorted. 'Sure, and fuck up its cash position. We'd be back where we started, a family-owned business at the mercy of those fickle bastards who are decision-makers in the banks, who are in turn at the mercy of their institutional shareholders. No, Oz my darling boy; noble as your motives may be, I'm not going to let you compromise us.'

'What are you going to do, then?'

'Nothing. When the transfer takes effect I'll sit tight and see what the Curator does. My guess is he'll do nothing at all.'

'What if he offers you the shares?'

'Why the hell should he do that?'

'Does Jack know that you know he's not your real father?'

She seemed to jump in her chair, then settled back into its thick cushions, her brow suddenly furrowed by a frown. 'I don't know,' she murmured. 'But unless Joe told him, I can't imagine how he would. You know I haven't seen him or spoken to him since he went away, but I can't say for sure that Joe didn't keep in touch with him. They were friends from way back, after all.'

'Has Jack ever tried to contact you?'

'Only the once, after he was committed to the State Hospital. I had a letter from him.'

'You never told me that.'

'You never asked me till now. But that's not surprising. Let's face it, Oz; if one of us has a reason to hate Jack Gantry it's you, rather than me. I found out everything he did, from Mike, and I know that Jan's death wasn't an accident.'

I looked away from her, across the pool, as I replayed in my mind's eye my last meeting with the maniacal Lord Provost, when he had justified himself to the last. I had wanted to kill him then, and if my friends hadn't been there to prevent me I might have done just that. I had never spoken of that night to Susie, and even if Mike Dylan had when he was around, I still didn't want to.

'So what did you do with the Lord Provost's letter?' I didn't ask her what it had contained.

'I sent it back to him, via the State Hospital superintendent, and told him that I wanted no further contact with him, of any sort. The superintendent replied; he said that he understood, and that he would take care of it for me. So far he's been as good as his word.'

'Long may it stay that way,' I said, a touch grimly, 'and long may the old bastard stay out there in Carstairs, enjoying his drug-infested porridge.'

I resolved to think no more of Jack Gantry, and to forget any notion of bidding for his shares in the group that still bore his name. Instead, I settled into my chair, smiled at my wife, and thought of my own Dad. I was due to give Mac the Dentist a phone call. I had still to tell him about Joe: I had put off doing that until I could give him the whole package, funeral arrangements and everything.

There was something else I probably had to tell him too. She had not been at the forefront of my thoughts since the bombshell in Motherwell had exploded, but Andrea Neiporte was still there. I had wondered whether to spill the beans to Mac or not, but I was coming down on the side of 'Yes'. If she was capable of tossing a can of paint at me, she was probably still capable of making trouble for him.

Jay had reported to me, that evening and the night before, that there had been no sightings of her on the video cameras at the entrance to the estate, or anywhere else for that matter. That was good; my guess was that the thing at the premiere had been her way of getting back at me for roughing up her old man. Still, I couldn't be certain, so Mac had to be told.

Susie, on the other hand, had not; she had written the incident off as a nutter at work, and there was no sense in making her any the wiser.

I decided to speak to my Dad as soon as Susie left for work next morning. That was first on my list. But what further action to take against the Neiportes ran it a close second.

# 10

I had intended to phone Mac the Dentist, but with a long, almost empty day stretching out in front of me I decided to give him the bad news in person. So, once Susie had gone, driving herself in the big Beamer, I told Janet that she was going to see her Granddad, and loaded her into the Freelander that we kept for knocking around the estate.

I'd have left it as a father and daughter outing, but Jay Yuille is a conscientious guy. He pointed out that he was employed principally as our bodyguard and that he could hardly be guarding them if they were seventy miles away. I have to confess that there have been occasions when I've found Jay's omnipresence just a wee bit intrusive, but I've always managed to keep those feelings to myself, since I'm the guy whose lifestyle made him necessary in the first place.

So I yielded to his insistence and let him come with us. I took the wheel, though, with him in the front passenger seat fulfilling the valuable function of picking Janet's toys up and handing them back to her each time she threw one on the floor. I drove sedately, because of the precious passenger, and because the Freelander, while it's a chunky motor, isn't exactly a flying machine.

The Forth Bridge was quiet heading north . . . it always is in the morning, but wait till the Edinburgh commuters head for home . . . and soon we were on the new road which heads for the East Neuk in more or less a straight line. Normally I'd have headed for Anstruther through Elie and St Monans, but there was a degree of urgency, in that Janet would soon be needing a pit stop.

My stepmother was at home when we arrived; she'd taken early retirement from teaching, and was only doing the occasional supply job. Things were completely natural between the two of us now, and I was grateful for that. Mary had been my mother-in-law before she'd married my Dad; Jan's death had shattered her as much as it had me. Afterwards she'd had to live with Prim's return to the scene, then our break-up. I hadn't been sure how she'd react to wee Janet, but she'd been a gem, accepting her as she would have any grandchild. As usual, she was all over her like a rash when we pulled up, unannounced. 'Why didn't you warn me?' she scolded me.

Janet had been to Enster often enough to have sussed out its main attractions. For example, there's a café on the harbour front. 'Ice-cweam,' was all she needed to say to Mary before she found herself loaded into her push-chair and heading for the town. Once again Jay insisted on going along, and this time I had no qualms about it, as the idiocy of bringing my daughter to a place where people might be after her father and grandfather began to dawn on me.

We had passed the Nciporte cottage on the way through Pittenweem, and I had pointed it out to Jay. He had said nothing, but a cold light had seemed to come on in his eyes.

When they had gone, I was left alone in my Dad's house, waiting in his kitchen for him to come through from the surgery, once he had finished mauling his twelve o'clock patient. I allowed him his usual twenty-minute average. I filled the kettle on the quarter-past mark, and five or six minutes later was stirring two mugs of coffee by the sink when I heard him walk in behind me.

'What the f . . .'

I turned to face him at the sound of his hearty greeting, a mug in each hand . . . and almost dropped them. There were dark circles under my father's eyes that I had never seen before. His broad shoulders seemed to droop as he stood there, and his pale blue nylon surgery tunic seemed to hang loose on him. I felt as if I was looking at a man I didn't know.

'No, Dad,' I said. 'That's my line.'

I handed him one of the mugs, turned him around and propelled him through to the living room. When he was sat in his armchair, I leaned forward in mine and looked at him, forcing him to look in my direction. 'You look like the picture in Dorian Gray's fucking attic,' I told him. (My Dad and I have never been anything other than frank with each other.)

63

'Thanks, son, for your vote of confidence,' he retorted. Even his voice sounded weary. 'You look pretty sharp yourself. Are you here alone?'

'No, I'm with you. Janet and Mary have gone on an ice-cream mission; Jay's with them.'

'Jay? Kevin bloody Costner, you mean, or should it be Frank bloody Farmer . . . whatever his name was in that bodyguard movie. He didn't do you and Susie much good at the premiere the other night.'

'Yes he did. He took most of the stuff. Jay's a good guy, so don't worry about us. What's with you? Have you been bothered by that American twat again?'

'Not him.'

'I didn't mean him.'

'She's English, remember. Yes, I had a call from her. It was . . .'

'Does she still want money?' I interrupted

'No, she didn't say any more about that. It was . . . it was unpleasant, that's all. She just screamed abuse at me, called me terrible names, said terrible things to me.'

'How many calls?'

'Two. One the day after you were here, then another a few days ago, the day after your premiere in fact.'

I heard a low growl, and realised that I was its source. 'Bitch,' I rumbled. 'I'm sorry, Dad: I made a mistake. I put the fear of God almighty into the husband, thinking that would be enough. Clearly, I should have done the same to her. That's not beyond redemption, though.'

Mac the Dentist shook his head. 'Don't make it any worse, son. Leave her alone, please.'

'I don't know if I can do that. It was Andrea Neiporte who chucked that can of paint at me at the premiere.'

His mouth dropped open, revealing his crooked, coffee-stained lower teeth . . . funny thing, but as far as I've seen, dentists rarely present good advertisements for their profession. 'Wh . . .' He looked stunned. 'How do you know that?'

'The police showed me a photo.'

I'll swear he went white under his tan. 'You didn't tell them who she was, did you?'

64

'Of course not.'

'Will they find out?'

'Not unless her mug's on the police computer and they do a check. They won't, though.'

My Dad stared at the empty fireplace. 'Let it rest, son.'

'It's hard for me to do that. The woman's tried to extort money from you; now she's persecuting you.'

'I know, I know. She's a nasty piece of work. But I set myself up for it. I should have stopped the procedure when Arthur was called away. Christ, I should never have done it in the first place. I should have told her that if she wanted a general she'd have to go to the dental hospital.'

'You mean there could be professional implications for you if the story comes out?'

'It's possible.'

'But that's ridiculous,' I protested. 'You've practised impeccably for thirty-five years.'

'Means nothing. If this goes public I could be for the high jump. So please, son. Let's just hope that she's got her frustration out of her system. Leave her alone.'

I had never seen him like this before, not even after my Mum's death, when he hit the bevvy pretty hard. That made me even angrier with Mr and Mrs Neiporte, but I heard what he was saying. 'Okay,' I said, eventually. 'I'll steer clear . . . until the next time she calls you, or shows up anywhere near me. She does that, and she gets a correction, as a friend of mine used to say.'

# 11

By the time Grandma Mary, Janet and Jay came back from the harbour, I had reassured my Dad as best I could. I'd also given him the bad news about Joe Donn. He was as shocked as I knew he'd be, and he asked me for the funeral details, insisting that he'd be there if it meant cancelling appointments.

I kept an eye on Mary over lunch, but she didn't seem worried about him. Sometimes, the closer you are to someone, the less likely you are to notice change, if it's gradual.

Once we had eaten, and Janet had been toileted, we got ready for the road. Rather than going straight back home, we took a detour over the hill to St Andrews. It was Friday afternoon, so Jonathan and Colin would be clear of school and I decided to give them a chance to see the wee cousin on whom they both doted. As I've said, I'm very attached to both my nephews, having become a bit of a surrogate dad since Ellen and Allan split up, but I keep a particular eye on Jonny. The older he's grown, the more of myself I've seen in him, and I'm determined that only the good bits are going to come to the surface. Colin, on the other hand . . . well he's just Colin. He's as wild as purple heather, but I've a strange notion that if either of them takes after his father and becomes a work-obsessed nerd, it'll be him.

There was a time when Allan Sinclair tried to be a normal family guy. My Dad and I took him golfing with us, but he was crap; he just didn't like the game. I tried him out at fishing, but all he ever did was fall in. He joined a five-a-side group at work, but broke his ankle. He even joined a rough shooting group, but after not very long they asked him to stay away for everyone's safety. Then the job in France came up; he moved Ellie and the kids out to a remote picturesque village, and left them there all day as he worked longer and longer hours. Finally, my sister did the inevitable; she moved out, went home to Fife and found a teaching job. Allan made a few noises, but the truth was that he was so wrapped up in his computer development work that he hardly noticed.

We found the lads where I'd guessed, kicking a ball around outside their mother's school, waiting for her to finish her week's admin so that she could knock off too. If Ellie was surprised to see us, she didn't show it, but she did button-hole me at the first opportunity. 'You seen Mac?' she asked. She's always been less reverent towards our father than me.

'Yup.'

'What's up with him? I was down there with the boys last weekend and he was like a bloody grizzly. Colin was mucking around, and he actually fetched him a clump round the ear. He's never done that before. I don't remember him ever laying a finger on either of us when we were kids. I hit the roof, of course; I took the boys home, and I haven't spoken to him since. I'm worried about him, though, Oz. Has he said anything to you?'

I hadn't been ready for that, and I was angered by it, but I busked it as best I could. 'Yes. He's got a bit of man's trouble,' I said, mysteriously, but as casually as I could make it sound. 'It's the sort of thing that comes with age, and it's nothing serious, so don't worry about it.'

'What, you mean getting up to pee in the middle of the night, that sort of man's trouble?'

'You get the idea.' Being a good actor is an advantage in many ways. 'Make allowances for him; give him a wide berth for a while if you think it's best. I'll give him a bollocking and tell him to make it up with Colin. He seems to be growing by the day too. Is he needing a new bike?'

'In-line skates,' she replied. 'You know, roller-blades. They're the rage in St Andrews right now.'

I slipped her a hundred from the roll in my pocket. 'Buy them and tell him they're from the Old Man. I'll get the dough off him next time I see him.'

She took it, but snorted. 'It'll cost him more than that. Jonny's still upset with him; you know how he looks out for his wee brother.' Without a word, I peeled off another hundred and handed it over. My Dad's tab was building up, and I'd make sure he paid it too. He hadn't told me about clouting the wee fella, because he'd have known for sure how I'd react. 'Colin's the safest kid in St Andrews, you know,' she continued, with a strange, soft, un-Ellie-like look of pride in her eyes. 'He's a little bugger, but he gets away with it, because none of his pals would dream of tackling Jonny.'

'Jonny? He's as nice a kid as you'd meet in a day's march. I've never seen him lift a hand to anyone.'

'He doesn't have to. There's just something about him behind all that niceness that says "Don't. You wouldn't really want to do that, would you." It's not threatening, but it's just as persuasive. You were the same when you were his age, you know.'

'Me?'

'Yes, you. Maybe you never realised it, but you were a man of respect at secondary school. Big Man on Campus, that sort of thing, although you never, ever threw your weight around. And of course at primary, you had me to look out for you.' A job she'd done very well, I conceded.

'Maybe it's me the lads don't want to cross now,' I suggested. 'Or big Darius. Are you still seeing him?'

My sister has a boyfriend. Darius Henke is one of the top performers in the Global Wrestling Alliance, a team-mate of my friends Everett Davis, Jerry Gradi and, of course, Liam Matthews.

'Yes, but not in St Andrews. I don't want to be the talk of the town. When he's free, I park the boys in Anstruther and we go somewhere nice. I've seen quite a bit of him lately, 'cos he's been on the injured list.' I'd heard that from Liam. 'Anyway, it's neither him nor you. Jonny doesn't stand in anyone's shadow.'

I looked across at him as we spoke. If anything, he seemed even taller than the last time I'd seen him, not that many days before; his features were taking on an adult cast and his shoulders seemed to be widening, taking on the bony look that comes with adolescence. 'Has he got a girlfriend yet?' I asked.

'There's someone in his year that he's friendly with, a lawyer's daughter. I don't encourage it, though. They're too young.'

I grinned at her. 'When they stop being too young, there won't be a fucking thing you can do about it. Want me to have a chat with him?'

It was my sister's turn to smile. 'There was a time, not that long ago, when I'd have said that would have been like sending him to the Casanova school for chastity. But you seem to have mellowed as a thirty-something. Aye, go on, if you want.'

'Bring them down to see us then. Come next weekend, in fact, before Darius gets signed off the crocks' list.'

Ellen pursed her lips, looking doubtful. 'Oh, I don't know about bringing Darius. We've never done the deed, so to speak, under the same roof as the boys.'

'Bloody hell, sister,' I laughed. 'Do you want me to have a talk with you as well?'

# 12

Joe's funeral was a strange affair from Susie's point of view. He was her father and yet she gave a sort of precedence to his sister-in-law Mira . . . her aunt, although I don't believe that she had any idea that she was. The crematorium chapel was full to overflowing; I knew that the old boy had been popular, but the turnout of colleagues, golf buddies, friends and neighbours took me by surprise. After the service was over and the curtains had closed . . . I always find that sort of send-off a bit theatrical . . . I took the precaution of calling the hotel in Bothwell that we had booked for the reception, and telling them to double the order of sandwiches.

True to his word, my Dad came through from Fife. He and Mary stayed close to Susie and me in the chapel, and we were well into the reception before I was able to isolate him for the word I wanted to drop into his shell-like. He took the rocket I gave him with appropriate contrition, promised to make a fuss of both Colin and Jonny, and even promised to send me a cheque for two hundred quid. 'Consider it a fine for being a grumpy old bastard,' I told him. 'And it'll be double for a second offence.'

I had hoped that Joe's send-off would draw a line under the unpleasantness in my life, and it did . . . for a day or two, at least. I worked on my movie script but enjoyed my break at the same time, getting a round of golf in at the new Loch Lomond course. It isn't too far from the estate, so I'd become a member. Pricey, but it's a great course.

I was able to play at home too; the previous owner of the place was a golf nut and he'd laid out three holes in one corner, well away from the house. It had been a real selling point as far as I was concerned. Old Willie, the gardener, grumbled about having to keep the greens cut, but he was a master at it. I'd even inherited a golf cart, an electric buggy which joined the ranks of my favourite toys . . . and Janet's too. The pair of us liked nothing more than jumping into it of a morning and cruising the place, and if you have a garden that's the size of a small county it helps to have something to get around in.

The estate's one deficiency, from a Janet point of view, was its lack of outdoor facilities. This was brought home to me by my younger nephew, when Ellie brought them . . . and Darius . . . for the promised weekend. 'You know, Uncle Oz,' said Colin, as he climbed up beside me for a trip in the buggy, 'it's a pity Janet doesn't have a proper playground.'

I blinked at him in surprise. 'What are you talking about, young man? This whole place is her playground. She's got a swimming pool, and a wee golf course and everything.' As I spoke I looked across the field and saw Jonny, with a better action than mine, hit a near perfect wedge shot to about four feet from the pin; as I watched him I decided I'd give him Joe's Callaways, since he looked good enough to handle them. The lad seemed to have set out on a futile attempt to teach Darius the basics of the game . . . it was bound to be futile because when you're six feet ten, golf is bloody nearly impossible.

'But she doesn't have a swing,' Colin countered, bringing my attention back to him, 'or a slide, or a climbing frame.'

'Which you would also find useful?' I suggested. He gave me a wide-eyed, innocent, 'Who? Me?' smile.

He had a point, though. When I mentioned it to Susie she agreed with him, and so we told Jay to hire a contractor and get it done. 'I'll build it myself,' he volunteered. 'Give me a shopping list of the things you want and I'll source them. Installation won't be a problem; it'll just be a matter of setting them in a solid foundation. We've got a cement mixer here and all the other tools I'll need.'

That evening Colin and I went net-surfing and found a website called 'rainbowplay', which offered a fantastic range of climbing frames, sandpits, picnic tables, club-houses, and even tree-houses 'for gardens that don't have trees'. I was as hooked as he was, so I called their enquiry number and ordered the lot, plus a small club-house for delivery to Ellie's garden in St Andrews. (What's the point of being a rich uncle if you don't act like one?)

71

That was a great weekend, a time of idyllic, undisturbed existence . . . and then the bombshell hit.

To be exact, it came through the front door of the Gantry Group headquarters building, in a padded envelope addressed to Susie and marked 'personal'. She'd have opened it too, only she didn't go to the office that morning, but straight to a site meeting at a major housing development that we had launched on the outskirts of Glasgow. This project was so big, it was more new town than housing estate, with retail units and a new primary school, towards which the Group was contributing a large chunk of money. It was called New Bearsden, and it was to have the prestige to match the original version, one of Greater Glasgow's swankiest suburbs.

The parcel lay unopened in her in-tray, on her secretary's desk, until, at just after eleven am, before the eyes of an astonished Denise, it gave a soft 'crump' (at least that's how she described it) and burst open of its own accord, sending a sheet of flame high into the air. By the time she stopped screaming and recovered enough composure to grab the nearest fire extinguisher, the package was reduced to ash along with the rest of Susie's morning mail, and the in-tray was a lump of melted plastic on a badly scorched desk.

Gerry Meek was the first of the senior executives on the scene. He had the presence of mind to do two things: one, lock the office door behind him so that no one else could see what had happened; and two, call me. Jay and I were in the car, the Lotus Elise that was another of my toys, in less than two minutes and heading for Thornliebank. Gerry had been for calling the police straight away, but I had told him to do nothing until we got there. Jay drove, and managed to break my unofficial world record for the trip. All the way there, one name kept repeating itself in my mind.

It must have showed on my face. 'That woman?' he asked, as we pulled up at the office. 'The paint-chucker?'

'I can't think of anyone else,' I told him.

He gave me a long look. 'Boss,' he murmured, barely above a whisper, but audible in the car's tiny cockpit, 'are you going to tell me the story?'

So I explained. Since I trusted Jay with my safety and that of my family, I felt that I could trust him also with the truth about my Dad's predicament. He listened, with neither comment nor question until I was finished. When I was he nodded his head and pursed his lips. 'Yes,' he exclaimed, 'I can see why they'd be frustrated, and why they'd want to get back at you. What do we know about this couple?'

I told him the little that my Dad had told me. 'He's a lab technician, is he?' he mused. 'Come on, let's see what he might have been up to.' He opened the car door and twisted himself out. I followed suit; I'm a bit bigger than Jay, so it took me a second or so longer.

I led the way inside and made straight for Gerry Meek's office. He looked scared, understandable in the circumstances. 'Before we go any further,' I began, 'is there anything about this company that I don't know about? Are there any secrets that you and Susie might have kept from me? Have any threats been made against the business? Have we crossed the wrong people?'

'No, Oz, nothing at all. I've been racking my brains for a reason for this but I can't come up with one.' He sounded desperate with worry. I wished I could put him out of his misery, but I couldn't.

'Let's see the mess, then.'

He took us through to Susie's outer office and unlocked the door. 'Where's Denise?' I asked, as we surveyed the black, soggy morass on the desk.

'I sent her home. She got the fright of her life. The thought of what could have happened if she'd opened that envelope . . .'

'It was addressed to Susie,' I reminded him, 'and marked "personal". Denise wasn't meant to open it.' I had been on auto-pilot until then, keeping everything under control, but in that instant a huge wave of rage surged through me. 'The bastard who did this is dead,' I said. 'As good as in the fucking ground.'

I hadn't been speaking to him, but I think I scared Gerry even more. 'Oz, we'd better get the police.'

'Why?' I snapped back at him. 'Because of a small accidental office fire that was put out inside a minute?'

'But it wasn't,' the finance director wailed. 'You know it wasn't.'

'I know fuck all of the sort. I'm looking at a pile of wet black ash here, that's all. Denise is a smoker, isn't she?'

'Yes, but not in the off . . .' He caught my look and stopped in mid-sentence.

73

'When's Susie due back?'

'This afternoon, I think. She said she'd have lunch with the guys at the site.'

'She hasn't called in? You haven't said anything to her?'

Gerry's expression was all over the place as he looked at me; he was seeing someone he'd never met before. 'No, she hasn't been in touch.'

'Good. That gives you a chance to get that desk out of here and off to the scrapper.'

'But what'll I tell Susie?'

'Nothing. That's my job. I'll decide what to tell her, but I do not want this incident going public. Understood?'

I've come to believe that life is a constant stream of irony, of gut-wrenching, jaw-dropping perversity. I'd no sooner given Gerry Meek the heavy message than the sound of sirens invaded the office, growing louder and louder until there was no doubt about their destination. I looked out through the Venetian blinds, and gave a crazy laugh as a police traffic car, all day-glo flashes and blue lights, drew to a halt right outside the window.

'Tell them we don't want any,' I said to Jay. No way could I trust Gerry to smooth talk coppers in his condition. The state he was in, give him thirty seconds and he'd have confessed to shooting Bambi's mother.

As Jay went off to talk to Mr Plod, I walked into Susie's office and sat behind her desk. My agitated fellow director followed me in, but I paid him no attention as I sat in my wife's chair and swivelled it around, looking out at the bright morning and trying to get a handle on what was happening. Eventually I formed my mental ducks into something resembling a row. I swung the chair round and turned back to Gerry. 'Before you packed Denise off home, did she say anything about the package?' I asked.

'It was in a Jiffy bag, apparently.'

'How was it addressed?'

He looked at me blankly. 'To Susie,' he exclaimed.

'No, man,' I said, forcing myself to be patient. 'Did she say if it was hand-written?'

'It wasn't. I saw it myself. The address was on a stick-on label; it looked as if it came off a printer.'

74

'Was it stamped or franked?' As I asked the question I realised how stupid it was. To send a letter-bomb with franked, and thus traceable, postage would be idiocy of a higher level than I'd ever encountered.

This didn't dawn on Gerry, though. 'I can't remember,' he replied.

'Do you remember the postmark? Did you see where it was posted?' He shook his head. 'Sorry, Oz.'

I waved a hand at him, to indicate that it didn't matter. At that moment, the phone rang on Susie's desk: I picked it up, hoping that it wasn't her. It wasn't; instead I heard Ali Speirs, the finance director's secretary, on the line. 'Gerry?' she asked.

'No, it's Oz. What's up?'

'I've got a journalist on the phone, Mr Blackstone,' she blurted out, anxiously. 'He says we've had a letter-bomb here. Is that why the police are outside?' I gave her boss a look of approval. He hadn't even told his own secretary what had happened.

'It's bullshit, Ali. Put him through here, but don't tell him it's me. Let him think he's speaking to Gerry.'

'Very good.' She didn't ask why; I guessed she knew him pretty well.

'Mr Meek?' a nasal, ingratiating voice exclaimed a few seconds later. 'This is Larry Moore, of the Red Hot News Agency. Have you got any comment to make about the bomb?'

'Well basically,' I began, 'I'm against all weapons of mass destruction, and I think that Robert Oppenheimer and his team have a hell of a lot to answer for. On the other hand, if the Pandora's Box of nuclear energy had to be opened, I suppose we have to be grateful that our side found the combination before Hitler did.'

There was a brief silence, and then Moore was back, less wheedling this time. 'Mr Meek, I was talking about the letter-bomb which was delivered to your office this morning.'

'Did you deliver it? If so, can you tell me where it is? Maybe then I can answer your strange question.'

'Mr Meek, are you denying that you had an incendiary device delivered?'

'I'll tell you what an associate of mine is telling the police even as we speak. We had a small outbreak of fire in the office. It was dealt with by our automatic system and by an alert staff member, and there was no need to involve the emergency services.' He started to speak again, but I cut him off. 'Now I've got one for you. Who fed you this crap?'

'We don't reveal sources, Mr Meek.'

'You couldn't reveal this one even if you did, because you don't fucking know it. You've had an anonymous call, Larry, haven't you, and you've seen a pound or two in it. Tell me, is there any part of the phrase "Taking the piss" that you have trouble understanding?'

'Are you saying this was a hoax call?'

'That's the first sensible question you've asked me.'

'But if it was, who'd make it?'

'That's the second, and it's one I'm going to be trying to answer for myself. But when I do, I won't be telling you. Have a nice lunch.'

I hung up on him, and looked up at the real Gerry Meek. 'Nobody else knew about the fire? Only you and Denise Scott?'

'Nobody. I just happened to be passing, and I heard the sound of the sprinklers, then Denise operating the fire extinguisher. When she told me what had happened, I decided it was best kept quiet till you got here.' He paused. 'But there's something else, Oz. Something I have remembered. The package was neither stamped nor franked.'

My eyebrows rose. 'Hand-delivered? A courier.'

'Could be.'

'Once the police have gone,' I told him, 'go and ask Danny.' The front of house act at Gantry Group head office is quite up-market, as befits a public company. We have night security, but during the day, from eight in the morning till five pm, there's a uniformed commissionaire, whose job it is to receive visitors and take deliveries. He's an ex-constable and his name is Daniel. 'You'd better give Ali the official version too, just as I gave it to that guy, and ask her to circulate it.'

I looked over my shoulder, out of the window. The two coppers had climbed back into their patrol car, and were leaving, a hell of a lot more quietly than they'd arrived. They had barely cleared the drive before Jay was back, his path crossing with Gerry's in the doorway.

'Sorted?'

He nodded. 'They bought it. They'll report it as a waste of police time. I asked them what they knew about the caller. All they knew was unidentified male.'

'They weren't the only ones to get a call.' I told him about Mr Larry Moore.

'What'll he do?'

'Flog his non-story for what he can get for it. It'll appear somewhere, I'm sure. I can see the headline, "Letter-bomb scare after fire at Glasgow firm". I just hope that none of the tabloids have the wit to tie this to the paint incident.'

'But don't be surprised if they do,' Jay warned.

'I won't be. I'm going to have to tell Susie, that's for sure.'

'Wise, boss. Now, what about these Neiporte characters? Are you sure about not bringing in the police?'

'Dead certain. It'd get out for sure . . . and think of those headlines when it did. "Film star's dentist dad in sex smear scandal".'

'You've missed your true vocation,' my bodyguard chuckled. 'You should have been a tabloid sub-editor. But you're right: that's how they'd treat it, and since half their customers don't read past the headline . . .'

I nodded, feeling the anger begin to swell again. I reached under the desk for a switch I knew was there, to make dead certain that Susie's private taping system, a hold-over from the Jack Gantry days that she hadn't bothered to remove, was switched off. 'I can't go near them again, Jay,' I said. 'I wouldn't trust myself. But I want this stopped in its tracks. No more incidents, no more threats.'

'No questions asked?' That was the key question in itself.

I looked him straight in the eye for more than a few seconds. 'None.'

# 13

As it turned out, Susie's series of meetings at the New Bearsden project took up the whole of her working day. When I called her on her mobile just after lunch, she told me she'd be coming straight home. When I told her what had happened at the office, her first thought after she came down off the ceiling was for Denise Scott. It didn't occur to her that she herself might have been lying in a burns unit somewhere, wondering if she'd be able to see again when they took the bandages off her face, and if she could, whether she'd be able to live with what was in the mirror.

It was only after she had called her secretary at home and satisfied herself that she was okay, that I was able to give her the rest of the story, and tell her how we had handled the police and the press. She didn't disagree with any of it; I was pleased that she accepted what I offered her as my reasons for playing it down. Given her early days as Gantry Group managing director, she was hyper-sensitive about its public image.

I'd thought about it, and if she'd really pressed me, I'd been prepared to tell her the truth, the whole story about the Neiportes and their attempt to blackmail my Dad, but it didn't get that far. The only thing she asked was why we hadn't told Goodchild Capperauld, the group's retained PR company, to handle it. 'There's public relations and there's crisis management,' I pointed out. 'Alison and her people are good at what they do on the positive side, but I've got no idea what they're like at scraping shit off walls.'

She accepted that analysis. Happily she didn't seem even to consider the idea that the incident might have been linked to the paint affair.

She asked how the package had made it through to her office. I was able to tell her that. Daniel, the commissionaire, had recalled it being delivered by a skinny cyclist messenger in a skin-tight suit, a plastic crash hat and wraparound sunglasses. The description fitted any one of a couple of thousand kids pedalling around the city. I knew that our chances of finding him amounted to zero, but I promised her that Jay and I would trawl round all the listed courier firms to see if we could trace the one that had made the drop.

I played it poker-faced, and went through the motions of beginning to trace the culprit. I asked her if she had had trouble with anyone recently, if she'd sacked any employees for misconduct, or incompetence, but nothing and nobody came to mind. 'It's probably just a one-off,' she pronounced, finally, 'but we'll have to increase security at the office from now on, for everyone's sake.'

'That's being taken care of,' I told her. 'Gerry's going to ask our security firm to supply a mail scanner. It'll be Daniel's job to put everything through it before it's distributed.'

'What about here?' she asked. I was pleased to see that she was beginning to show a degree of concern for her own security.

'We'll have one here too. Jay or I will screen everything. You don't touch it, okay?'

She snorted. 'We'll see about that.'

As I'd feared, the story did make the press next day, but it was the *Herald*, rather than one of the tabloids, and so it was written up as a hoax call, rather than a genuine emergency; happily the police confirmed that. 'Maybe you should go into the crisis management business,' Susie suggested, as she read it over breakfast. She had a real point there, had she only known it, but I chose to laugh it off.

The mail scanner arrived next morning, but Jay wasn't there to set it up. He had gone off on what I had told Susie was a couple of days' leave, to deal with a family emergency. I didn't tell her that the family in question was mine. She said something pointed about bad timing, but she liked Jay as much as I did, so she didn't push it. When I said I'd told him to take as long as he liked, just to make sure that he got the problem sorted, she nodded agreement.

I plugged the scanner in and gave it a test run with an envelope loaded with coins; in the instant that it slid down the shelf of the machine and through its sensor beam, the alarm went off with a clang.

I found the volume control and turned it down, then switched it off. The truth was I didn't expect to have to use it in earnest. I was damn sure who the pyromaniacs were and that they were about to receive the sort of warning that they really would take seriously.

With that done, it looked as if I was in for a long solitary day. Having decided that our daughter should prepare for the arrival of her brother by learning to mix with other kids, we had found a playgroup in Rhu that looked ideal for the purpose. She and Ethel had headed off there just after nine for what the head teacher . . . if that's what they're called in kiddie corrals . . . had called 'enrolment and indoctrination'. Our nanny had snorted at that one, but Janet hadn't batted an eyelid. All she was focused on was the word 'play'.

Left with only old Willie, the gardener, for company, I did the obvious thing and phoned the golf club to check whether there was a tee time available. There was indeed, provided I was prepared to share it with an overseas member, newly arrived from the south of France and hungry for action. I gave him all that he could handle, and a little more besides; he took his three and two cuffing in good part, and proved to be an entertaining lunch companion as well.

When I got back, I checked my e-mail, finding the few spam messages that had made it through my filter . . . 'No, sir, I don't need emergency finance.' 'No, sir, I don't want to see people who look something like famous people in unusual sexual positions.' (I'm a bloody actor for Christ's sake; I've seen *real* famous people in unusual sexual positions) . . . and a 'How's it going, buddy?' message from Miles Grayson.

I've become such an e-mail nerd, I almost didn't bother to check my voice-mail. It was almost by accident that I saw the light flashing on my telephone. There were two messages. One of them was from some enthusiastic girl telling me that I'd won a voucher worth a thousand pounds towards the cost of a luxury fitted kitchen . . . The first time an enterprising company decides to cold-call people and say, 'We've got this really good product that we're prepared to sell you at a fair price,' they'll make a bloody fortune . . . and the other was from Ewan Maltbie, asking if I could call him back.

It was either him or the fitted kitchen girl, so Maltbie won . . . if only narrowly.

Although I was returning his call, his secretary made me hold on for five minutes, listening to 'Sultans of Swing' . . . could there ever be a better choice of telephone music for a law firm than something by a band called Dire Straits? . . . before he came on the line himself. 'Mr Blackstone,' he began.

'I never imagined you could play guitar like that,' I said.

'Pardon?' he replied, sounding bemused. Solicitors? Getting the joke? Forget it.

He went on. 'I want to talk to you about Joe's personal effects. I'll be putting the house on the market this week. However I expect a quick sale. I've already had two notes of interest from other firms in the town, and once it's advertised I expect a lot more. As you know, I'm bound to sell all the furniture . . . all that is sellable, that is. However I wondered whether you and Mrs Blackstone might like to go through it first, to see whether there's anything you'd like to buy privately, before it goes to auction.'

I couldn't imagine that there would be, but I decided to accept the invitation anyway. 'We'll take you up on that, Mr Maltbie. There's one thing that I'd certainly like to look at, and that's Joe's computer. It's just possible that he had items on it that relate to the Group. If that's the case then I'd like them erased . . . or I suppose the company might buy it, as an indirect contribution to the charities that will benefit from the sale.'

'Mmm,' I heard Maltbie mutter, 'I don't recall Joe ever saying anything about having a computer, but if you'd like to check, I have no problem with that. When would you like to visit?'

'Gimme a minute,' I told him. Susie and I keep a master diary on our computers: I was still switched on, so I was able to consult it quickly. 'If you don't hear to the contrary,' I said, 'we'll make it tomorrow afternoon, say two thirty. That seems to be the only opening this week.'

'That will suit me. I'll arrange for a member of my staff to meet you at the house.'

'Not necessary; we'll collect the keys from your office.'

'No, no, I insist. You're both busy people.' I smiled as I thought about my day. 'Oh, by the way,' he continued, 'I was sorry to read about the incident in Mrs Blackstone's office on Monday. It's a blessing no one was hurt. We can never take too many precautions in our offices these days, you know. It just takes one moment of care-lessness . . .' He paused. 'Mind you, I can understand why the papers were prepared to believe that hoax call. There are some funny people around these days.'

'Too bloody right, mate,' I muttered, so quietly that I doubt whether he heard me.

'The Gantry Group's not having the best run of luck just now, is it?' I heard him say.

'Eh?'

'I said you're having a hard time just now. First poor Joe, going in such a tragic way. Now a fire in your office. If one didn't know they were both sheer blind bad luck, one might almost think that someone has it in for you.'

I blinked as he said it. I'd been so focused on the paint-chucking incident that I'd gone straight there for a connection. But Ewan Maltbie didn't strike me as a tabloid reader; he probably didn't even know about that. It's amazing what you can see when you're not wearing blinkers.

# 14

After I thought about it some more, though, I didn't buy into the lawyer's suggestion. There was no threat to the Gantry Group: we were major employers and well up there among the business flavours of the month. On the other hand, there had been a threat to my Dad, a physical attack of sorts against Susie and me, and we knew who was behind both of them.

I did give a moment's thought to calling Jay on his mobile and telling him to go easy on the Neiportes, but I decided to let him get on with it. I didn't know what he was going to do, but I guessed that it would be along the lines of my own call on Walter, only a bit more scary. We hadn't discussed what to do if our bluff was called, but I had worked it out for myself. I was going to pay them, but I was going to set it up so that the exchange was filmed, and so that it was made very clear that it was an extortion payment.

I half-expected Jay to be back before we left for Motherwell. He wasn't, but I gave it no thought. Susie had come home for lunch with me and our daughter, now a fully enrolled and indoctrinated pupil at the Daybreak Nursery, and loving every minute of it.

When we left for Motherwell, with Susie at the wheel this time, we took a more direct route, crossing the lonely Erskine Bridge to avoid the west of Glasgow, then picking up the M8 and heading for Edinburgh, although we wouldn't get anywhere near it.

The Kingston Bridge was busy, as it always is during the working day, but at least the traffic was moving, albeit slowly. As we rolled across, I found myself glancing up towards the skyline on my left, to the distinctive building where Susie and I had lived. Prim and I had lived there too, for a while, and before that, Jan and I had died there . . . or at least she had, although part of me, maybe the good part, had gone with her. Now that I had cut that place from my life, I realised how badly I had needed to do it, but that something had held me back for too long. Closure is a word used by many people who don't really know what it means. I only came to understand myself, when I turned my back on that cursed place.

I gazed up at the familiar floor to ceiling windows that looked down on me and the rest of the city centre. As we came as close as we would, before the bridge dipped down and took us out of its sight, I could just make out the figure of a man standing where I had stood so often, looking down as I had done. For all I knew he could have been looking at Susie and me. I had no idea who he was, whether he was a good or a bad man, a happy or a sad man, and as I looked up at him, tiny in the distance, I realised that I didn't give a fuck, either.

We rolled on under the Charing Cross flyover; when we emerged into the daylight on the other side, the traffic, as it always does there began, to pick up speed. By the time we passed the great forbidding bulk of Barlinnie Prison, one of the most famous divisions of what is known to some as the Windsor Hotel Group, we were pushing the limit.

Ewan Maltbie's office junior was waiting for us when we arrived at Crawford Street. She said that she'd been told to wait with us and lock up after we were done, but I wasn't having that. I told her that we'd lock up and drop the keys off. She left, a little doubtfully, but the proud possessor of an Oz Blackstone autograph, which I'd scrawled on the back of a photo she'd brought with her.

I could tell right away that Susie felt strange to be alone . . . husbands don't count as company . . . in her father's house, for the first time in her life. 'Do you really want any of the furniture, Oz?' she asked.

'I don't give a toss,' I replied, honestly. 'If you see anything you'd like, make a note and we'll buy it from the estate, but to be truthful, I said we'd come simply because I thought it was something you'd want to do.'

She smiled up at me. 'You're a big softie, you know: but you were right. Even though there's nothing here I'm going to want, other than the crystal Joe left me, it's something I needed to do. It's important that I feel like someone's daughter. Understand?'

'Sure. You take a wander around, and I'll go and look for Joe's computer.' As I walked into the living room, I noticed that the display cabinets that had housed the crystal were empty, and that two big tea-chests marked 'fragile' stood in the middle of the room. Two golf bags, their hoods zipped up, lay on the floor beside them; our legacies, Susie's and mine, from father and father-in-law.

But no computer. There was a table under the window that looked out in to the back garden, but there was nothing on it. I thought back to the last time I'd been in the house, before Joe's death. No, it hadn't been there then either. Somewhere else, then. '*Phone lines, Osbert,*' I said to myself. '*It must be near a phone point for the modem.*'

There was a phone in the hall. An extension lead ran from the jack point. I followed it upstairs to Joe's bedroom, where a phone sat on the bedside table. Another cable, a DIY effort this time, ran from that point. I traced it round the skirting and back to the door, but there it disappeared under the carpet. I went out to the landing and looked around, but I saw no wire resurface. I opened the nearest door, but that was the bathroom, so I tried the one next to it. Sure enough, just inside that door, the phone cable ran up the skirting and along the top, loosely, for Joe had been stingy with the staples.

No doubt the room had once been a bed-chamber, but its single-man owner had transformed it into a study. One wall was lined with shelving, there was a television set in one corner, with a video beneath, and beside the window, where the phone cable ended, there was a desk with a swivel chair. On the desk there was a phone handset . . . but no computer. 'Don't tell me he used an internet café for his e-mails,' I whispered to myself. But then I looked at the box where the cable terminated.

It was fitted with an adaptor, turning one output into two. One of the sockets held the plug for the desk phone, but the other was vacant.

The desk had deep drawers on one side, and a cabinet in the other. I opened each in turn, expecting to find a laptop, but all I saw were personal files, assorted stationery items and a collection of movies on video. I looked at the titles: Joe had been a closet Clint Eastwood fan, it seemed.

Still, though, there was no computer. I reckoned that my internet café notion must have been right, for all the double socket, and I was about to give up, when my eye was caught by a cardboard container on the lowest of the bookshelves; it was open on one side and I could see the spines of the volumes that it held. I picked it up and shook them out into my hand. They were all soft-covered; one was a registration book for Windows 2000, another was a manual for Microsoft Word, and the third was the owner's handbook for a seriously powerful Shoei laptop, complete with a fifteen-inch LCD screen and the fastest Pentium processor on the market.

I opened every drawer in that room again. I went back into Joe's bedroom and searched it, not once, but twice. Finally I went back downstairs and opened every drawer and cupboard there. Susie came in from the garden as I was going through the sideboard. 'What are you doing?' she asked.

'Looking for Joe's computer.'

'Maybe you were wrong. Maybe he didn't have one after all.'

'He had this.' I showed her the manual.

'Someone's had it away then,' she pronounced. 'Someone who's been in the house since Joe died.' She paused. 'Unless he lent it to someone.'

'Get real, love. Would you lend anyone a two thousand quid computer?'

'I suppose not. But maybe he did. You just never know.'

I did know something, though. I knew that Ewan Maltbie's throwaway line about a connection between Joe's death and the fire at the office might not have been as far-fetched as I had thought.

86

# 15

I reported the missing computer to Maltbie when we took the keys back. I had mentioned its existence in the first place so I felt that I had to. I hadn't seen his self-assurance shaken before. 'Are you sure about this?' he asked me, in a tone that said as clearly as words that this was a great inconvenience and that he wished it would go away.

I didn't like my word or my intelligence being questioned. 'I'm sure Joe had a spare telephone jack point in his study upstairs. I'm sure I've received e-mail from him in the past. I'm sure this was in his bookcase.' I tossed the owner's manual on to his desk. Then I reached into my jacket's inside pocket. 'Even you can be sure about this,' I told him, as I unfolded a sheet of pink paper and laid it in front of him. 'I found it among Joe's personal files.' The solicitor picked it up and peered at it through his half moon glasses. It was a receipt, from PC World, for the purchase around eighteen months before of a Shoei 1900 laptop computer, with optional extended warranty.

'Damn,' he said, earnestly. 'What am I going to do with this?'

'You're the bloody lawyer,' I replied, amiably. 'You tell me.' He frowned at me. 'But if you want a hint,' I continued, 'there's a detective superintendent called Tom Fallon up at police headquarters. You might report it to him.'

'You really think so?'

'Too right. This isn't a box of paper-clips that's missing; it's a valuable piece of kit.'

He made a small tutting sound. 'Do you want to report it, then?'

'Bugger that,' I exclaimed sincerely. 'I'm not the beneficiary here, the nominated charities are, and you're the executor, so you do it.'

'But he'll want to question my staff. It'll be very inconvenient.'

'He's as likely to question his own bloody staff. They've had more opportunity than your people. But the first thing he'll do is something I didn't have time to. He'll check with PC World, to see whether the machine's in for repair, and if they don't have it, he'll go through Joe's papers for a receipt from another specialist. It's only after he's exhausted those possibilities that he'll start a theft investigation.'

'You really think I should inform him?'

'No, Mr Maltbie. I insist that you do.' As I looked at him I realised that his imagination didn't stretch beyond the walls of his own office. The absence of the computer changed everything. Yes, it was possible that the machine was in a repair shop. Or maybe, as Susie had suggested, Joe had lent it to a friend. But neither of those explanations solved the riddle of the missing CDs.

According to the PC World receipt, Joe's laptop had been fitted with a CD rewriter, with which he'd have been able to copy files, music, and the like. When I'd gone back upstairs after searching the living room, I'd found in the cupboard in his desk a box of blank Sony CD-RW data storage disks. The trouble was, there were only four in the box, and there should have been ten. More than that, the four were all still in their plastic wrappers, not just unused but unopened.

I had looked for the missing six disks as carefully as I'd looked for the computer; they were nowhere to be found. I'd even checked his CD collection, in case he'd been downloading or copying music. Sure, maybe Joe had lent those to a pal as well . . . and maybe not. And sure, maybe a bent copper had nicked the laptop . . . but almost certainly not.

The theft of the computer shone a completely different light on Joe's death. Fallon couldn't overlook it, but the trouble was, a few days before we'd sent the old boy up the chimney at Daldowie, so any reopened investigation would be hamstrung from the off.

Of course there was another angle. If Joe's death was to say the least suspicious, as I thought it was, did it connect in some way to Susie's letter-bomb, that I'd been so quick to lay at the feet of the Neiportes? Clearly, that was another line of investigation for Fallon . . . only I'd covered the bloody thing up. Perhaps I'd have been able to talk my way out of it, but I had a feeling that telling porkies to the police might not be all that good for my career.

# 16

When we got back from Motherwell, just after five, I saw that Jay's car was parked outside his cottage. I wanted to speak to him, urgently, but it had to wait, for Janet was demanding quality time with her parents, and Ethel was showing signs, for once, of being run off her feet.

So the three of us changed into swim gear and jumped into the pool. Susie and I are both strong swimmers, and we had made a point of teaching Janet, even before she could walk. She was a natural, with no fear of water, and although we still made her wear flotation armbands, she didn't really need them. She and her mother splashed about, while I did a few lengths, then climbed out and pressed some serious weights on the exercise machine in the corner of the pool-house.

When I was finished, so were they, wrapped in towelling robes and looking so cute, the pair of them, that I'd have swelled to bursting point with pride if I hadn't had some very serious matters on my mind. I took a quick cold shower then went upstairs to change.

When I was ready I called Jay from the bedside phone. 'I'm going to hit a few golf balls,' I told him. 'Fancy?'

Susie was in our bedroom by that time, sorting out her clothes for the evening, while Janet trotted about, still in her robe and flip-flops, chattering happily to herself. I waved to them both on my way out, but they barely noticed me.

I picked Jay up in the buggy and headed over to my mini course. Neither of us said a word on the way there. I stopped in the middle of the first fairway we reached, dumped a bucket of practice balls on the ground and started hitting nine irons to the nearest green. Jay took a seven iron and began whacking away . . . he has one of the clumsiest golf swings I've ever seen.

After a dozen or so shots, I looked across at him. 'Well?' I asked.

'The problem has been resolved,' he said.

'Effectively?'

'It doesn't get any more effective.' He was looking at the green, but I could tell he was seeing something much further away. I felt a chill sweep over me, far, far colder than the pool had been.

'What are you saying, Jay?'

'Nothing.'

'Are you telling me those people are dead?' I gasped. 'I know I said something along those lines at the office on Monday, but there is such a thing as a figure of speech. Come on, man. What really happened?'

He glanced at me. 'We agreed there would be no questions.'

'I know, but . . .'

'You gave me no specific orders.'

'I know that too.'

'That's how it was and that's how it has to stay. We must not discuss this.'

'But Jay . . .'

This time he looked me in the eye, dead in the eye. 'You don't want to know, boss. Believe me. Just take it from me that your family will have no more trouble.'

I turned away from him and took out my four iron, aimed at a green further away, and let fly. The ball started on the flag, but soon developed an extravagant slice. 'Fuck,' I cursed, quietly, and not only at my shot.

'There's been another development,' I said. I told him about the missing laptop.

'Probably the coppers, boss,' he murmured, when I was finished.

'I don't believe that. You might divert a case of whisky from a recovered hijacking, but you don't take a computer from an accident victim's home, knowing that the whole fucking place is going to be inventoried for his estate.'

'You might if you were stupid enough.'

'I don't buy into that.' I hit another four iron: this time it stayed straight and landed on the green about ten feet from the flag.

'Nice shot,' Jay conceded. 'So you're getting round to telling me you think Joe's death wasn't an accident, and that whoever did it stole the computer?'

'That's about it.'

'And you're going to suggest that the letter-bomb might have been sent by that person, and not by the Neiportes?'

'Possibly.'

'That'll come as a great comfort to them, but it won't change anything.'

'What do you think?'

For the first time, Jay gave me something resembling a smile; it was a pretty grim one, though. 'You really want me to tell you?'

I nodded. 'Go on, I can take it.'

'Then I think you're letting the movie business fuck up your head. You're treating life like a script. Joe's death was accidental. His laptop was either lost or stolen from his house, or his car . . . the fucking things are portable after all . . . before his death. The Neiportes sent Susie that letter-bomb. End of story.'

I frowned at him, then I made myself laugh, wondering if it sounded as hollow as it felt. 'Maybe. Okay, probably. Sod it, yes. You're right.'

All at once, his shoulders seemed a little less tense. He actually hit his next shot more or less towards the green. But as I looked at him, I could not help but wonder whether Jay really believed his version of events, or whether he was making himself believe it, because he needed to.

# 17

I've found that the older I get, the more I'm able to compartmentalise. If I have worries or troubles, I can isolate them and put them in boxes, to be taken out and looked at every so often. Rest of the time, I show the world my smiley Oz face, the one that looks out from the billboards outside cinemas and moistens the underwear of ladies throughout the English-speaking world . . . or so a rather overenthusiastic Canadian reviewer wrote after my first Skinner movie.

Whenever the contents of these secret compartments, these emotional safe-deposit boxes, start battering to be let out, I have a routine for handling it. I go into the nearest gym and batter the hell out of myself; if you ever want to gauge how stressed out and worried I am, here's a handy tip. Squeeze my biceps: the harder they are the more there is going on in my head.

This relationship was actually news to me until Susie drew it to my attention. As I've said, she is the only person alive who can read me like the complex book I have become. It was a couple of weeks after Jay's 'family crisis', and well more than half-way through my break between movies when she asked me, one night as we were in our bathroom, getting ready for bed, 'Are you worried about this next project of yours?'

I looked at her blankly as she removed her eye make-up; she had chosen an inappropriate moment, my Braun toothbrush not quite having finished its two-minute cycle. When I had, and when I'd completed my obligatory anti-plaque mouthwash . . . once a dentist's son, always a dentist's son . . . I said, 'No. Not at all. What made you ask that?'

'You've been shifting a hell of a lot of weight lately.'

'Uh?'

'You're never out of the gym. Every night I've come home from the office lately, you've been in that pool-house working out.'

'I've got to be fit for *Mathew's Tale*,' I reminded her. 'It's a pretty arduous part.'

'Oz, you are fit; the way you've been flogging yourself lately, anyone would think you're training to fight Mike Tyson. I'll bet Liam and Darius don't train as hard as you, and they're professional athletes. So? What's on your mind?'

'Why should there be anything on my mind?'

'Because it's your classic behaviour pattern. You were like that when you came back from Spain, after that thing with the house out there, and the policeman, then when you came back from the States after Prim ran off with that guy, then when there was that problem on your first Skinner movie.'

She was right, of course; it hadn't dawned on me until that moment, but she *was* right. I remembered one particular session in Edinburgh, when I had gone to the gym with Liam, and he had put me through hell, working all of the anxiety and aggression out of my system.

'Okay,' I told her, finally, as I worked the truth out in my head, 'it's the aftermath of that letter-bomb incident. It's been getting to me. If you hadn't been at Bearsden that morning . . .'

'I'd have told Denise to go ahead and open all my mail.'

That hadn't occurred to me at all. I felt a sudden flash of relief, followed by guilt at the thought of what might have happened to the secretary if the thing had flared up in her hands.

'Maybe, but the mere fact that it happened. Makes me angry, makes me anxious.'

'But we've got security in place now, at the office and here, and there have been no more incidents. We thought the thing was a one-off at the time and that's the way it's been. The only effect was a wee slide in the share price when the story hit the *Herald*, but that's corrected itself. You know what the stock market's like. Most of these analysts have about as much logic in them as do bloody astrologers.'

She made me smile, as the thought of '*Smith and Jones, stock-brokers and fortune-tellers: tarot cards by appointment*' ran through my mind. 'I suppose. Okay, I promise, from now on, I'll only worry about the next movie, and about the impending arrival of our son.' I looked down at her as she stood beside me, naked in front of her mirror. 'Speaking of whom, dear, your profile is changing by the day.'

'Don't I know it,' she muttered. 'This is going to be a big lad. I was nowhere near this size at this stage with Janet.'

'You still look fantastic, though.' It was true, she did.

What was not nearly so certain was the promise I'd just made. I'd said I'd stop worrying about the letter-bomb and its aftermath, but that was going to be a hell of a lot easier said than done.

As time passed, I'd thought about what Jay had said to me, about my actor's imagination. I had forced myself to think as he did. The police had looked into the disappearance of Joe's computer, but without success. However a check of his insured property had revealed that a Piaget watch and a valuable carriage clock were also missing. The supposition they had reached, as Tom Fallon had explained, was that the thefts had happened not before, but after Joe's death. This was far more likely, since the house had no alarm system, and since PC 'Cash' Money had admitted to CID colleagues that she might have left the kitchen window open after the house had been locked up on the day Joe's body had been found. Details of the watch and the clock, plus the serial number of the computer, had been circulated with no success at that point, but the underlying, unspoken message was that no way did the police see grounds for reconsidering the official verdict of accidental death.

The probability was clear. The attack on me at the premiere had been, we knew for sure, the work of Andrea Neiporte. The incendiary had to have been her also; the fact that her husband had worked in a university science lab and so had access to chemicals was a pretty damning pointer. Top that off with the fact that everything had been peaceful since Jay's trip to Fife.

No, it would not be easy to put all that out of my mind, for it sure as hell hadn't been until then. For the previous few days, I had been looking at the *Courier* website, the electronic version of the newspaper that covered Tayside and Fife. I had scrolled through every issue, looking for stories of missing couples, until, just the day before, I had found one. It wasn't much, not the sort that other papers were going to follow up on. All it said was that Fife police were looking for information on the whereabouts of a Pittenweem couple, Mr and Mrs

Walter Neiporte, after Mrs Neiporte's mother had reported them missing. Subsequent checks had revealed that the couple had both been absent from work for several days. The police spokesman was quoted as saying that there was nothing to indicate suspicious circumstances, and that a number of bills remained unpaid, the implication being that the couple had done an old-fashioned moonlight.

But I knew they hadn't. I didn't know exactly what had happened to them, but I could guess it hadn't been peaceful. I knew also that I was responsible. As Jay had said, I hadn't given him any direct orders; that was his way of telling me that any unfortunate consequences, if they developed, would stop with him. There would be a cost, I supposed, but I was a rich man.

Except . . . Gerry Meek had been there when I had made a very specific threat in Susie's office, and he had heard it. If the police were to interview him . . .

The plain fact of the matter was that I was more than a little anxious. I didn't give a monkey's dump about the Neiportes. As I saw it they had tried to ruin my old man's life, and if their own had been trampled as a consequence, that was tough on them. I'm a believer in retribution, make no mistake.

Yet a mistake had been made, and I had made it, when I had allowed things to get out of my direct control. I had come up against bad people before, and on a couple of occasions I'd been forced to do something about them. In each situation, I'd asked myself one question: 'What's the downside for Oz?' On each occasion the answer had been, 'None', and I'd done what I'd considered to be right at the time.

This was different, though. I'd let someone else do my dirty work, and thus I'd put myself in his power. I trusted Jay, but my life was literally in his hands. And what a life. I looked at how much I had to lose: my career, my marriage, my children, and my wealth, not to mention my liberty for about half of my remaining life expectancy.

No wonder I was knocking ten bells out of my exercise equipment. No wonder my body looked and felt as though it had been carved out of marble. No wonder I had awakened, sweating and on the edge of panic, on each of the last several nights. No wonder the dark edifice of Barlinnie Prison loomed large in my thoughts.

No wonder I was beginning to look at Jay Yuille in an entirely different light. If he ever became a problem to be solved, I was damn certain that he was one I wouldn't delegate.

# 18

There was no sign, though, that Jay was looking at me any differently. He behaved towards me in exactly the same way he had before the Fife episode. That had not been mentioned since, or even hinted at. As the days and weeks went by without further mention of the Neiportes in the *Courier*, or any other newspaper, my bad dreams began to ease, and I began to feel more secure.

In the last few days before shooting began on *Mathew's Tale*, I decided to go up to Enster to visit my Dad. I hadn't seen Mac the Dentist since Joe's funeral, or heard from him, and I wondered how he was. So I stuck my clubs in the passenger seat of the Lotus . . . there's nowhere else for them to go, and headed east.

As it turned out he was in good form all round, even on the golf course, although my new, home-tuned game was too much for him in the end. After our round, we paid a return visit to the Golf Tavern . . . it's more my style than the Elie club-house . . . where the atmosphere was much easier than on our previous visit.

I didn't raise the subject of his problem: I'd never intended to. But he did. Just as I was finishing my pint of orange squash and picking up my second crab mayonnaise roll, he reached across and squeezed my arm. 'Thanks, son,' he said, quietly.

'For what?'

'For helping me through that thing, for putting some backbone into me and showing me the way.'

'Nada,' I muttered. I assumed he'd read the *Courier*, although he didn't say.

'It wasn't nothing at all. It was . . .' He paused. 'It's a funny thing, Oz, we go through our lives thinking of ourselves as role models for our children, and then a day can come when we realise that they've outgrown us, and that it's the other way around.'

'Bollocks,' I responded, cheerfully.

'I don't know about them,' he remarked, and the moment had passed.

'How's Susie?' he asked me suddenly. 'How's Janet? And how's my next grandson?'

'The first one's still working her socks off, although I'm trying to get her to slow down. The second seems to have appointed herself class captain at her nursery school. The third may actually be an elephant, going by the size of his mother.'

He laughed. 'Naw, he's a Blackstone male, that's all. You were exactly the same. Your mother was like an elf with Ellie, but she was like a fucking pillar box when she was carrying you.'

'Don't say that to my wife, for God's sake.' I looked across at him. 'How about your other grandsons? Fences mended?'

'With Colin, certainly. He's a corruptible wee sod, right enough; those skates did the trick: them, and a sincere apology. As for Jonny, he still acts a bit different towards me. Sometimes I wonder if it'll ever be the same with him.'

'Probably not, Dad, but don't put it down to what happened. Jonny's growing up fast; the absence of a father has . . . I won't say it's robbed him of his childhood, but it's accelerating his adolescence. I've got great hopes for him, you know. He's a special kid.'

'He's you.'

'So Ellie says, but he's not. If he was I'd know everything that's in his head, but I don't. There's something in him that wasn't in me when I was his age. I see it in the way he looks at his mother, and his brother. It's a sort of worship.'

'You mean you didn't worship me?' my Dad asked, quietly.

'You're a fucking dentist,' I reminded him. 'There have been, and are, people on this planet who've worshipped cows, birds, cats, the Sun, the Moon, their ancestors, living emperors, money, precious stones, graven images, actors, musicians, racing cars, and the people who drive racing cars. But never across the great span of human history and endeavour will you find a case of anyone worshipping a fucking dentist.'

He was still chuckling when he waved me off, after I had driven

98

us back to Anstruther in his Jag and said 'So long' to Mary. I could hear his laughter all the way home. I had been lying, of course. I did worship him.

# 19

Although movie-making's a high-pressure business, I always like to get back to work. There may come a day when I'm blasé about the whole business, but I'm a way short of it yet. I love turning up for a new project, meeting my fellow actors, the guys and gals behind the scenes, the caterers, and even the publicity people.

I have to say that since I've moved out from under Miles Grayson's hugely generous and protective wing, I've enjoyed it even more, since I'm beginning to feel like a real actor, as if I'm with my peers. That even includes Ewan Capperauld, the British star most respected by everyone in the business, including himself.

Ewan has played just about every type you can name, and played them all brilliantly. For all that Miles did a great job in the part, I was sorry that in the end Ewan didn't get to play Bob Skinner, for that role could have been written for him, or he for it. But in my professional opinion, he's at his best whenever he plays the bad guy. Of course that may be true of all good actors, for as they'll often tell you, the villain is usually the meatiest role in a movie.

That isn't necessarily the case with *Mathew's Tale*, for the hero part, my character, has loads of meat about him, but Ewan's guy, Sir Gregor Cleland, an amazingly nasty baronet, is one of the 'best' baddies I've ever encountered.

'How's it been with you?' I asked him, after we'd greeted each other at the first cast meeting. You can never be sure how Ewan's going to react at times like that. He has a habit of dropping unconsciously into whatever character he's playing; on this occasion, Sir Gregor was still in his box, for he answered affably.

'Fine, thank you. I've been working my butt off, though. I've just come off a month playing Hamlet at Stratford-on-Avon. The offer was made, and I decided to do it one last time, before I got too ridiculously old for the Prince's costume. The Bard's a progression for an actor, you know. One starts with Hamlet and Henry the Fifth, then moves on to Richard of Gloucester and his kin, until finally, one is offered Lear. That's when you know you're over the hill. Have you ever done any Shakespeare, Oz?'

There was a time when I'd have thought he was taking the piss if he'd asked me that . . . and probably he would have been . . . but not any more. Now I'm taken seriously, even by people as eminent as him.

'As a matter of fact I have,' I told him. 'I played Romeo, once; Jan, my first wife, played Juliet. Doesn't count, though. It was at school.'

'Of course it counts. It all goes on the CV, my lad.'

'Speaking of wives,' I began, a shade tentatively.

'The divorce is final,' he replied. Ewan's private life had turned chaotic a while back; that was what had forced him out of the Skinner movies.

'Sorry.'

'Thanks, but don't be.'

'Are you still seeing Natalie Morgan?' She had been the start of his trouble.

'Not for a while. I've been going around with Rhona Waitrose.'

'*You and the Scots Guards*,' I thought, suppressing a smile. Rhona was known as one of the friendliest girls in town; I'll never forget the night she turned up at my place for a spot of 'rehearsal' wearing nothing but a raincoat. Neither will she, I suspect; Susie had turned up just after her.

'Nat's totally committed to her company now.' Actually, I'd known this, for Natalie Morgan had succeeded Susie as Scottish Business-woman of the Year, after succeeding James Torrent, her late uncle, as head of the office supplies giant that bore his name. 'You should keep your eye on her, Oz,' he added, quietly.

I looked at him, surprised. 'Why? She doesn't fancy me, does she?'

Ewan gave a deep theatrical chuckle. 'Far from it. She hates you, actually.'

Surprise turned to astonishment. 'Me? What have I done to deserve that? Come to think of it, I seem to recall saving her life once.'

101

'That counts for nothing. She blames you for getting involved in that business in the first place. Don't ask me why, but she does.'

I shrugged. 'I can live without her love.'

'I'm sure you can, but that's not why I say you should keep an eye on her. She's a very ambitious lady, and she is not content simply to run her company in its present form. She wants to use it as a base for expansion by acquisition, and one of her main targets is the Gantry Group.'

I whistled. 'Is it now? She's wasting her time then. Susie has a controlling interest in the business, and I can tell you now, selling out ain't in her plans, or in mine.'

'There are minority shareholders, though, aren't there?'

'Yes, but very much a minority.'

'Nonetheless. I don't know a lot about company law, but if a significant offer came in, your wife might be told that she had an obligation to all the shareholders to accept.'

'Who'd tell her?'

'The courts, possibly.'

'Do you know this is going to happen?' I asked him.

'Not at all,' he insisted. 'I know that the thought has crossed Nat's mind, that's all, because she told me. Talk to Susie, Oz. If I were you I might be thinking about buying out the minority interests and taking the company private again.'

I could see the logic in that, and the sense; I even knew how it could be financed. But then I thought of Jack Gantry, and his newly recovered interest in the Group, and realised that it wouldn't be as easy as it sounded.

# 20

To say that Susie did her nut when I told her about Natalie Morgan's ambitions would be akin to describing the Eiffel Tower as a big television aerial. I've seen her angry before, but her reaction was one of sheer unbridled fury.

'The bitch,' she yelled. 'That arrogant, conceited, jumped-up twat!' I was glad that I'd delayed telling her until Ethel had taken Janet off to bed. 'She thinks she's going to take over my company? In her fucking dreams she is! She's a bloody glorified photocopier sales girl and she thinks she can turn me over? Let her try, that's all. Let her bloody try.'

'What are you going to do about it then?'

That silenced her for a while. 'Nothing,' she said finally. 'Nothing that I'm not doing already. I'm going to build up the Gantry Group until it's absolutely invulnerable, and until no conceivable offer could ever match the company's potential.'

'How about buying out the minorities?'

'And hamstring myself financially? If I did that I'd wind up working for venture capitalists, and that is something I'll never do. It's an option I rejected when we went public. No, my love,' she said, tight-lipped. 'I'd go in the other direction first. I'd make a hostile bid for her.'

'Torrent's big, Susie. You'd have to do the deal with shares; you'd lose personal control of an expanded business.'

'I know,' she conceded. 'And there's another consideration. I don't want to be a photocopier sales girl.' I was pleased to see that her brain was starting to work again. 'Just because Natalie Morgan thinks that diversification is the way to go, doesn't mean that it is. So let the bitch come, and let her try to swallow me. She'll choke.'

It was a while before the subject was raised again over our dinner table. Her anger abated, and her judgement restored, Susie did a couple of typically well thought out things. She hired a firm of investor relations consultants to raise the profile of the business in the City, and she filled the vacancy on the board created by Joe's death by appointing Sir Graeme Fisher as non-executive chairman of the company.

Fisher is said to be Scotland's only genuine billionaire, having built his fortune, along with a formidable reputation for plain speaking, in the direct insurance business. He once said, famously, that he did not know a single Scottish company, other than his own, of which he would consider becoming a director, and so, when Susie sweet-talked him into joining the board of the Gantry Group, the announcement made the front page of the *Financial Times*, and was reported in every other business newspaper in the UK.

Graeme Fisher's appointment was as big a surprise to me as it was to the rest of the country. Susie didn't discuss it with me at all. I could tell that she was up to something, and for a while I worried that she had changed her mind about having a go at taking over Torrent. She told me eventually, though, five minutes before she told Gillian Harvey and Gerry Meek at a board meeting, held on a Saturday morning to fit in with my filming schedule.

*Mathew's Tale* was in its early weeks of shooting and was going well; I loved my part, finding that I could associate with him better than with any character I'd ever played, better even than Andy Martin in the Skinner movies. Make-up was a bit of a bugger, since 'Mathew' had a war wound, a sword-cut across his face sustained when fighting against Napoleon, and that had to be put on every morning. It was worth putting up with that, though, for the sheer pleasure of working on the project, and the great luxury for a film actor on location of being able to commute from home.

When Susie broke the news of her coup, my first reaction was to take a small huff that I hadn't been consulted. That cut no ice; my wife told me firmly that this was a decision for her alone, without being coloured by anyone's personal prejudices. Gerry Meek's first reaction was nervousness; our new chairman had been backed in his own business by a very high-powered finance director and he was worried that he might try to introduce him. Gillian Harvey wasn't worried at all; on the contrary, she was both astonished that Susie had pulled it off, and dead chuffed by the personal cachet that serving on a board chaired by Fisher would bring her within the bank.

The appointment was formalised there and then. On the following Saturday morning, at another board meeting, I had my first experience of Sir Graeme Fisher's famous plain speaking.

Our new chairman was a slightly built man in his late sixties, totally bald and with piercing blue eyes. At first sight, it occurred to me that he would have made a perfect James Bond villain. This was confirmed when he spoke. 'Ladies and gentlemen,' he began, in an unreconstructed Lanarkshire accent, 'I want to make one thing clear from the outset. I'm not here as a figurehead. I've agreed to chair this business because I believe that it has potential and can go on to achieve a mass not far short of the company with which I've been associated until now. I hope I don't need to tell you that it's my job as chairman to represent the interests of all the shareholders and to ensure that they achieve maximum value for their investment in this business.' He looked at Susie through those unblinking blue eyes. 'That means, Miss Gantry, that I don't give a damn about the size of your shareholding, and that I will not allow you to pursue policies which I believe may be holding the company back. This is a publicly quoted company, and I will not let it play by private company rules.'

This was too much for me. 'Excuse me, Sir Graeme,' I interrupted, 'but I was under the impression that last week we appointed you as chairman, not managing director.'

He didn't even look in my direction. 'I'll come to you in a minute, Mr Blackstone.' I wanted very much to reach across and twist his head round to face me . . . and then maybe twist it a bit further than that . . . but for Susie's sake I sat there like a scolded schoolboy.

'You may not like what I'm saying to you, Miss Gantry. You may even think you've made a terrible mistake and be tempted to correct it at once. If that is the case, of course I'll go at once. However, I don't need to tell you how that would be viewed by the business community, especially after the publicity which greeted my appointment. Now, do we understand each other?'

Susie drew in a deep breath; I feared that when she exhaled it would burn off his eyebrows, leaving him totally hairless. But it didn't. Instead, she nodded. 'I understand you, as long as you understand that I am indeed managing director, as my husband pointed out, and that the day-to-day running of the business will remain mine.' She paused, and gave him a sweet smile. 'And as long as you understand that if you ever threaten me again, implicitly as you did just now, or explicitly, I will blow you out one second later.'

For the first time, Graeme Fisher blinked, then he too smiled. 'Agreed.'

Then he turned to me and the smile was gone. 'Mr Blackstone, you're a shareholder as well as a director, I understand.'

'True,' I said, coldly. I had decided that I did not like the man, and I wasn't about to disguise the fact. 'An unpaid director,' I added.

'There's no virtue in that,' he retorted. 'If you're contributing, you should be rewarded. Now let me ask you something: if a situation arose where your wife and I had a disagreement, and let's say, her position threatened your interests as a shareholder, who would you support?'

'Her.'

'So you're saying that your first duty as a director is loyalty to your wife?'

'I'm saying that I know my wife, and her abilities, better than anyone on this planet. I don't know you; I only know what you've achieved in another business. If it was a matter of choosing between your judgement and Susie's, then based on experience, I'd back hers.'

'Mmm,' the old knight muttered, 'commendable, maybe, but still not exactly objective. Mr Blackstone, I'll be as direct as I can be. Other than support for your wife, I can't see a single quality that you bring to this table. I've looked at your CV and I can't find a thing on it that qualifies you to be a director of a listed company. Son, this might have been a family business once, but it's gone beyond that; it did as soon as it offered shares for public subscription. I have an instinctive dislike of husband and wife teams in this situation; I don't like pillow talk, or any other discussions between directors to which the rest of the board aren't privy. So, what I'm saying is that I'd feel a lot more comfortable chairing this board if you weren't a member.'

'You're asking me to resign?'

'I am indeed.'

'And if he doesn't?' said Susie, heavily.

Fisher looked at her and gave her another flicker of a smile. 'Don't worry, Miss Gantry, there was no implied threat there. If he doesn't I'll chair it uncomfortably, although I will ask you both not to discuss agenda matters outside the properly constituted forum for such discussions. That is, round this table. Fair, I think.'

'Fair,' my wife conceded.

I reached an instant decision. 'It's okay, Chairman,' I told him. 'You won't need to bring your haemorrhoid cushion to meetings. I'll resign, on one condition; that you don't seek to replace me with a nominee of yours, or with anyone else who is not acceptable to Susie.'

'I wouldn't dream of doing such a thing.'

'Fine,' I said, although I didn't quite believe him, and stood up. 'See you in the car,' I said to Susie, who was frowning up at me, seriously.

'What the hell did you do that for?' she demanded, when she joined me forty-five minutes later.

'It seemed like a good idea at the time. Maybe I can't support you as a director, but I sure as hell can as a husband. Besides, no way am I going to let that guy tell us what we can and can't discuss in our own bedroom.'

She grinned at me. 'You're not as dumb as my chairman thinks, are you?'

# 21

As the weeks went by I began to think that maybe Sir Graeme Fisher wasn't as smart as he thought, either. Susie gave me blow-by-blow accounts of her meetings with him, and of the board meetings to which I'd given up access. The overall impression that I formed of the guy was that he was efficient, but maybe, just maybe . . . listen to me, criticising a guy who's made a billion from scratch . . . not quite as comfortable in the construction industry as he had been in the world of insurance and finance. All the initiatives still seemed to be coming from Susie, but, that said, we both had to concede that with him in the chair, the share price hit an all-time high, around one sixty-five a share, and stayed there.

As Gerry Meek had feared, he did secure the appointment of another accountant to the board, but only on a non-executive basis, and only after Susie had given her approval and her vote. The nominee, Philip Culshaw, had been, until his retirement, Scottish managing partner of one of the big three accountancy firms. Since then he had been collecting directorships and playing golf. By a coincidence he did the latter at my new club, and I had met him there, having drawn him in a Sunday medal. When Fisher offered him a directorship of the Gantry Group . . . without consulting the board first, incidentally . . . he had been shrewd enough to call me before accepting, to ask how Susie would view it.

'As long as you're not in Fisher's pocket, Phil,' I told him, 'she'll welcome you.'

Culshaw's appointment turned out to be the best move Fisher made. Far from being a Trojan horse, introduced by the chairman as a first step to axing Gerry Meek, he had been nothing but supportive of the finance director. His presence, even more than Fisher's, seemed to add to the bank's confidence in the business, so much so that for the first time since her appointment, Gillian Harvey missed a board meeting to take a holiday.

There were other benefits too. Where Graeme Fisher has contacts at the very top of British industry, and in Government too, Phil Culshaw is a mover and shaker who operates and has contacts at all levels. I didn't appreciate this, though, until one Saturday on the golf course ... that was all I had available by that time. The extended location work on *Mathew's Tale* was coming to an end, finally, and we were approaching the point where the team would transfer to a sound stage in the south of England. I hadn't expected to play at all, but he had called me a couple of days before, to invite me to share his tee time at Loch Lomond.

We were approaching the turn and I was two down; Phil's a consistently tidy twelve-handicapper, and my lack of recent practice, even on my small private course, was showing as I struggled to play to single figures. On the ninth green he applauded silently as I rolled in an eight-footer for a half, then fell into step beside me as we headed for our buggy and the tenth tee.

'Have you been hearing any whispers, Oz?' he asked me.

I looked at him, puzzled. 'What? Like voices in my head, you mean? I can't say that I have.'

'I'll bet you have,' he chuckled. 'You're a deep one, Mr Blackstone.' I let that pass. 'No, what I meant was have you heard any rumours about the business?'

I thought about it as we rolled along towards the tee; the course was busy and there were two games waiting in front of us. 'No,' I told him, as we took our place in the queue. 'I can't say that I have. But I wouldn't expect to, Phil. I don't move among the chatterers any more; at least I don't at the moment, with this movie I'm on. Why? What have you heard?'

'Nothing specific,' he said, quietly. 'Nothing I can put my finger on. But there's something up.'

'What makes you think that? It can't be pub talk. I don't see the affairs of the Gantry Group being common conversation pieces in the Horseshoe Bar.'

'No, it's not that.' He hesitated. 'The thing is, Oz, my old firm has acted for people in the past who've been a bit schizoid in business terms. By that I mean their core companies have been solid and entirely above board, but there's been other stuff behind them.'

'That sounds familiar,' I told him. 'You could have been talking about the Gantry Group, in the old days.'

'You get my drift. Well, a few days ago, a whisper floated back to me from one of my former partners that the subject of the company had come up in casual conversation with one of these gentlemen. Nothing specific was said, but my former colleague was left with the impression that his client knew something.'

'Why?'

'Because the man said, casually, that he wouldn't be buying any shares in it any time soon.'

With a struggle, I began to paint a mental picture of what he was saying to me. 'You mean that the Group may be a target for gangsters?'

'That's an implication that could be put on it.'

'Well it's one that won't wash. You're a director, man. You must know that we've never been asked for protection in connection with any of our jobs. We've never been approached by phoney security firms offering their services, or else. When Susie took over she cut off all the dirty bits of the group. It's pristine.'

'I can see that from inside,' he admitted. 'But wasn't there an incident, not long before I joined the board? Something involving a small fire in the office.'

'So what?' I frowned at him, looking more than a bit defensive, I suspected.

'So, the word was that it might not have been accidental.'

'But it was. Read the *Herald* if you don't believe me.'

'Since when did one believe everything one reads in the press? The suggestion's been made that it wasn't, and isn't it true that there were anonymous calls to the press and the police alleging as much?'

'A stupid staff member.'

'That won't wash with me, my young friend. Nobody was sacked after it, or disciplined in any way.'

'Nobody was traced.'

'Did anybody ever try?' he asked, dryly.

'Leave that aside, though, Phil. There have been no incidents since that one.'

'None that you know of.'

'But I would, and so would you.'

'Maybe yes, maybe no.' He glanced across, we were next up on the tee. 'My concern is this, Oz. If anybody wanted to have a go at the group, mount a hostile takeover, say, they'd have little or no chance given the share price. The underwriters wouldn't support a bid much above the existing levels and the board would be quite justified in recommending rejection. But if the share price was to be seriously undermined . . .'

I got his drift. Actually I'd had it for a while; I'd simply wanted to make him spell it out. 'And who the hell would do that?'

'The Torrent Group has been credited recently with an interest in acquiring Gantry.'

'Come on, Phil. I know Nat Morgan. She's an aggressive character and I don't like her much, but you will not make me believe for one second that she'd conspire with criminals to undermine the share price of a public company.'

Culshaw tapped his big hooked nose. 'You're assuming something there, my friend.'

'And that is?' I asked patiently.

'That Ms Morgan is the only player in Torrent, and that she makes all of her own decisions.'

'You mean she isn't? I've had a check done on her. I know who's on her board, I know who all her major financial backers are. She's the boss, Phil.'

He laughed. 'You, of all people, can't be that naïve. You don't have to be a director, or a major shareholder in a business, to have a fundamental influence on the way it's run. Oz, you're walking proof of that.'

As I took in what he was saying, a name seemed to burn itself into my forehead. It didn't help. If anything it made me more confused than ever. Why the hell would Ewan Capperauld want to undermine the Gantry Group?

I didn't have time to dwell on it, though. 'Come on,' said Culshaw. 'The tee's clear at last.'

# 22

He's a cunning sod, is our Phil. I knew damn well that he'd raised the subject of hints and rumours surrounding the Gantry Group in the middle of our round as a bit of added insurance . . . as if being two up at the turn wasn't enough. He could just as easily have waited until we were back in the club-house before bringing it up.

As it happened, it backfired on him. Instead of destroying my confidence it helped me focus. I saw the golf ball as an enemy, and I knocked hell out of it for the rest of the round. I was two up myself after fifteen and closed out the match with a tap-in par on the seventeenth.

Back in the bar, we let the subject of Natalie Morgan and her possible ambitions lie. I didn't forget Phil's warning, though; on my second pint, I brought it up. 'All that stuff we were talking about on the course: I take it you're going to tell Fisher.'

'That'll be a bit difficult,' he replied. 'My information came through a professional source, so no way can I let it be minuted. Telling you about it seemed like the best thing to do; you seem like the sort of guy who might do some digging, rather than just waiting for it to happen.'

'Noted,' I said. 'Now, there's something I've got to ask you, behind the mighty chairman's back. I've told Susie that she is going to take maternity leave, and damn soon, just like any other working mother. When Janet was born, Gerry Meek deputised for her, but this time there are too many financial balls in the air for him to combine her job with his own. So we were wondering . . . would you fancy being acting managing director? It wouldn't be for long, mind.'

When Susie and I had discussed an approach to Culshaw she'd been sure he'd turn us down; his golf meant a lot to him. For once she was wrong.

'I'll do it,' he said, with barely a second's thought. 'If anyone is playing silly buggers, they may be counting on a vacuum at the top. I take it Susie will raise that at next week's board.'

'Yes. She'll present it as her appointment. She thinks Fisher fancied the job himself, but no way is she going to let him take any executive decisions.'

The shit had hit the fan, though, long before the board gathered seven days later.

Only a day after Culshaw and I had our chat, Susie and I were at home, watching that silly *Monarch of the Glen* thing (she likes it), when the phone rang. I don't like it, so I answered.

'Oz Blackstone?' asked a voice at the other end. It was a journalist; I could tell by the very tone of the woman's voice. *'Which member of our cast has done what, to whom, and with what?'* Those were my first weary thoughts as I said, 'Yes,' in a tone of my own that was meant to convey in a single affirmative just how pissed off I was at having my Sunday evening interrupted.

'It's Jenny Pollock here, from the *Daily Record*. It's your wife I'd like to speak to actually.'

I switched into protective mode in an instant. 'Not a chance. Susie's tired, she's fairly pregnant and on top of that she's watching telly. I'm not putting my life at risk by telling her the *Record* wants her.'

'But it's important, Oz.' I've noticed this about celebrity; it puts people you've never met on automatic Christian name terms. 'I'm working on a story that involves the Gantry Group and we're planning to run it as tomorrow's lead.' That got my attention, but I wasn't about to let 'Jenny' know it.

'The Group employs media relations consultants,' I told her. 'They're called Goodchild Capperauld. You've got Alison Goodchild's number on file I'm sure, but if not I'll give you it.'

'I don't want to talk to PR consultants on this, it's too important. If you won't let me speak to your wife, I'll just have to call Sir Graeme Fisher and ask him about it.'

*'And Christ knows what he would say in a crisis!'* I thought. 'You're missing the obvious,' I told her. 'I will not disturb my wife, but you can talk to me if you like.'

113

'Do you have authority to speak for her?'

'Don't be fucking dense. Now, what is it, this story of yours?'

Jenny Pollock took a deep breath and then dived in. 'I believe,' she began, 'that the Gantry Group is in the first stages of a major housing project to the north west of Glasgow.'

'That's right. It's called New Bearsden, and I'd say that major was an understatement.'

'It's the biggest development of its type that you've ever undertaken, yes?'

'And then some.'

'Can you tell me something about the house types?'

'It's a mix, from apartments aimed at singles, to substantial family houses on large plots. Believe it or not there's a shortage of high-amenity housing in that area.'

'I believe it; I live there myself. In fact I've been to the Gantry sales office to have a look at what you'll be doing. I don't think I'll be going back, though, in the light of what we'll be running tomorrow.'

'And what's that?' I was still trying to sound bored, but it was proving difficult.

'I have information that several notorious alleged criminals have bought some of the biggest and most expensive houses on key parts of the estate. Let me try some names on you: Mark Ravens, Jock Perry and Kevin Cornwell. Have you heard of them?'

Word for word, Phil Culshaw's strange half-warning replayed itself in my head. I decided to lie. 'No, should I?'

'You should read the *Record* more often, Oz.'

'Jenny, if I could read it less than not at all, I would.'

'Very funny.' To her credit, she laughed. 'All those guys, as I'm sure you know, are alleged to be among the ring-leaders of organised crime in Scotland. They're popularly known, in the tabloids and on the street, as the Three Bears. Between them they control virtually the whole of the greater Glasgow area, including Paisley. Their activities include protection, through bogus security firms, reselling stolen goods, including cigarettes and alcohol in huge quantities, money laundering and, naturally, the drugs business.'

Of course I'd heard of those guys. Mark Ravens had actually tried to sell his 'security' services to the Global Wrestling Alliance, until a

114

meeting with Everett Davis and Jerry Gradi had convinced him that on this occasion at least he should think small. The Three Bears were serious enough, though, and in their own playgrounds they had been known to do some nasty things.

'All three of them, I'm told,' the reporter continued, 'have bought little palaces on the New Bearsden estate. Furthermore, I've also had information that several of their associates are buying in there as well.'

'And what have you been told might be behind this?' I asked her.

'It's only a hint,' she said, 'but . . . Remember the stories a while back about Northern Irish guys trying to muscle into the drugs business in Scotland.'

'Vaguely.'

'Well the word is they haven't gone away, and that the Three Bears have decided to get together for added security. The story we're going to run tomorrow is that they're planning to turn Gantry's New Bearsden estate into a sort of Glaswegian mafia compound. I want to ask your wife two questions, that's all. Did she know about these purchases, and what's she planning to do about them?'

'I'll answer those questions for her,' I said. 'I'm still not letting you speak to her. So, first; she doesn't know a thing about this story of yours, and second; she plans to find out whether it's true, or just the usual load of mince. You can phrase the last bit any way you like, Jenny.'

She chuckled down the line. 'I'll say she's launching an internal investigation first thing tomorrow, if that's all right.'

'Fine, for it won't be a lie. Where did you get all this stuff anyway?'

'I can't tell you that, Oz.'

'I know where you didn't get it. It didn't come from Ravens, Perry or Cornwell; those guys don't talk to the press, and they don't hire media relations advisers either . . . although if they did, I've a fair idea who'd pitch for their business.' I took a chance. 'It's not them, so it's gossip from someone out to harm the Gantry Group. If I dropped the name Natalie Morgan in your ear, what would you say?'

There was a pause, only a couple of seconds, but to me it was very significant. 'I wouldn't say anything, because I couldn't. If I betrayed an informant's confidence, even under oath in the witness box, I'd never work in journalism again. I'll tell you this, though, Oz. I honestly do not know the source of this story . . . the informant and the source are not necessarily one and the same . . . but if I was you, on the basis of what I've told you, I'd say that Susie has to have a mole in her company.'

# 23

That's what she said too, once I'd related everything that Jenny Pollock had told me . . . *Monarch of the* Bloody *Glen* had only five minutes to go when I came back into the drawing room, so I let her watch it to the end before giving her the bad news.

'I hate firing people, Oz,' she murmured, 'but when I find out who's passed this information to that Morgan cow, their feet won't touch the ground.'

'We don't know for sure it's her who's the informant,' I reminded her. 'Jenny Pollock didn't say that it was. It's possible that someone in the sales office spotted the three names, put two and two together, made four and then a few more, and called the *Record* off his own bat.'

'True,' she conceded, 'but whatever happened there's going to be heads rolling. These three guys are the biggest hoods in Glasgow. They're bloody celebrities, almost. If this is true . . . you never know, it might be all balls . . . someone should have spotted the three sales and tied them together. I'm going to start right at the top of the project team; Des Lancaster's jacket's on a shaky nail, I'll tell you.'

'You'd better start with your chairman,' I suggested. 'I don't think that Pollock will phone Fisher, but you never know. In any event, you can't let him learn about it from the tabloids.'

Reluctantly, she agreed with me, and looked out Sir Graeme's home phone number. I sat beside her as she told him what would be making next morning's headlines, in case he wanted to speak to me. He didn't, though; clearly he still preferred to think of me as a non-person. All he did was shout a lot, so much that Susie held the phone away from her ear.

'If you wish,' she said. She murmured a couple of things I couldn't hear, then exclaimed, 'You don't have to spell out the consequences to me, Graeme. I'm well aware of them, and I have my own thoughts on that aspect too.' She slammed the phone back into its cradle.

'He wants to conduct the investigation himself,' she told me, 'with Gillian Harvey as a witness. I don't mind that, when I think about it. It's probably better that the interrogation's done by someone who doesn't know the people involved.'

'What was the last bit about?'

'The share price. New Bearsden's a huge project, Oz, it represents a massive financial commitment on our part, but it's been a gamble I've been happy to take, because there was no way I could see it being a loser. But if this story drives the buyers away, it will mean big trouble. We might have to downscale the project, cancel contracts under penalty, God knows what.'

'It couldn't bust the business, could it?'

'No, but it could put us back to square one, and make us vulnerable. That's why Ms Morgan has to be behind it.'

I couldn't argue with that.

By the time that Jay dropped me at Glasgow Airport to catch the sparrow-fart London shuttle, en route for Shepperton Studios, the *Record* was on the streets. Worse, all the other papers had picked it up for their last editions and BBC was running it on the morning news as well.

The follow-up phone calls had started a few seconds after the first copies of the *Record* had found their way into the hands of its competitors. Naturally, we were prepared for them; Alison Goodchild had been briefed . . . as I had expected, I had tracked her down with Ricky Ross; their strange, on-off relationship had survived for longer than either of them had anticipated . . . and had programmed our phone to divert all calls to her number.

That didn't mean that we had a peaceful night, though. Susie was approaching the really uncomfortable stage of pregnancy, where sleeping with her was like sleeping with a bag of rabbits. (We have a very big bed, but she always seems to drift towards the piece that I'm on.) Add to that the fact that she woke me several times to ask me what I thought of so-and-so on the payroll, and whether he or she might be the mole.

At five minutes to four, when all was still dark outside, even in early summer Scotland, she had convinced herself that Denise Scott was the prime suspect, and that she had set the fire in the office herself, then tried to leak the story to the media. She hadn't convinced me, not by a long chalk, but I grunted and rolled on to the last few square inches of unoccupied space on what I laughingly thought of as my side of the bed.

This was not the ideal preparation for my first day's studio shooting on the *Mathew's Tale* project. Nor was the news I received in the limo that picked me up from the execrable Heathrow, when I used my WAP mobile to check the Gantry share price. The London Stock Exchange had only been open for a couple of minutes, but in that blink of an analyst's eyelid it had fallen by just over thirty per cent.

I called Susie, because I knew that she'd have beaten me to the punch. 'What do you think?' I asked her.

Her optimism surprised me, especially after her night of paranoia. 'Not too bad,' she replied. 'Fisher said we should expect at least a forty per cent mark-down in value. Apparently the City has a wee bit more faith in me than my chairman; the new price is based on the brokers' assessment rather than on actual trading. I don't expect there to be much, not initially at any rate.'

'When there is I'm buying,' I told her.

'Don't be daft, Oz. I don't want you to do that.'

'You're not going to stop me. I'm going to instruct my brokers to pick up any stock that's offered, and I'm going to have the investor relations consultants let it be known that I'm doing it. I'm going to be seen to support you, honey, whether you like it or not.'

She laughed. 'You'd better be careful, then. If things get worse you could wind up owning all the minority shareholding.' And then she paused. 'Of course if it did get that bad you couldn't lose; as soon as a takeover bid came in the price would go up. You could sell out to Natalie Morgan and make a right killing.' She paused again. 'Here, Oz, you're not the mole, are you?'

When I thought about it, I realised that it wasn't a bad scam, but I protested loudly into the phone until she apologised for her bad taste joke. 'By the way,' I asked casually, after I had allowed myself to be mollified, 'you're not still harbouring dark thoughts about Denise, are you?'

'No,' she admitted, 'I'm not. That was unworthy of me too. Denise is as loyal as they come. But if it was her, it would say a lot; for example that I must be a really crap managing director if my own PA plotted to get rid of me.'

'Which you're not. You're brilliant, even if you are a grumpy wee witch at times. Now you just let Fisher and Harvey earn their exorbitant directors' fees by running their investigation, unimpeded by you. Your job is to see whether you can cancel the house sales to these three hooligans and to their henchmen . . . assuming that the *Record* story's true, that is.'

'I'm ahead of you,' she told me. 'I was going to get hold of Greg McPhillips first thing, but he beat me to it. He called just after you left in fact. So did Des Lancaster, the project manager. The story's accurate, okay: Ravens, Perry and Cornwell, the Three Bears, are all purchasers, but in their wives' names, not their own. As for the henchmen, we can't say for certain who they are: the development's been selling very well off the plans and there are a lot of buyers.'

'What did Greg say?'

'Nothing good, but nothing I didn't expect. If we could prove that there was a conspiracy here, we might have a chance of cancelling the contracts, but we'll have the devil's own job doing that. All of the three actually do have more or less respectable front businesses, and none of them have any significant criminal convictions. As for their wives, they all raise money for bloody charities. They've all signed contracts and paid deposits; the next obligations lie on our side now. They can pull out, on forfeiture of their deposits, but we can't. As things stand, if we just gave them their money back and told them to piss off, they could sue us . . . unless we cancelled the whole project, which I will not, no, cannot do.'

'So what are you going to do?'

'My instant reaction is to give them their money back, tell them to piss off, and take my chances, but I'll take serious legal advice before I do that. These people may not care to launch a civil court action.'

'No,' I snorted, 'they may just blow up your office instead. These are gangsters, Susie.'

'Ach, they are of a certain level, that's all; there's bigger than them. The Lord Provost was, for a start. I don't give a damn about them, really. Let's try and put it in perspective, now the initial shock's worn off. Think this through with me, Oz. What's happened so far?'

'First, the letter-bomb,' I said, 'leaked to the press.'

'Right. We dealt with that at the time and it did no damage. Next?'

'The Three Bears buy into the New Bearsden project, and that fact is leaked. This time it has done damage to the company.'

'True, but that doesn't need to be a conspiracy at all: the three of them might each have fancied the project separately and bought with no collusion. But someone's come upon the fact and leaked it. I don't think that the McMafia give a bugger about us. They're not our real enemies. The person who's feeding the press is, and the way I read what Jenny Pollock said to you, that wasn't done by a mole within this company, but by someone who's paying them.'

'So how do we deal with the New Bearsden situation?'

She gave me a small laugh. A good sign; when Susie's sense of humour is working, she's on the ball. 'This time we can't do what you did with the letter-bomb, and just lie about it. I see another option, but we use it calmly and quietly. Subject to the legal advice I mentioned earlier, what I intend to do is indeed to give our three dodgy clients their money back. But I don't intend to tell them to piss off. I intend to ask them, through our legal advisers, so that we can't be accused of defaming anyone, how much it would take for them to agree to piss off. What do you think?'

'Good old-fashioned bribery? That usually works, I'll grant you. But remember, love, these guys are among other things in the protection racket. If you give them a bung to go away, what's to stop them pulling the same dodge on every housing project you undertake in the future?'

'We'll see them coming next time.'

'But will you see their cousins, or their mates, or just some punter they've picked up in a pub and paid to front for them?'

'Maybe not, but I'll deal with that as and when it happens. This is today's crisis, and old-fashioned bribery, as you call it, is our best chance of knocking it on the head. Got any better ideas?'

I did, but I doubted whether Everett and Jerry would co-operate. 'No,' I said, 'if you think that's your best shot, take it.'

'I will, but there's something else: our real enemy. Fisher and Harvey can look for the mole, but we need to do more than that. I want to follow my instincts, Oz. I want Natalie Morgan tailed; I want to know everyone she has contact with. I want her phone tapped if it's possible; I want to know everyone she speaks to. But I don't want the instruction to come from within the company, in case our mole finds out about it. Do you think Ricky would do it?'

'Not the phone-tap. He won't do that because it's illegal. But as for the rest of it, I'm sure he will. He used to work for Torrent, remember, until Natalie's Uncle James sacked him. He's got a long memory, has ex-superintendent Ross. I'm sure he'll take the job.'

'Okay. You instruct him. Tell him we'll pay for it privately.'

'Susie,' I protested, 'I'm working here.'

'Oh? Where are you now? That doesn't sound like film studio noise in the background.' I owned up to my surroundings. 'Okay, call him now. Get him on the case.'

'If it'll make you happy,' I conceded. 'Kiss our daughter for me, and I'll call you tonight. Go carefully, though.'

I called Ricky straight away, catching him at home. 'It's you,' he growled. 'Thanks a fucking million for last night; the phone never stopped till three in the morning.'

'That'll teach you to sleep with a PR consultant. I've got a job for you now, though.' I filled him in on Susie's requirements; as I had expected, he jumped at the chance to get one back at Torrent. Ross Security had been embarrassed by its public dismissal by the company, and probably a little damaged financially as well.

'Who gets the reports?' That was all he asked; we didn't discuss money, legal parameters, or anything else.

'Susie: at home, though, not in the office. I'll be down south for a while.'

I left him to it, and spent what little was left of the trip to the studios in Middlesex on the phone to my bankers, to see how much ready cash I had to play with, and then to my brokers to tell them I was a buyer for any Gantry shares that came on to the market . . . but in small lots. I didn't want to boost the price too quickly; there might be a profit to be made, at the end of the day.

I did something else too, as soon as I got to the studios. I checked the schedule to see whether Ewan Capperauld was on set that day . . . I knew he wasn't in any of my scenes . . . and when I found out that he was, sought him out in his dressing room. He was in surprisingly fine form, for a Monday morning. I asked him what had brightened his day, but all I got was a mysterious smile.

The Gantry story hadn't made the London press . . . they really are insular bastards down there . . . and so I had to fill him in on the details. When I had finished I asked him something, straight out. 'Are you still seeing Nat Morgan?'

The smile came back. 'No. As I told you, I'm horizontally occupied in other quarters at the moment.'

'*Rather you than me, mate,*' I thought.

'You haven't seen her at all lately?'

'No, nor spoken to her for at least three months.'

'When you were on speaking terms, did she ever talk about Susie, and the Gantry Group?'

'Did she ever not? I'm afraid your wife is something of an obsession with the lovely Nat. She's a business megalomaniac, you know; it's something she seems to have inherited from that appalling uncle of hers. She wants to build Torrent into a corporation that stretches from sea to shining sea.'

'Do you think she's up to it?'

'Not a chance, m' boy. Between you and me she's better in bed than in the boardroom. Your Susie would have her for breakfast in a business battle.'

'Did she ever mention having any contacts within the Gantry Group?'

'Not that I recall. The only things she ever said about it were derogatory, and you don't really want to hear them.'

'I sure do.' In the distance I heard an assistant director call my name, but I ignored him. They're best left alone anyway.

'It was personal,' Ewan said, 'petty stuff. I ignored it, really. She would say that Susie had inherited her position and that she had no vision of her own. She suspected that she was still taking orders from her father, for all that he was locked away. She said that Lord Provost Gantry and her Uncle James had been men who had understood each other.'

I didn't know they'd ever met, but Jack Gantry certainly got around. 'Do you have any idea what she's up to these days?'

'Trying to do you down, from the sound of it.'

'I meant personally.'

'So did I,' he laughed, and then was suddenly serious. 'As for the other, I don't know. The truth is, Oz, the last time I heard from Natalie, she called me to say she didn't want to see me any more. Her affections now lie elsewhere, I'm afraid.'

'Any idea where?'

He shook his head. 'Not the faintest.' He grinned again. 'And now my boy, you really must go. That assistant director is almost hoarse shouting for you.'

# 24

I wasn't the most popular man on set that morning; my discussion with Ewan had held up shooting, and delays can be more expensive in the movie industry than almost anywhere else in the world. But I made up for it by being flawless.

I had worked on my scenes the day before, and refreshed them on the plane . . . once I'd finished reading the newspaper coverage. Concentrating as hard as I ever have in my life, I was able to put everything and everyone else out of my mind and, literally, become Mathew Fleming from the moment I walked on to the sound stage until the moment the make-up woman took off my dramatic facial scar at the end of the day's work. Louise Golding was on top form too, and all our scenes were first takes . . . a rare occurrence on a Paul Girone movie, as I'd found out already. By the time we were finished, not only had we made up for my delay, we'd bought time for one of Ewan's key shots to be wrapped up.

They had booked the cast . . . apart from Ewan and Scott Steele, who both live in London . . . into a hotel in Surrey, a secluded country house just south of Guildford, down the A3. There was still some commuter traffic around when we left Shepperton, and so we didn't get there to check in until almost eight.

I'd been snacking on set, and, frankly, Louise and I had both seen enough of the excitable M. Girone for one day, so I asked for a poached salmon salad to be sent to my room, and went off there straight away, to phone Susie.

'Good day at the office?' she asked me, just as the room service waiter wheeled in my salad on a trolley. I bunged him a fiver and he left, nodding and muttering thanks. There was a bottle of Martin

Codax, a nice Spanish Albarino white wine, in an ice-bucket; I poured myself a glass as I answered.

'It was fine, and it just got better; my dinner's arrived.' (Scottish people do not have 'supper'.) I described the plateful on the trolley, and sipped the wine; not bad at all.

'Lucky you,' said my wife. 'I had macaroni with Ethel and Janet.'

At once I felt envious, and homesick, so I forced myself back to the serious stuff. 'How did it go with the lawyers?'

'I've been told to make no public comment.'

'Not even to me?'

'Don't be daft. Greg McPhillips spoke to his tame QC, and her very firm advice was that we should say absolutely nothing at all to avoid any risk of defaming the purchasers of these houses, who are not, she reminded me, Ravens, Cornwell and Perry, but their wives. She gave the okay to my proposal that we offer to buy them out of the deal, but she insists that any contact must be in print, and that she drafts all our correspondence. That's where we're at.'

'When will she have finished the first letter?'

'Tomorrow, she hoped.'

'What's been the effect of the stories on the New Bearsden project?'

Susie snorted; I could see her frowning as clearly as if I was looking at her across our desk. 'Just as we expected,' she replied. 'Total and utter catastrophe. Sales have been trotting along at nine or ten a day until now. Today we didn't have a single visitor to the sales office, other than journalists demanding to see the site plan so they could pin-point the three plots in question; I've had to tell Des Lancaster to close until further notice. Worse than that, though, we've had umpteen phone calls from buyers, straight people who've reserved plots, wanting to know whether they'll be living next door to drug dealers, and we've had at least half a dozen formal contacts from solicitors advising that their clients want to cancel, without financial penalty.'

'How have you dealt with them?'

'Stalled them, for now. We've reserved our position and said that we'll respond at the beginning of next week.'

'I don't suppose we've had any contact from the Three Bears?'

126

'Funny you should ask that. Mummy Bear Perry called Lancaster and accused him of blackening her good name in the papers. Bizarre, eh?'

'You said it.' I forked up some poached salmon. 'Alongside all that, how's the Star Chamber going?'

'What?' She laughed. 'Ah, you mean Fisher's uncompromising, in-depth investigation, as he's quoted as saying in the *Scotsman*. So far, it's achieved the resignation of Des Lancaster's secretary . . . which she was subsequently persuaded to withdraw, after Des gave her a made-up apology from the chairman for the rudeness of his questioning . . . and it's prompted one of the New Bearsden site agents to adopt an aggressive attitude. That's how Sir Graeme described it. The way Gillian Harvey tells it, the guy . . . he's Irish: Aidan Keane . . . said that anyone who accused him of deceit or disloyalty would be eating all his meals with a straw for the next six weeks. Other than that, though, there's been nothing.'

'How many suspects are there?'

'As many as might have walked into Des's office and had a look at the sales list. He's a bit cavalier about things like that, is our man. Fisher's already saying he's got to go. He may be right, but I'm not going to give him the satisfaction of admitting that straight away. I'll wait till the smoke's cleared a bit, then I'll transfer him to head office, swap him with Brian Shaw, the purchasing manager, job for job.'

'You really don't like sacking people, do you?'

'No,' she admitted. 'Des is a nice man, and besides, I've met his wife.'

'You'd better not ever buy a football club, love. You'd make a lousy chairman.'

'I've got much more sense than to buy a football club, ever. I'd be as well chucking pound coins into Loch Lomond.'

'There is another way. If you bought a club, you could start by taking all the overpriced, overpaid, clapped-out foreign players that are keeping young Scots out of the game, weighing them down and chucking them in. The financial consequences might be the same, but it would be much more satisfying.'

'I'll still pass. You buy it instead.'

'I might, but I'm fully committed, buying in Gantry shares.' I'd checked with my broker on the way to the hotel; I'd acquired another fifteen and a half thousand shares in the course of the day. That had pleased me; it was a relatively small number, so it meant there hadn't been a stampede to sell.

I heard Susie wince. 'Are you sure about doing that?'

'Dead certain.' I filled her in on the result of my day's trading, and that seemed to cheer her up.

She changed the subject, slightly. 'Did you speak to Ricky?' she asked.

'Yup. He's on-side. He'll report to you as soon as he has something. I did some detecting on that front myself, though.' I told her what Ewan had admitted, about the end of his liaison with Nat Morgan.

'She's got a new man?' Susie exclaimed, surprised. 'Now there's a thing.'

'It happens: look at us, for example.'

'Maybe, but this must be some guy.'

'Why?'

There was a long silence on the other end of the line; the longer it lasted the more puzzled I grew. Then Susie broke it, with an incredulous vengeance. 'You're an actor,' she exclaimed, 'and you ask me that? Remind me: which character are you playing in this project, Dumb or Dumber? He must be some guy because, whoever he is, she's chucked Ewan Capperauld, no less, for him.'

128

# 25

The more I think about it, the more I believe that Susie's success in business is due not just to her judgement and her ability to make big financial decisions without flinching, but to the breadth of her vision. Sticking to gender stereotypes . . . politically incorrect, I know, but it's purely for illustrative purposes . . . she acts like a man, but thinks like a woman. Expressing it more acceptably, if I can, she has a degree of foresight that I certainly don't possess, nor do any other guys I know.

The only person in my life who's come close to matching it was Jan, but in my eyes, Jan's on course for canonisation, so I suppose I should stop using her as a comparison.

I broached the Natalie subject again with Ewan later in the week, over a steak sandwich in the cafeteria during a break between scenes. He was in Sir Gregor mode, and was pretty grumpy, so I didn't press it too hard, but it was pretty clear to me that his ego had been bruised by the ending of the relationship.

'You really don't know who the new guy is?'

'Not a clue,' he said, bitterly. 'She didn't say. I suppose she thought that I might have acted in current character and challenged the chap to a duel.'

'Pistols at dawn, and that?' I laughed. 'Ewan, you're a fucking brilliant actor, but can you shoot straight?'

'I won the rifle shooting cup in the cadet force at school,' he said, archly.

'And did the targets shoot back?'

He scowled at me.

'If I ever hear who he is,' I asked him, 'do you want me to tell you?'

'I wouldn't be in the slightest interested,' he replied, then a faint, out-of-character smile flickered across his face. 'Unless he happened to be extremely short-sighted, in which event I might just consider a duel.'

'You'd still want to load both guns yourself, though.'

'Absolutely. No point in taking unnecessary risks.'

'In fact, on the day it might be advisable to use a stunt double.'

He beamed. 'You are getting the hang of this business.' He paused, looking at me slightly sideways. 'Tell me, Oz, are you one of nature's duellists? Would you defend your honour with your life?'

I laughed at him. 'I'm in your camp. I might defend it with yours, but I'd be a bit more careful with mine. I'll define my attitude for you, if I can. A lawyer I know once told me that at its heart, his business is about kicking the other guy in the balls as hard as you can. That's how I see it. I think of duellists as outrageously stupid. The notion of giving someone a sporting chance, an even break, is anathema to me. In such circumstances I would use every advantage I had. Like my lawyer pal, if I was properly prepared and the chance arose, I would put the boot in in a micro-second and the other guy would not get up.'

Ewan frowned. 'Why do I get the impression that you are not speaking hypothetically here?' he murmured.

'I am, I am,' I assured him, even though he was close to the mark.

'Nonetheless, I shall make a mental note not to cross you. As for Miss Morgan,' he continued, 'she and her new paramour are no longer of any concern to me. Nor, incidentally, is Miss Rhona Waitrose.'

'Don't tell me she's chucked you too?' I spoke without thinking, although if I had thought I'd probably have said the same thing. I like Ewan, but it's my mission in life to keep his ego in check.

For a moment he became Sir Gregor again. 'As if,' he exclaimed. 'No, I found the lady a little young, and to be frank a little overeager. As it happens, I terminated that relationship.'

'And now?' I asked, for I sensed there was something else coming.

Ewan said nothing, but glanced across the cafeteria towards Louise Golding. I heard myself gasp. 'My Lizzie, you swine? My childhood sweetheart? If I had a glove on me I'd strike you across the face. Pistols at dawn it shall be.'

'Much better than a kick in the balls,' he exclaimed, loudly enough for Louise and her hairdresser to look up from their coffee and across at our table.

I left it at that; clearly Ewan knew nothing about his successor as Nat Morgan's love interest, nor, personal pique aside, did he seem to care. I wouldn't have cared either in his shoes; Louise Golding is built like a Greek goddess, even if her breath isn't all it should be for the morning close-ups.

For the rest of the week I was a model professional. I take my job seriously, and I've learned already that the more conscientious you are, and the more co-operative you are with directors, the more work you'll be offered. That's certainly proved true in my case, so far at least. Scott Steele told me once that in his first three years as an actor, he worked for a total of four months. Any inactivity I've had up to now is of my own choosing, or to be more accurate, mine and Susie's.

As the days went by the crisis in the Gantry group seemed to get no worse. The share price improved, if only a little, but no more shares came to the market. It was Wednesday before Greg McPhillips' tame QC came up with her letters to the lawyers acting for each of our three problem buyers. Susie didn't trust the fax for the purpose, so instead she sent me an e-mail file, which I downloaded on to my laptop.

The draft seemed flawless to me, given my incomplete knowledge of Scottish legalese. It was for Greg McPhillips' signature as company secretary and it referred to recent publicity in the tabloid press. While not commenting on, it said, far less concurring with the descriptions of the business activities of each of the buyers' husbands, it was a regrettable fact that the stories were having an adverse effect on the trading of the Gantry Group.

It went on to ask whether in the circumstances the solicitors' clients would be prepared to withdraw from the missives agreed for the purchase of the houses in question. The Gantry Group recognised that this would involve each buyer having incurred abortive expenses through no fault of their own. It was prepared to meet these costs in full and to offer an additional payment of five thousand pounds to each of the three.

I called her as soon as I'd read it. 'Seems fine to me,' I said.

'What do you think of the compensation offer?'

131

'Sensible. It's not so big that it'll encourage them to see it as a precedent.'

'Mmm,' Susie murmured. 'That's what I thought, but I don't know if it'll work. Greg's spoken to the Perrys' solicitor. He hinted that we'd be making them that sort of an offer to go away, but he got a dusty answer. The guy was non-committal at best: apparently he muttered something about damage to his clients' reputation.'

'That's a fucking laugh,' I commented, 'considering that Jock Perry has a reputation as one of the biggest crooks in Glasgow.'

'Maybe so, but Greg's reading is that they'll see they've got us by the shorts, and that they'll be looking for more than five grand.'

'Will you go up? Did the QC have a view on that?'

'She feels that ten grand would be safe, but that if we went much higher it would begin to look like bribery, and would set the sort of precedent we discussed . . . not just for ourselves, but for other builders. She's right about that one too; I've had a couple of my rivals on the phone already. On the face of it they've been expressing their sympathy, but really they're shitting themselves about how we handle it, and how it might affect them.'

I thought of some of Susie's rivals: it seemed to me that most of them cared about nothing more than the number of units they could build to the acre. As for the quality of their product, they were all in our wake. 'It'll affect them badly, I hope,' I told her.

'I'm sure you do, but I have to live with these people. I'm on the board of the House-builders' Association, remember.'

'You could always resign.'

'If I play this wrong, I'll have to.'

'You won't: it'll be fine. How's the witch-hunt going?'

'No suspects,' she replied, 'but Aidan Keane's resigned. He told me that there wasn't room for him and Fisher in the same company, and that since he'll be easier to replace, he's going.'

'Are you going to let him?'

'I'll have to. I can't sack Fisher for conducting a zealous investigation.'

'Not even if it's overzealous and fruitless?'

'Not even.'

'What about the Keane guy?' I recalled meeting him once at a Group party; I hadn't liked him much. His eyebrows met in the middle and he struck me as aggressive, just as Fisher had found him. 'Could he be your mole? Could he be going before he's caught? Could his outrage just be a smokescreen?'

'I don't think so, but I can't be sure,' she admitted. 'I suppose that if he goes to work for Torrent he'll move to the top of the list.'

'Speaking of Torrent,' I asked, 'have you heard anything from Ricky Ross?'

'Mmm, yes,' she said, with a new urgency in her voice. 'Have I ever. I was going to get round to that. He called me an hour ago. Nat Morgan had a very interesting lunch meeting today, in the Atrium Restaurant, in the Saltire Court office block, in Edinburgh.'

'Saltire Court? That's full of lawyers, accountants and fund managers, isn't it?'

'So I believe. And there were two of them at Morgan's lunch table. There was her lawyer, Duncan Kendall, from Kendall McGuire, the top corporate firm, and her accountant, Alan Williams. But not just them,' she added, quickly. 'There were others; there was Marvin de Luca, a director of Industry Partners, the major league venture capital firm, and Hew Bothwell-Brody, a major league stockbroker who commutes between London and Edinburgh. Then there was Sir Nigel Lanark, the merchant banker.'

I could see them in my mind's eye, all those thousand quid suits trying not to ogle the tall, olive-skinned, chocolate-voiced client. 'What was the significance of that?' I asked. 'It sounds like just another expensive lunch to me.'

'No, love, that was no ordinary lunch. If it had just been Kendall and Williams, I'd have thought so, but not with the other three there. Those guys are all players, financiers, the sort of people you'd want around you if you were planning to go into a takeover battle. I think Nat's getting geared up for action, and I'm in no doubt about what's being planned.'

'Do you think one of those guys might be her new man?' I asked.

'I asked Ricky that, but he said there was no sign of it; Natalie arrived and left on her own. He also says that he knows that de Luca,

133

Kendall and Lanark are all married, and that the stockbroker's a poof. Your friend has quite a database.'

Idly, I wondered what it would say about us. 'Do you think she'll move straight away?' I asked.

'No,' Susie replied, firmly. 'Not yet. I haven't told you about the sixth player at the table. It was Angela Rowntree.'

'And she is?' I knew that name from somewhere, but I couldn't pin it down.

'Managing director of Sapphire Investment managers.'

'Oh shit.' I knew that name; Sapphire controlled six of the biggest investment trusts in Scotland, and their total holdings included eighteen per cent of the stock of the Gantry Group. 'They were sounding her out?'

'Exactly. But she didn't bite; not yet, at any rate.'

'How do you know? Have you spoken to her?'

'No, and I can't, because I don't know about the meeting, do I? I know because our Ricky, clever bastard that he is, had one of his guys at a table across the restaurant, recording the conversation with a very small, but effective, directional mike. He said that Lanark asked her how she would feel about a takeover offer that valued the Gantry shares at significantly above current market price, subject to one hundred per cent acceptance. Angela told him that if it was significantly above the market price as it stood before the bad publicity on Monday, she'd probably expect the board to recommend acceptance, but that if it was simply based on the price as it stands today, she'd hold off to see how I managed the current crisis. She also said that Lanark and de Luca would be crazy if they underwrote a bid based on last week's price, and they had to agree with her.'

I thought about this. As I saw it, Susie had breathing space; a few days at least, and if she could manage to buy off the Three Bears, she should put herself in the clear. I said as much.

'Yes,' she agreed, 'provided that we don't have any more unforeseen disasters lurking in the undergrowth. I'm still uncomfortable, though; I'm more than half expecting one of those disasters, but I haven't a bloody clue where it's coming from.' She sighed, un-Susie-like. 'Oz, don't get big-headed about this or anything but I wish you were here.'

134

'Friday afternoon,' I promised her. 'I've seen the schedule for the rest of the week, and with a bit of luck I should be able to catch a flight around lunchtime.'

'Good,' she murmured. 'It's not just all this crap, you know. Even without it, I'd be missing you anyway.'

As it turned out I was able to keep my promise to my wife . . . but not before fate had lobbed an even bigger grenade in my direction.

# 26

The shooting schedule worked out, and with the blessing of Paul Girone, I left Shepperton in the limo at midday, heading for Heathrow and the first Glasgow shuttle of the afternoon. I called Susie from the car; the letters to the three gangsters' lawyers had gone out from Greg McPhillips' office the night before through the legal mail network, but she told me that none of them had responded.

'Okay,' I told her. 'Maybe you'll get a reaction this afternoon. If you do you can tell me when you get home tonight. I'll be there before you, assuming that British Airways doesn't mess me about.'

For once, the world's favourite airline didn't; the shuttles were running to time, and I was able to check in, grab a sandwich and a Coke, then walk straight on to the plane. The complimentary news-papers were running low at the foot of the air-bridge. All the *Herald*s had been snaffled by the earlier flights, but since we were heading for Glasgow there were still a few copies of the *Scotsman* to be had. I picked one up as I boarded.

I had had an early start on set. I belted myself into my window seat, leaned my head back, and fell asleep almost at once. When I awoke, we were on the climb, passing through the first layers of wispy cloud, looking down on Windsor Castle. As far as I could see there were no standards flying; Her Majesty must have been at one of her other palaces that day. I thought to myself that maybe it was time for Susie and I to buy a second home. For all that we lived on a pretty large property by British standards, we had a simple lifestyle for a movie star and a millionairess.

I was contemplating the alternative charms of France and Florida when the guy in the aisle seat leaned across the empty middle berth, on which he had dumped a jacket, a palm-top computer and a thick briefcase. 'Excuse me,' he began. 'But you are Oz Blackstone, aren't you?'

I glanced at him; he was in his thirties, podgy around the face, though not grossly overweight, and from the look of the sweat marks under the arms of his blue and white striped shirt, he had run to catch the plane. He was clean-shaven, and his dark hair was controlled by some sort of gel, from which a single bead of sweat had escaped and was running down his left cheek. I'd have taken him for a salesman . . . of palm-top computers perhaps, for I've never met anyone who actually uses one of the fiddly wee things . . . only he was wearing braces. In my experience only lawyers hold up their trousers with braces these days; I guess it's born of the extreme caution for which their profession is famous.

'A bleary-eyed and half-asleep Oz Blackstone,' I told him, 'but yes, that's me.'

He chortled. 'A hard night on the town was it?' he asked, jovially. (An incredibly rude question to be asking a complete stranger when you think of it, but it comes with the territory I inhabit these days, and I've learned to roll with it.)

'You know what it's like for us actors,' I told him. 'We have to do the round of the nightclubs to keep the children of the paparazzi in their private schools.' I caught the look of uncertainty as it came into his eye. 'Actually it was a hard morning in a film studio,' I went on, 'from which I'm escaping for the weekend to see my wife and daughter. It is actually possible to be in my business yet not be a piss artist.' I made myself smile at the guy as I finished. There's no point in snubbing people, even though it's what you'd really like to do.

'I wish it was possible in mine,' he exclaimed, full joviality restored. 'My name's Wylie Smith, by the way, middle name Henry, which causes the odd laugh among my colleagues these days.' I thought about this for a second, then remembered the newsagent, book shop and CD chain. I remembered also a Hearts goalie who raised a few laughs in his time as well, but they all do if they play long enough. Just ask the big guy with the ponytail.

'Which firm are you with?' I asked him.

He stared at me as if I had just told him the date of his birth, his

137

mother's maiden name and his inside leg measurement. 'You know me?'

'I don't think so.'

'Then how do you know I'm a solicitor?'

'It's a fifty-fifty chance on these flights, and you don't look like a footballer.'

His crest seemed to fall very slightly. 'I am, though. I play for my firm's team. We'd a match last Sunday in fact: played the Faculty of Advocates. Lost two nil.'

'You let them win?'

'There were two judges in their side: we thought it wise. Oh yes, and to answer your question, I'm a partner in Kendall McGuire.'

'*Now there's a coincidence.*' I almost said it aloud. Instead; 'I thought you were based in Edinburgh.'

'We are: Edinburgh and London, that is. I've been in the London office since Wednesday morning, and now I'm going to Glasgow for a meeting with a client. After that, I'm off home.'

I decided that I wanted to browse in W H Smith for a little longer. 'You're a pretty specialist firm, aren't you?' I asked him.

'Very. Nearly all of our practice is corporate, although we do handle some very specialised private client work, people we call Hinwies.'

I knew the term but I played dumb. 'Come again?'

'H. N. W. I.,' he spelled out. 'High Net Worth Individuals.'

'Ahh,' I said, reclining my seat as the captain switched off the seat belt sign. 'It's nice to know that Susie and I have an acronym. We're a bit beyond Yuppieness.' I waited for his chortling to subside. 'You've never acted for Gantry, have you?' I asked.

He blinked, then gave me a slightly confused look; you might even have called it apprehensive. 'Ah, the Gantry Group,' he exclaimed, when he caught on. 'No we haven't. Not yet at any rate, but strange things happen in the business world, so you never know. Who are your legal advisers at the moment?'

'McPhillips and Company . . . and Greg's a mate, as well as being company secretary, so I wouldn't hold my breath if I was you. But you've got a pretty chunky client list anyway, don't you?'

'Oh yes. As I said, we're absolutely blue chip. We've acted for some of the biggest names in Scotland, and beyond.' He reeled off three insurance companies, a bank and two major manufacturers.

'Don't you act for Torrent as well?' I dropped it in gently to see how far the ripples would spread.

'Not as far as I know,' WHS replied.

'*Then your senior partner's keeping secrets from you,*' I thought, '*or you're lying in your teeth.*'

'Ah. I was told you did; I must have been misinformed.'

'We'd like to, of course,' he volunteered, 'just as we'd like to act for the Gantry Group.'

'I think those two might be mutually exclusive.'

'Oh? Why should that be?' He looked surprised.

On the other hand, I did my best to look mysterious. 'Can't say, I'm afraid.'

'*Let him take that back to Duncan Kendall and see what they make of it.*'

'I have met Natalie Morgan, actually,' Smith volunteered. 'She's quite a spectacular lady, isn't she?'

'I've met her too. I don't like her . . . actually. She's not as bad as her uncle, though. Now he was a real cunt.' I don't like the 'c' word, but when I thought of the late James Torrent, it just slipped out. 'Where did you encounter Nat?' I asked the question in the hope that the solicitor's professional discretion gene might be a wee bit faulty, but he had said as much about her as he was going to, especially knowing that I wasn't a fan.

'Socially,' was all he volunteered, then he changed the subject. 'That was a rather unfortunate business for the Gantry Group at the weekend.'

'Unfortunate,' I agreed, 'but not crippling. Greg's dealing with it.'

'I'm sure he is. Still, if there's anything Kendall McGuire can do for you . . .'

I smiled at him as cheerfully as I could. 'Well . . .' I began, starting a look of anticipation in his eyes, '. . . if any of the Three Bears happens to figure on your Hinwie client list, you could ask them to fuck off and buy somewhere else.'

The flight attendant chose exactly the right moment to interrupt our discussion. WHS accepted his lunch tray; I passed on mine but took a small bottle of red wine, then settled down with my *Scotsman*.

The lead story was a banner heading about the latest cost estimate for the Holyrood Parliament building. The subject ceased long ago to excite me . . . and the rest of the Scottish nation, I suspect . . . but for the broadsheets it's an ever-ready club with which to batter the fledgling legislature about the ears, and to demonstrate to the world that our celebrated national parsimony is alive and well. I read it nonetheless, whistling in spite of myself at the numbers they were claiming.

The back page seemed to be in the same spirit, a ritual castigation of our unfortunate rugby players in the light of their latest mauling in the southern hemisphere. It cut no ice that it was only the constant press carping that had driven the Scottish authorities to fill the team with grand-maternal Aussies and Kiwis who couldn't quite make their own national sides. It cut no ice that rugby union isn't even our third choice as a national sport; genuine, round-ball football, golf and bowls all come before it. They had been gubbed by a side with ten times the resources, but they were still a national disgrace.

I was annoyed, and a bit scunnered . . . there's a real *Sunday Post* word for you . . . when I fought my way to pages two and three, folding the pages awkwardly, it being a real bugger to read a broadsheet on a plane while trying to balance a glass of wine on a tray table.

My crabbitness . . . another from the D C Thomson lexicon . . . lasted for as long as it took me to cast my eye on the lead story on page three. The headline read 'Fife police struggle to identify pig farm couple'.

My gasp must have been audible, but fortunately W H Smith had just spilled a piece of chicken cacciatore down his trousers and was otherwise occupied. I got a grip of myself quickly, and focused on the story.

'*Senior detectives in Fife,*' I read silently, '*admitted last night that they had so far failed to identify human remains found yesterday on an intensive pig farm near Arncroach in East Fife.*

'*The bodies, believed to be those of a man and a woman, were badly decomposed, making it difficult for police to estimate how long they had been there. Asked for a comment, Detective Inspector Tom Reekie, of North East Fife CID, said that, initially, the deaths were being treated as suspicious, until cause of death could be established.*

'*A post mortem examination will be carried out today in Edinburgh by a team including a pathologist and a forensic anthropologist.*

'*Inspector Reekie confirmed that identification was impossible at this stage, but that a number of possible lines of inquiry were being pursued. He said that other forces, not only in Scotland but throughout Britain, had been advised, so that they might check their missing persons files.*

'*However it is understood that Fife police themselves are pursuing the possibility that the bodies might be those of American-born Walter Neiporte (37), and his wife Andrea (29), who have been missing from their home in the fishing village of Pittenweem for several weeks. Police sources said that relatives of the couple were being contacted in the USA and England, so that DNA samples might be obtained for comparison testing.*

'*Neighbours of the missing couple described them last night as "strange", and "distant", although work colleagues described Mrs Neiporte as a "popular, friendly woman".*

'*The farm where the bodies were discovered, Lesser Saltgate, is operated by Mr Sandy McPhimister, of Kincraig. It is one of several that he owns in the area and has been the subject of repeated complaints from neighbours concerned about lack of supervision, the standard of husbandry, and about smells coming from the premises.*

'*It is understood that the bodies were discovered by SSPCA inspectors called in after complaints were received of a particularly foul smell. They were said to have been concealed in the troughs and covered in pig feed.*'

The last part made my stomach turn over: I imagined that Walter and Andrea had become part of the food chain.

The stories were accompanied by head and shoulder photographs of the missing couple; instantly a cold fist gripped my stomach. It didn't go away until I had convinced myself that hers was so dated and so grainy that there was no chance of Ronnie Morrow, assuming he read the story, picking her out as the woman who had chucked the paint at Susie and me. Mind you, I had to work hard to convince myself.

# 27

Jay Yuille was waiting for me at Glasgow Airport, with the engine running as usual in the hope that the police and the security people wouldn't give him a hard time. I tossed my bag on to the back seat, then climbed into the front beside him. I don't like acting the toff at the best of times, and I wanted to see his reaction close up when he saw the *Scotsman* report.

He didn't bat an eyelid; he scanned the story then handed me the paper.

'What's this, Jay?' I asked him as he pulled away, waving to a copper who was peering through the glass at me in the front passenger seat. Automatically, I waved at the guy too. As I did so I saw Wylie H Smith rushing off towards the taxi rank: remembering the way he'd been sweating on the shuttle, I hoped he didn't sit too close to his client . . . for both their sakes.

I turned back to my minder. 'Looks like a domestic tragedy to me, boss,' he replied, quietly.

'For sure, but . . .'

'But nothing, Oz: I've seen cases like these before. People get involved in something, thinking they're on to an easy mark and that they're smart enough to control the situation, take their profit and bugger off. But they're not that smart, and all of a sudden they find out that they're not in control. When that happens, the consequences can sometimes be terminal.'

'But this isn't any old case, is it?'

'It is as far as you're concerned.'

'Come on, Jay, let's stop pissing about. I sent you after these people and we both know that.'

I saw his nostrils flare slightly. 'No, sir. This is how it was. You

142

perceived a threat to your security, you did not want to go to the police, so you *asked* me,' he leaned on the word, 'to look into it. You did not *send* me anywhere. That's the way it was.'

'Not exactly.'

'Yes, Oz, exactly. You'll recall also that we agreed no questions would be asked about my methods?'

I nodded. 'Yes, I remember that.'

'Well don't fucking ask any then,' he said, quietly.

'You mean I have to live with this, and that's it.'

'Yup, live with it. That's more than the Neiportes are doing. Tell me something; do you really give a shit that they're dead?'

I felt my mouth twist. (Being me, I probably filed the gesture away subconsciously for use on a future movie. The truth is that art imitates life, not the other way around.) 'No,' I admitted. 'Not one tiny turd.'

'The truth is that your only worry is that it might come back to you.'

'I suppose.'

'Then stop worrying. It won't.'

'You certain of that?'

'Dead certain, you might say.' He glanced across at me as we headed west along the motorway. 'But that's not really your only worry, is it? You're scared you might have replaced one threat with another; the Neiportes with me.'

Scared wasn't quite the word, but I murmured, 'Maybe.'

'Then don't be. I came to you recommended, didn't I?'

'Yes, highly.'

'Well you remember that. The report you got on me included the word "loyalty", and it wasn't used lightly. I work for you, Oz, and you pay me well. I'm a specialist, and I set my own parameters. When you ask me to do something I'll do it, and I promise you I will never use it to gain any sort of leverage over you. If you want to give me a bonus down the line, that's up to you, but I will never ask you for one.' He took his right hand off the wheel and reached across. 'Fair enough?' he said.

I took it and shook it. 'Fair enough.'

'Good. So no more questions.'

We could hardly talk about rugby after that, so the rest of the journey back to the estate was spent in silence. When Jay dropped me at the house, it was empty. Susie was still at work, Ethel and Janet were away on a Daybreak Nursery outing, and the contract cleaners weren't due until the following Monday. The only sound I could hear was that of a mower in the distance. I guessed that Willie was quickening up the greens on the golf course.

I dumped my bag, which held the few clothes I'd brought back with me, mostly for the wash, and changed into a pair of swim shorts. I did a hard half-hour on my gym equipment, enough to work me out, but nowhere near enough to change my body shape, then swam for a bit to cool off. All the time I was thinking, at first about the Neiportes and how the police investigation would go, but gradually I found myself turning back to the week's first crisis, and Susie's three rogue house-buyers. If they'd had a couple of people bumped off and dumped on a pig farm, they wouldn't be bothering about it afterwards, I reckoned.

I was still in the pool when the phone rang. There was a hands-free unit near at hand, so I heaved myself out and picked it up just before the automatic answer cut in. 'Yes?' I said, breathing only a bit harder than normal.

'Oz, is that you?' It was my Dad, and he sounded agitated. It didn't take a quantum physicist to know why.

'It's me.'

'Have you seen the papers?'

'Yes, of course, it's tragic, isn't it. Those poor people . . . and from Pittenweem too, that's assuming they are who they think they are.'

'Oz . . .' Mac the Dentist said heavily, but I talked right over the top of him.

'Look Dad, I know you're upset, with the thing happening on your doorstep, but I really don't have time to talk to you just now.' I hung up on him.

We all have paranoid tendencies, but they're multiplied many times over when we have things to hide. At that moment all I could think about was Princess Diana, Prince Charles and their various bugged telephone conversations, which surfaced so embarrassingly in the tabloids. I could tell that my Dad was on his mobile, out in the garden, I imagined, and I'd been using a phone that worked on a radio signal.

144

The last thing I wanted was a detailed conversation being intercepted by some radio ham in Auchtermuchty and sold to the press.

I dried off, went through the house to the office conservatory, and called his surgery number on a more secure line . . . I'm reasonably certain I'm not on the MI5 surveillance list, and I know he isn't.

'I'm free now,' I said, breezily, when he answered. I checked my watch; it was five minutes short of four. 'Fancy a few holes at Elie? If I leave now I can get there for quarter to six.'

# 28

Susie wasn't best pleased when I got home at ten thirty. I'd left her the briefest of notes as I'd rushed out, forgetting that I'd said I'd pick her up from the office. I'd fixed that by calling Jay from the road and asking him to collect her in the Freelander . . . she was getting too big to drive comfortably, or even safely . . . but she still had a petted lip on her when I walked in.

There was only one thing to do, and that was to kiss it better. 'I'm sorry,' I said when she had softened. 'It was a spur of the moment thing; I hadn't seen my Dad for a while, and the way things are I wasn't sure when I'd have another chance.'

'It's all right,' she whispered. 'You're a big softy, that's all. Truth is I envy you. I wish I could bugger off on the spur of the moment to see my father.'

I wrapped her in my arms again. 'I know, love, and I'm so sorry you can't. But, here, you can nip off and see mine any time you like. How about that?'

She smiled. 'I like the thought of that. I'll go and see Mac any time . . . just as long as I don't have to sit in his dentist's chair that is.'

'No chance of that.' Like me, and many of our generation, Susie has perfect teeth. Macabre I know, but in that instant I found myself wondering how they'd identify us in a plane crash.

She might not have enjoyed visiting my Dad that afternoon, though. He'd been as agitated as hell when he'd arrived, a couple of minutes after me even though I'd come from the other side of the country and he'd come from Anstruther. I'd said nothing to him as we'd changed, although I could see him boiling.

He'd demonstrated his discomfort by carving his tee-shot out of bounds, then barely clearing the hill with his second, causing the

146

starter to avert his eyes in sympathy. (I, on the other hand, had popped a three-iron over the top, nice as you like.)

He took it until my par putt rattled into the cup, and no longer. 'Right!' he said.

But I shook my head. There's a thick plantation behind the second tee, and you never know. I hit a nice five wood; there's no need to risk a full driver, although my Dad did and found the rough. I won the second with a bogey five . . . I took too much club for my second, knocked it through the green and had to chip back up . . . and only then did I turn to Mac the Dentist.

'Nothing, Dad,' I told him. 'You have nothing to be concerned about.'

'But son, what the hell have you done?'

I gave him my best incredulous look, hoping that it would fool him. 'What are you saying? Just fucking think about what you're saying here?'

He reddened before my apparent anger. 'But . . .'

I didn't let him go on. 'What makes you fucking special?' I asked him, as I took a seven iron out of my bag and tossed my ball on to the ground behind the marker posts. 'What makes you think you have to be the only person they've blackmailed? These were nasty people; neither you nor I have any idea what else they were into. The only thing we know is that somewhere they've messed with the wrong guy and wound up dead for their bother.'

I took a deep breath, focused and hit a gentle faded shot to the front of the third green. Then I turned back to him. 'There was nothing unpredictable about that. What is incredible is that you actually think it was me who bumped them off.'

'No,' he protested. 'I don't think that. But you know people, son; that sort of people. That was my first thought.'

I didn't want him to get any nearer the truth, or I'd have had trouble keeping up my act. So I shut him up, as Jay Yuille had silenced me.

'And your last,' I said, icily. 'I warn you, Dad, don't ever talk to me about this again, or it'll be many a day before you and I stand up on this tee again. Let the police get on with their investigation, for I promise you it will not come back to you. If they phone you looking for dental ID, send it to them without a word. Yes?' I snapped. He nodded, looking at the ground like a chidden schoolboy.

'Right. Now in case you've forgotten you're two down and I've got a twenty-footer for a birdie waiting down there.'

'How did your golf go anyway?' Susie asked.

I smiled. 'My Dad played shite. Never won a hole; he didn't even manage a half till the sixth.'

'That's not like him. He'll be losing to Jonny next.'

'He does that already.'

'I suppose so. I always forget how big he's getting.' She squeezed my arm as we lay on the couch, nursing a couple of glasses of Gran Sangre de Toro . . . one of the best sleeping potions we know. 'Sorry I was grumpy when you came in. It's been a trying week.'

'I know it has, love. Did you go for your check-up, by the way?' She nodded. 'All okay?' She nodded again, but avoided my eye. 'Susie?' I demanded.

'It's nothing. My blood pressure was a bit raised, that's all. Only a wee bit, honest.'

I put down my glass and turned her to face me. 'What did your consultant say?' I asked her, a little urgently I guessed, for she twisted in my grasp.

'Och, Oz, it's all right, really. She said she'd keep an eye on it, but it was only a couple of points up.'

'Well it's getting no higher. That's it; now that Culshaw's agreed to deputise for you, you're off on maternity leave as of now.'

'I knew you'd say that. I'm all right, really, and so's the baby.'

I made her look at me again. 'Susie, my love, I usually think four or five times before trying to lay down the law to you, but not this time. You are out of there.'

She must have been tired, for she gave up the fight. 'Okay,' she conceded. 'It'll take me a few days next week to hand over to Phil, but once that's done, I'll stay at home.'

'You mean that?'

'I mean it; cross my heart.' She settled down beside me again on the couch. 'Now, how was the rest of your day?' she asked. 'Anything interesting happen?' She giggled. 'Apart from making a movie, that is.'

'As a matter of fact . . .' I told her about my encounter on the Glasgow plane with Mr W H Smith of Kendall McGuire.

'There's a coincidence,' she murmured. 'I wonder how he managed that?'

'What?'

'To get sat next to you.'

'Aw come on, that was pure chance. You can't just go to the check-in and ask to sit next to someone.'

'Maybe he saw you check in, then went up and asked for the same row.'

'No way.'

'Oh no? Were all the window seats taken?'

I thought back to the flight. The plane had been less than half full. 'No, but not everyone likes one. Anyway, the guy was sweating like a horse when he got on board, as if he'd had to run for it.'

'That means nothing. You know how hot that departure lounge can get.'

That was true enough, I conceded; it had been like a furnace at lunchtime. Then I stopped myself. She was as paranoid as I was. 'Maybe so, but I still don't think the guy was a plant.'

'Maybe he just saw you and took a chance.'

'Forget it. He didn't strike me as that smart.'

'What did you talk about?' Susie asked.

'Football at first, then business. Actually, when I think of it, I began the business chat. I clocked him as a lawyer; it was only after that that he told me who he was with. We got talking and I asked him who they represented; the interesting thing was that he denied any knowledge of a Torrent link.'

'That was a lie for a start, if he's a partner like he said.'

'I don't think so. I'm an actor, remember; I should know when someone's hamming it up. Has it occurred to you that Duncan Kendall might have been representing someone else at Natalie's Atrium lunch?'

'It might have, if Ricky hadn't told me that she's been to his office half a dozen times over the last week or so. No, love, that confirms what we already knew; the bitch is at it. They're playing it really close to their chest, especially if Kendall's keeping secrets from his partners. Did you talk to the guy all the way up to Glasgow?'

149

'No, he told me that he'd met Nat Morgan socially, I gave him my opinion of her, and that more or less terminated our discussion.'

Susie grinned. 'I should imagine it would have. Now, are you going to ask about my day?'

'Yes. Consider yourself asked.'

She pinched her nose. 'Four highlights, really. First, your son has been kicking hell out of me all day.'

'Good for wee Mac. Now you know what sleeping with you's like just now.'

She gave me a mock frown. 'Second,' she said, heavily, 'about three tons of crated up playground equipment arrived this afternoon. So you and Mr Yuille can spend this weekend drawing up a plan of how it's going to look, and deciding where you want to put it.'

'We more or less know already. We just need to size the stuff up.'

'Fine, you do that. Oh yes, and your sister phoned, wanting to know, and I quote, "what the bloody hell" she's supposed to do with her delivery . . . I told her to get a local builder to set it all up for her and Uncle Oz would pay. Highlight three, we've been invited to a posh Scottish Enterprise Dinner on the Saturday after next, in the Old Course Hotel in St Andrews. I've said we'll go, provided I'm not in labour. I've turned down the accommodation they offered, though. It was just a double en suite, so I'd rather stay with Mac and Mary.'

'Me too. And fourth?'

'Mrs Perry's lawyer called Greg. He said that he thought our offer was an insult, but that he'd consult his client and see how insulted she felt.'

'Did Greg get the impression she'd find ten grand less insulting?'

'He didn't know. All he said was that we'd have an answer by Monday or Tuesday.'

'Let's hope it's the right one.'

'Fuck 'em if it isn't. I'm past caring. Last and finally, but this isn't a highlight. Fisher's investigation has ended, like the dampest of squibs. He's cost us a good agent and a couple of foremen who've gone as well as Aidan, but he hasn't got near finding our mole.'

'If there ever was one,' I muttered.

'What do you mean by that?'

'I don't know,' I confessed. 'But it's been a week. You'd have thought he'd have popped up for air by now.'

'Are you saying that this might not have been information leaked, but something set up from the outside all along?'

I shook my head, trying to clear it as much as anything else. 'To be truthful, my darling, it's been a long, hard week. I don't have a fucking clue what I'm saying.'

# 29

We didn't have to wait till Monday or Tuesday to find out the reaction of the Three Bears' wives to the compensation offer. That fine organ, the *Sunday Herald*, told us twenty-four hours later.

It had been a quiet Saturday; Jay and I had obeyed orders and completed our detailed planning of Janet and wee Mac's playground. It was going to look pretty good, I reckoned, and I had no safety worries with the equipment. It was all first class and solidly put together . . . Clyde-built as they used to say, when that meant something.

We had done more than that, actually. I had helped him fit a new double gate to the back entrance to the estate, making sure that the lock worked and that the bolts held it secure. It's not that it's used much, indeed hardly ever, but there's some pretty danger- ous boggy ground near Loch Lomond, and the track which leads from the gate down to the road runs through some of the worst of it. It's said to be virtually bottomless; when they were building the new golf course, they lost an earth mover . . . and almost the course architect himself.

So, you see, the entrance had to be secure not to prevent people from getting into the estate, but to prevent small people, like my reckless nephew Colin, Janet, and her wee brother eventually, from getting out.

With that job done, Jay and I hit a few golf balls, then I headed back to the house to take Janet for a swim. At first I couldn't find her, until I wandered towards the office conservatory and heard her chirping away us usual, but being 'shoosh'-ed, by Susie. As I walked in, I saw that my wife was on the phone, and from the look on her face I did not fancy being the person on the other end.

At once, I thought about her blood pressure. 'Who's that?' I asked.

She said a quick, 'Hold on,' then covered the mouthpiece. 'Press. *Sunday Herald*,' she whispered.

I reached out a hand. 'Gimme the phone.'

'No!'

'Susie, you're red in the face. Please give me the phone and make me happy. Take Janet to the pool and let me deal with this.'

She shrugged, then gave me a quick smile. 'I like it when you're masterful.' She handed me the phone.

'Hello,' I said, 'this is Oz Blackstone. My wife's pregnant and she isn't taking business calls today. Now who is this, please?'

'It's Arnott Buchan, *Sunday Herald*, and she was taking business calls a minute ago.'

'Not any more, Mr Buchan. You can either phone Alison Goodchild, our PR consultant, or you can try it on me. Susie's effectively on maternity leave from now on.'

'Do you speak for the Gantry Group, Mr Blackstone?'

'I speak for my wife, mate, and she is the Gantry Group.'

'That's a sweeping statement. I don't know if Sir Graeme Fisher would agree with you.'

'I could give a fuck about that.' Irony is almost as difficult to convey over the phone as on the printed page, but I think I managed it. 'Do you want to carry on this discussion, or call Alison?'

'No,' said the reporter. 'I'll speak to you. It's about the New Bearsden situation. I've spoken to the lawyers acting for the Three Bears.'

'That's not quite accurate,' I pointed out. 'Those three gentlemen are not the purchasers. For reasons best known to them, all three of the deals in question were done in their wives' names.'

'Yeah,' said Buchan, 'but we both know the score, Mr Blackstone. It's all about asset sheltering, isn't it.'

'Call me Oz, everyone else does. And you said that, not me. The fact is, I don't care what it's about. I only know that the publicity surrounding these purchases is harming the Gantry Group.'

'Is that why your wife's lawyer tried to bribe them to withdraw?'

'Your lawyer wouldn't even let you hint at that in print. Because of the tabloid furore we've found it necessary to ask these ladies if they'd be prepared to withdraw from their agreements, and we've offered them a small premium. Effectively we've offered to buy those plots back at terms advantageous to them.'

'That may be how you put it, but all three of them, and I've spoken to them separately, claim that you've stigmatised them and their families.'

I laughed; I didn't mean to, it just came out. 'That's bloody rich. We've never discussed these purchases, other than in private. We've never said anything about these three people to any reporters. The offers that were made were and remain, on our part, confidential, lawyer to lawyer. The only people doing any stigmatising are you guys in the media, in the way you've run the story, and the three families themselves, in feeding you with quotes.'

I paused. 'Stigmata's a dangerous topic for them anyway; I seem to remember a story a while back about a guy whom your sister newspaper, the *Herald*, said had fallen out with Mark Ravens. Does it ring any bells with you?'

'I think so.'

'I'll bet it does. They found the guy alive, but nailed to a wall in a flat in Paisley. Crucified. A crown of barbed wire jammed on his head. He'll bear the stigmata, the marks of the Cross, for the rest of his life.'

'What are you saying to me?'

'Nothing you can ever print. I'm just telling you not to get fucking sanctimonious with me, mate. Now what do you want to say to me? What's the bottom line on this story?'

'Okay,' said Buchan, 'I take your point. What I was in the middle of telling your wife is that all three families . . .'

'Are we speaking Sicilian here?'

'Nice one, but no comment . . . that all three families have rejected your offer. They intend to proceed with their purchases, on the basis that, as respectable business people, they have as much right as anyone else to live on what you yourself claim will be the finest modern housing development in Scotland. Their solicitors have also told me . . .'

'Wait a minute.' I interrupted him. 'Are you saying there's been collusion here? Are the three acting in concert?'

'As far as I'm concerned, Oz, they're acting separately. I've asked each of them that same question, and they've all denied it.'

'As they would.'

'Maybe, but it'll be down to the Gantry Group to prove otherwise. What they've each said . . . individually . . . is that they're not prepared to back out at any price. They've also said that if the Gantry Group attempts to withdraw from the agreements unilaterally, or tries to pull any tricks like redesigning the development to take these three plots out . . .'

'*Damn it!*' I thought. That had been an option under discussion.

'. . . they will go straight to court to seek interdicts preventing them. I should tell you that each of the three lawyers expressed complete confidence that they would be granted.'

That was our legal advice too, but I wasn't going to tell the *Sunday Herald* that.

'Can I ask you a few formal questions, Oz?'

'Sure.'

'First, can you confirm that such offers were made to the three buyers?'

'Yes, in the terms I expressed to you earlier. In the light of media coverage, which I'm sure the families found as unfortunate and embarrassing as we did, we've offered to buy the plots back, at a premium.'

'What's your reaction to the rejection of that offer?'

'If that's true, and it won't be till our lawyers hear from their lawyers, I'd say that it's unfortunate too.'

'Finally, in the light of their threat to go to court, what does the Gantry Group intend to do next?'

'The board will discuss that next week.'

'Will New Bearsden go ahead?'

'Too bloody right it will.'

'What about Sir Graeme Fisher's investigation?'

'What happened to "finally"?'

'There are always a few more.'

'The investigation's over.'

'Has it resulted in any disciplinary action?'

'Go and take a look outside the New Bearsden site office, or the

Gantry Group HQ building. If you see any heads on poles you can run the photo on page one.'

'I'd heard that one of the heads might belong to a guy called Aidan Keane.'

'You've been drinking in the wrong pub, then. Aidan's resigned, but he's neither suspected of anything nor accused of anything.'

'I hear he's got a new job, though. He won't start for a few weeks, and it's not official, so much as I'd like to I can't run it.'

'What's that, then?' Suddenly I was interested.

'Mr Keane's going to be property manager for a pub chain called Caiystane Inns.'

'Never heard of them.'

'Wouldn't have expected you to. But if you look it up, you'll find that the chairman and managing director is a Mr Mark Ravens.'

I whistled. 'Thank you for that, Arnott,' I told the journalist. 'Now, if you'll excuse me, I must go and see if I can find a pole.'

# 30

I filled Susie in on most of my conversation, but I didn't tell her about Aidan Keane's rumoured new employer. That information I kept for Phil Culshaw, when I phoned to ask him if he could take over as acting managing director with immediate effect. Susie had agreed that they could manage without a formal handover, and that if there was anything on which he needed her advice he could either call her or drive out to the estate.

He and I discussed Aidan Keane, then we linked in a three-way conference call to Des Lancaster. The poor old project manager had been enjoying a quiet day in his garden till we ruined it for him.

'Are you sure about this?' he exclaimed when I told him about his departed lieutenant.

'It came from a journalist, but I don't think he'd have volunteered it if he wasn't pretty sure of his sources. I gave him some straight answers; I think it was his way of thanking me.'

'I can see it now,' said Des, slowly. 'Aidan acted as a negotiator sometimes; he closed the deal with Cornwell, and that was why Sir Graeme asked him some heavy questions, but he had nothing to do with Perry or Ravens, so he was stood down as a suspect. But when I think about it, he was in a position to keep the three sales files well apart, to cut down the chances of any connection being made.' He sighed. 'On top of that there's his writing.'

'What do you mean?' asked Phil.

'There's a master lay-out of the project on a wall of the sales office; every time a sale's made, the buyer's name's supposed to be written on that particular plot. Aidan was responsible for making sure it was kept up to date. The trouble is, his blooming handwriting is very close to being illegible. For example, on the board, "Ravens" looked more like

"Rawlings" and "Cornwell" and "Perry" looked like they were spelt with an "a" rather than with an "e". Oh dear.' Lancaster sighed again, even more deeply. 'Sir Graeme will have me this time, when he hears this.'

'No he won't,' I told him. 'Fisher's had a week to look at that board himself, and ask questions about it. You're in the clear, Des.'

'I don't know, Oz. The truth is, I'm almost at the end of my rope with this job. I think I may well chuck it anyway.'

'I'll tell you what,' said Phil. 'How would you feel if . . .' He floated the idea of the job swap with Brian Shaw that Susie had discussed with me.

'Do you think Brian would go for that?' Des exclaimed, not quite managing to disguise his eagerness.

'I wasn't planning on asking him,' said the acting managing director, dryly.

We were better prepared for the breaking of the *Sunday Herald* story than we had been a week earlier. Our QC had given us a plan that covered every contingency, including the one that had developed, and a copy had been given to Alison Goodchild, for her to use as a briefing book.

It said that the company would act in the best interests of all its shareholders, and reserved the right to take any action it considered appropriate. Effectively that meant reserving the option of cancelling the three sales and taking the chance that the threat of court action was a bluff, knowing at the same time that if it wasn't, the likelihood was that we were in for a kicking.

What I was not prepared for was the verbal kicking I received from Sir Graeme Fisher once the story had appeared in print.

'What the hell do you think you're up to, boy?' he shouted at me, as I sat at the breakfast table with a slice of toast in one hand and the phone in the other. 'You're not a director of this company and you don't speak for this company. What's this nonsense you're quoted as saying? "*My wife is the Gantry Group*?" You're making it look a damned laughing stock, and you're making me look a laughing stock.'

I kept my face straight through his tirade, because Susie was sitting across the table and I didn't want her to get wind of what was happening.

'You don't need any help there,' I told him, smiling.

His tone went up a notch or two, attaining incandescence. 'You impertinent young . . .'

'Shareholder is the word you're after, I think.'

'Then listen, shareholder. If your wife is stepping down as managing director, for whatever reason, the first body that has to be told is the Stock Exchange, not the *Sunday* bloody *Herald*. You've broken a fundamental rule, son, but it's me who's going to have to apologise for it. Do you know what I'm thinking now? I'm thinking that it might be in the best interests of the company, by which I mean all the shareholders, if rather than allow your wife to go on maternity leave, I suspend her formally from duty because of the way she's handled this crisis. Allowing you to speak to the press is reasonable evidence, as I see it, of a serious lack of judgement on her part, justifying such an action on mine. I propose to take independent legal advice . . . not your pal McPhillips . . . and if he agrees that I have a right to do that, I will.'

I wasn't sure whether Susie sensed what was happening or not, but she chose that moment to slip off her stool at the breakfast bar, gather Janet up in her arms, and leave the room.

The change in my tone of voice must have surprised Fisher, just a little. 'Now listen to me, you old bastard,' I hissed. 'Get your ego in check and remember your place. If you don't assure me right now that what you've just said was all bluff and bullshit there will be a special board meeting before this day is out. I will attend that meeting as my wife's proxy and the only item on the agenda will be your resignation as chairman.'

'On what grounds?'

'On the grounds that I don't fucking like you. If you think I'm not serious, just try me out. Now I'll tell you two things. One, if you ever call me "boy" or "son" again, your age won't stop me slapping you silly. Two, if you ever threaten my wife again, nothing will protect you. Now this is what you're going to do. You'll instruct our brokers to make a statement to the Stock Exchange that Phil Culshaw has taken over as acting chief executive of the group during Susie's absence on maternity leave, but that she will be available to him for consultation and advice. That'll impress the analysts. What you've just proposed

159

would scare the crap out of them, and the bankers and every independent sharcholder.'

I had to pause for breath; that's how angry I was. 'You've got five seconds,' I continued, 'to let me hear you say "Yes", or I call Greg as company secretary and have him call that meeting. And don't waste one of those seconds thinking I'm bluffing. One, two . . .'

Fisher said, 'Yes,' on the count of four, although it came across as if he was choking.

'Sensible,' I said. 'By the way, what do you think of Aidan Keane as the mole?'

'He's a hot-head, but I'm certain it wasn't him.'

'Wrong.' I hung up on the Knight of the Realm.

'Was he indeed?'

I looked over my shoulder; Susie was standing in the doorway.

'How much of that did you hear?'

'I came in on "I don't fucking like you". I've been wanting to say that to him since the first day he took the chair. He's got to go.'

I shook my head. 'No, not now he's got the message. It would be a bad move at this point. You have to show unity. The share price will take a big enough thumping tomorrow as it is.'

# 31

I wasn't wrong about that: when the market opened next morning all the week's small recovery had been wiped out and a further ten per cent had gone from the company's value, knocking the shares below their original flotation price of one pound.

I was in Middlesex when I found this out. Paul had scheduled an early start for the second week's shooting. I knew it wouldn't be a brilliant opening, but I wasn't prepared for Ernie Nichols, my broker, phoning me to ask if I was sure I still wanted to buy Gantry shares.

'Of course I do,' I told him. 'This crisis will all be sorted in a couple of days.' Optimism was essential, I felt, even though I didn't feel much.

'It's not a bright picture,' he warned me. 'If sales on your new development are as poor as they were last week . . .' That statement could have been lifted from a master-class in diplomacy. There hadn't been any sales; a hastily put together market research programme had told us that in addition to public concern about living next door to gangsters, many potential buyers had been put off by the fear that if they bought in New Bearsden they might come under police scrutiny themselves.

'The analysts aren't too keen on your wife's decision to step aside either. They feel that it sends the wrong message. Even at this stage you couldn't persuade her to stay in post, could you?'

I told Ernie that I was the guy who'd insisted that she step aside, and that he should stick to buying and selling. He did that, okay. By midday I'd acquired another hundred thousand Gantry shares from small private investors who'd lost their bottle.

But the small fry weren't the only ones to head for the hills.

I was on-set in the afternoon when I had a message to call Phil Culshaw, whenever I could. I was between takes, so I called him on my mobile at the office. 'What are you doing just now?' he asked.

'Nothing. Why?'

'I meant are you shooting funny scenes or heavy drama?'

'The latter.' And how: my character and Ewan's were having their final confrontation.

'That's all right then. What's the worst thing that could happen to the company in the present situation?'

'Saddam Hussein and Osama Bin Laden could buy adjoining villas?'

'Worse than that.'

'George W Bush fancies a weekend retreat in New Bearsden?'

'You're getting there. Sapphire's selling out. Angela Rowntree called me this morning. She told me that she doesn't see the situation being resolved any time soon, if ever, so she's taking what she can get right now and investing elsewhere.'

'So why haven't her shares come on the market?' I asked. 'Ernie Nichols would have told me if they had.'

'She's accepted a private offer, and you're not going to like it when I tell you who the buyer is. Not that you can't guess.'

'Natalie Morgan. Torrent PLC.'

I heard Phil's sudden quiet grunt. 'Got it in one. You're not surprised then?'

'No. In the light of what you told me a while back, Susie and I have been tracking Ms Morgan. She met with the Rowntree woman last week.'

'I don't imagine I want to know how you found that out.'

'No, you don't. Has the deal been done, or can I make a counter-bid?'

'It's done. Anyway, you don't have that sort of money.'

'I have friends who do.'

'Ah, but would they put it at risk?' He had me there: Everett Davis owes me, but not that much. 'Anyway,' he continued, 'it's academic. The deal's done. Sapphire has accepted an offer of one pound thirty pence per share, and that's not all that far below the Gantry price before the nonsense began. Ms Rowntree didn't say, but I'm assuming

162

that the price will be paid in new Torrent shares, and that she'll simply be exchanging an investment in one company for another.'

'Damn it.'

'No, Oz, that reaction's too mild. I had Nat Morgan on the phone half an hour ago. She told me that given the size of her holding, she expects a seat on the board. I've also had a call from Fisher. She's made the same demand to him and he supports her. Do you want to tell Susie, or shall I.'

'Neither of us will. I don't want her blood pressure raised by a single point, and that news would send it up the scale. You tell Morgan what Susie would if I'd let her. Remind her that she owns about eighteen per cent of the company, and that's not enough to make demands. When she owns fifty-one per cent she gets a seat, but not before.'

'It may come to that, Oz,' Phil warned. 'Almost certainly this is a precursor to a full bid, contingent on one hundred per cent acceptance.'

'Yes, and Susie has sixty per cent and she'll reject.'

'Not so easy. There's another twenty-two per cent out there.'

'Some of that's mine.'

'Yes, but how much?'

'I dunno for sure,' I admitted. 'but it'll be short of one per cent.'

'Minimal. That leaves another twenty. Okay, Joe Donn's six per cent might be out of the reckoning, but that leaves fourteen. Morgan will only need about half of that on her side. If significantly more than half of the minorities want to accept, and the company's advisers deem that a bid of one thirty is the best price attainable, Fisher will recommend acceptance.'

'You mean he'll sell the business out from under Susie's feet?'

'Yes. And I'd say the court would back him if it had to.'

'Where's the escape hatch?'

'Susie resigns her executive position and a successor is appointed. As an ordinary shareholder, she can reject the offer. But, and it's a big one, if she does that her shareholding is such that she could be forced to buy out the minorities.'

'Yes, we had anticipated that one. Do you see any daylight in this?'

'If she took the offer Susie would be a big player inside Torrent. She could make a real nuisance of herself.'

'That's not her scene, Phil.' I thought, as quickly and as broadly as I could. 'Listen, you're chief executive, and it has to be your decision, but if I was you I'd make the bold move now. We've been nice to these chancers for long enough. I'd tear up the Three Bears' sales and call their bluff.'

'And what if they sue?'

'That possibility is the reason why the share price is on the floor, so I don't see that it can do that much more damage. But if they don't . . .'

'Then we've won and it goes back up. You're right, of course. But as a responsible managing director, can I put the business at such a risk?'

'Which is the bigger risk? Doing that or doing nothing and letting New Bearsden turn into a financial disaster? Phil, I'll bet you a million quid right now that the day Nat Morgan takes control of Gantry she'll make those three hooligans a modest offer for their plots and they'll accept.'

He was silent for a while. 'You really think she's behind them?'

'I'd stake your life on it, mate.'

Culshaw laughed. 'In that case, I've got no choice. But . . . and I really don't want to know how you do it, it would be very nice if you could get me some proof of that.'

But I was in no position to start gathering proof, was I, not four hundred miles away from the action, on a sound stage in Middlesex. I was doing what I could by remote control, of course; Ricky's operatives still had Natalie Morgan under surveillance, and after Arnott Buchan's tip on Saturday, I had asked him to organise a tail on Aidan Keane as well, using close-mouthed Glasgow people who knew the territory. Common sense told me that I couldn't do any more if I was in Scotland, but I wasn't happy being away from Susie at that time, and that was the truth of it.

My anger must have come through in a big way on camera that afternoon, for my big scene with Ewan was another one-take wrap, and after it the Great Man Himself actually complimented me on my work, telling me that for all his years of experience, I'd actually scared him a little. The way I felt, I was surprised I hadn't scared him a lot.

I shouldn't have done it, I know, but I couldn't stop myself. Before we went our separate ways, Ewan back to his London base and I to mine in the hotel, I asked him if he still had Natalie Morgan's private number. If he was curious, he didn't show it: he just produced his Filofax, copied it on to a blank note sheet, tore it out and handed it over to me.

I had been in Nat's flat once. It's a penthouse, perched on a block in Ravelston in Edinburgh. I could picture it as I dialled her number, and her, prowling around like a great cat. Make no mistake, if I'd known her in my single days . . . and even in some of my married ones . . . I'd have fancied spending more time there than I had, and exploring one of the rooms I hadn't been in. I still wouldn't have liked her, but I was never one to let that get in the way of a memorable shag. From the moment we'd met I'd been irked by her arrogance, as no doubt had she by mine. We were two people destined never to hit it off, whether we were physically attracted to each other or not.

The phone rang out, until an answering system cut in. The voice on the message wasn't hers. It was male, and it sounded familiar: it didn't take me long to realise that the guy telling me that Natalie Morgan wasn't home, but that I could leave a message, was none other than Ewan Capperauld. She might have chucked him, but she still kept him on her tape to impress callers.

That's what I told her too, when I started to record the invited message, that she had more than a little bloody cheek. I hadn't got very far when she picked up the phone. 'Well hello, Oz,' she exclaimed. 'I'll be happy to ditch old Ewan, if you'll do me a replacement. I'd love to have your husky Fife tones answering my calls. What can I do for you, my dear?'

It had taken her about ten seconds to get under my skin. Her voice was different; maybe that's what triggered it off. I was used to Nat sounding cold and aloof. She'd never teased me in her life before. But now there was a chuckle at the back of her throat, and as she spoke I could see her smiling.

'You know very well what you can do for me, Natalie. You can get your greedy, ambitious doe eyes off my wife's company.'

She laughed again. 'Thanks for the compliments, darling; I could always tell you liked my eyes. I rather like yours too. When you look

165

into them and ignore everything else there's a coldness about them that's very impressive. It's rather sad that you've become Susie Gantry's lap-dog.'

'Rottweiler would be a better description, as you're going to find out if you keep trying to hurt Susie.'

'That's good,' she chuckled. 'I prefer you when you're not trying to be nice. I have to confess I've seen all your movies, and when they let you be the bad guy, it really turns me on.'

'Keep pushing your luck then, and see how moist you get. I'm not kidding. This move of yours is not welcome, either on a personal or a business level. It doesn't make any sense either. You know sweet eff all about the construction and property businesses. If you want to expand Torrent, why not stick to your own sector? That's what your uncle would have done. By the way, I don't know if I ever told you this, but I thought he was a shit as well, and I'm glad he's dead.'

'Oh come on, Oz! James may have lacked business vision, but he did have his good points.'

'Name one.'

'When he died he left everything to me.'

I laughed; sort of. 'He didn't leave it, he was taken away from it. He was a greasy, grasping, avaricious . . .'

'Lecherous?' she said. 'Yes, how about lecherous.'

'Fine, if you want. Tell me, 'cos I've always wondered? Did you and he . . .'

Hard as I was trying, I couldn't seem to rattle her. She tutted at me. 'Unworthy, Oz, unworthy. He'd have liked to, of course, but I never gave him the opportunity.'

'You mean it wasn't necessary, you were his heir anyway?'

'Got it in one, darling. Now you, on the other hand; I loathe and detest you also, but . . .'

'Forget it, girl. You'll never feature in my will.'

'That won't ruin my day. So come on, Oz, tell me. I hear you're calling the shots behind the scenes these days, now that little wifie is off practising fecundity. Am I getting my seat on the Gantry Group board?'

'I wouldn't give you a seat on a scout camp latrine, gal.'

She laughed again, louder than ever. I judged it to be a little forced.

'You are a mean bastard, aren't you. You're a name, though. I may still offer you a place when I take over.'

'Dream on.'

'I am. We announced it this afternoon. Torrent is making a formal bid for one hundred per cent of the share capital of Gantry. It'll take us a week or so to prepare, but we've advised the Stock Exchange already. Your shares have recovered a little, but with that thug Culshaw inviting court action on the company, I'm still certain of success.'

'You're crazy. I'm a private shareholder, and I'll never sell.'

'I'm advised that the court will see you as acting in concert with your wife; it'll force you to sell also. Come on, Oz, do a private deal with me now and I'll make you a director. I heard you were really wounded when dear old Graeme forced you off the board. He's on my side, you know. He was a great friend of my uncle.'

'You shouldn't have told me that, Nat. He's been hanging on by his nails anyway, but now he's history.'

Suddenly I had had enough. 'No more crap; here's the deal. You drop this nonsense, or I will break you.' She started to chuckle but I cut her off. 'In half, girl, in half, and I always keep my word.' I paused for a second. 'So you take that warning to heart, and you take it somewhere else as well. Take it to whoever's behind you. I know you, you see; you don't have the vision for all this. You couldn't set up the Three Bears to buy into New Bearsden, or use Aidan Keane to cover it up till the trap was ready. For sure, there's someone behind you, and you know what? I'm going to fucking have him as well.'

# 32

I really was itching to be back in Scotland, but a contract's a contract, and my being in Middlesex was keeping a lot of people in work. So I resigned myself to working as hard and as well as I could in the hope that I might be able to sneak some more time off at the end of the week.

One of my great grandmothers was Irish and I suspect that she may have had a touch of leprechaun blood in her veins. Whatever it was, be it a four-leafed clover, a lucky charm or just plain random chance, the extravagant luck of the Blackstones worked for me again, just when I needed it.

For virtually all of the rest of the week, the scenes we were due to shoot involved, among a few others, Louise Golding and me. I was on set at eight sharp next morning, still seething over my clash with Nat Morgan, but word perfect on my lines and ready for action. I strolled into make-up and sat in my usual chair, in front of my usual mirror, ready to have Mathew's facial scar applied for the day, only to see Paul Girone reflected behind me instead of Liz Ostrakova, the make-up artist. Not only that, but he looked uncharacteristically hesitant.

'Oz,' he began, a trace of French showing as always in his accent, 'how's your schedule?'

I looked at him blankly in the mirror. 'You know what my schedule is, man. You're the director. You draw it up, remember.'

'No, I mean how is your schedule after this project? What do you have lined up?'

'I take a break as usual . . . nicely timed for the birth of my second child . . . then Roscoe's got me in a project in New York. Why, do you have something to offer me?'

'Maybe, as it happens, but not so soon, and that is not why I ask. If this production was to overrun, it would not be a disaster, yes?'

I turned in my chair. 'It would not be a disaster, no, as long as it didn't overrun up to my next commitment. A bit of a pisser, I have to admit, but not a disaster. What's the problem anyway? Has the writer come up with some extra scenes?'

'God no!' he exclaimed. 'This movie is long enough as it is. No, the problem is that Louise Golding has come up with spots. In English I think you call it the chickenpox. She will not be able to work for two weeks.'

'Can't you reschedule? Shoot other scenes to cover her absence?'

He shook his head, sorrowfully. I could understand that; what he was saying was going to cost someone . . . an insurance company, but maybe not . . . a lot of money. 'I tried to work something out, but almost everything we have left involves Louise, or Ewan, and I have released him till the middle of next week, to do some location work on his next movie. There is nothing for it but to close the project until Louise can come back to work, like I say, at least two weeks. You can go home if you like. I'll call you next week, to confirm that it's okay to restart the week after that ' He paused. 'How about you, have you ever had this thing? I'm told it's highly contagious.'

'Spreads like wildfire, man, but I'm okay. I've had the whole round of childhood ailments, so I'm immune.' I grinned as I got out of the make-up chair. 'You'd better keep your fingers crossed that Ewan is too. From what I gather, he's been closer to Louise than either you or me.'

As it turned out, if Paul hadn't taken the decision to fold there and then he would only have been delaying the inevitable. Twenty-four hours later, the focus puller, the best boy . . . a girl, by the way . . . Liz Ostrakova and the key grip were all as spotty as Louise. By that time, though, I was back home, keeping a distance between me and Janet, until Ethel convinced me that someone who'd had the disease couldn't be a carrier afterwards.

Once back home, I was able to tell Susie what had been happening in the company, although by that time it wasn't news to her. My clumsy attempt to have Jay intercept and mislay the business news-papers had been pointless, since she had simply gone on-line, then

169

bent Phil Culshaw's ear and later mine because she'd been kept in the dark.

That persuaded me that it was probably better for her blood pressure to be in the know than to find out later, so before I left to meet Ricky Ross in Glasgow, I told her what I was planning.

We met just after midday in the Ubiquitous Chip, a celebrity hang-out close to the headquarters of the BBC in Scotland. It was Wednesday lunchtime, but it was still early, and so the place was quieter than I'd seen it. Glancing around, I saw a familiar ex-footballer . . . you know who I mean; he's everywhere . . . an evening news presenter with a lady that I hoped was his wife, given that they were holding hands, and one half of a television comedy duo, having what looked like a serious lunch with a journalist, or so I judged from the small tape recorder that was placed on the table between them. Its red record light was showing: I pointed to it and Ricky got the message. To be on the safe side, we moved to a table further away. I didn't want our chat to wind up in a reporter's audio notebook by accident.

Once the ex-footballer and I had exchanged autographs, Ricky and I got down to business. 'Morgan?' I asked him.

'We've been tailing her as instructed, and as far as I can tell she hasn't caught on yet. It's been bloody dull for my people, following her from one business meeting to another. It's been time consuming too. You're going to have some bill when this is finished.'

'If you get me a result it'll be worth it. What about her sex life? Have you found the mystery man?'

'What mystery man? The woman's fucking celibate . . .' I smiled at this contradiction in terms, but he didn't pick it up '. . . as far as I can see,' he told me, 'unless she's shagging her lawyer or her accountant, because they're the only guys she's seeing consistently. She did make one trip to Glasgow yesterday, to a private address, not an office, but she only stayed for about an hour, and then she was off home again. Barely time for any meaningful action. Besides, Natalie's never struck me as the sort who has to travel to get seen to.'

'Who did she visit?'

Ross shook his head. 'I'm sorry. We didn't find that out. It was an apartment block, with a secure entrance, and there were no names on the door outside, only numbers. It could have been anyone in there.'

'Did she go in with a key?' I asked.

'No.'

'Okay, if she goes back there again, tell your guy to be close enough to see what number button she pushes.'

'He's already told, don't worry.'

'Good. What about Aidan Keane? Has he gone anywhere near Ravens?'

'No, but he'd be really bloody stupid to do that so quickly, Oz, and that's assuming your reporter pal's story is right.'

'Maybe, but you're tailing him, yes?'

'Yes, of course we are. Keep your hair on. Tell you what, I'll get you an up-to-the-minute report.' He took out his mobile, pressed some keys and held it to his ear. 'Avril?' he said. 'Where are you?' Five seconds passed, time enough for Ricky's confidence to evaporate. 'Did you get the number?' A few more seconds, time enough for his forehead to furrow. 'Magic. You'd better get back to his place then, and wait for him to show.'

He put the mobile away and looked up at me. 'He's out of our sight. Avril was watching him, as normal, from her car. He left his flat in Crow Road, heading towards the bookie's on the corner, where he's gone every day this week at the same time. Only this time a motor pulled up beside him on the pavement, the back door opened and he got in. Avril was going to follow, but just as she was pulling out, a vehicle cruised past her going slow, with the driver looking out as if he was trying to find an address. By the time her exit was clear, the target car was out of sight. It could have been heading for Scotstoun, or the Clyde Tunnel, or the expressway.'

'The number?'

'The slow car blocked her view. It was an old model Vectra, that was all she could tell me. Sorry.'

'You should be. It sounds to me as if she was rumbled; that second car could have been there to block her deliberately. It makes me wonder whether I should give you this next job.'

Ricky sniffed. He looked huffed. 'Suit your fucking self. What job?'

'We're playing call my bluff with the Three Bears,' I told him. 'I want them all tailed, every one of them. If there's collusion, and I'm sure there is, we have to be able to prove it.'

'Are you sure about this, Oz? You don't mess with these boys, not on their side of the street.'

'They shouldn't have come on to mine. Tail them. These guys are supposed never to meet and never to speak to each other. If they do, I want to be able to prove it.'

'The case won't get to court, if your scenario's right. Nat'll have paid them off before then, as soon as she has control of the Gantry Group.'

'I don't want to prove it in court. I want to prove it in the press. When they meet up, I want pictures, location, the lot. Your best people, Ricky, no more Avrils.'

'She was unlucky, Oz.'

'In that case I want your luckiest people.'

Ricky sighed. 'Okay. Actually, when I think about it, the job's not as dodgy as all that. If any of my people are spotted, the targets will probably assume they're the Scottish Drugs Enforcement Agency. These guys are used to being tailed by the polis.'

That was a problem I hadn't anticipated. 'In that case the SDEA had better know what we're up to, just in case they do have active surveillance on the Bears. Have you got a contact there?'

He nodded. 'Of course, loads of them, but the crime co-ordinator's the best bet. He's an old mate, from the Tayside Force. If he does have an operation underway, I could probably persuade him to pull it for a few days, as long as we feed him anything we turn up.'

'Fine. Go to it,' I told him.

'What about lunch?'

'Who said anything about lunch?' I asked him. 'I'm meeting Phil Culshaw here for lunch. You get your show on the road. If you get me the results I'm after, I'll buy you the biggest bloody lunch you've ever had, in the restaurant of your choice.'

He glared at me for a second, but he couldn't keep it up, and his grin broke through. Ricky's a pro; he knew it was urgent. 'If you really mean that,' he said, 'there's a place in Barcelona called the Seven Doors. And we'll fly there club class, thank you very much.'

'Deal. Now piss off.'

He did, and Phil Culshaw took his place at the table five minutes later. This time I asked for the menu.

'I didn't expect to see you here this week,' he said. 'I was surprised when Denise gave me your message.'

I told him about the spotty actor. 'It's fortuitous. Gives me a chance to put some things in place.'

'And to check up on how well I'm doing in Susie's absence.'

'Not even I would have the nerve to do that, Phil. But how's it going?'

'As anticipated. McPhillips and Company had the expected letters of protest this morning.'

'Did they return the cheques, though?'

'No, they didn't go that far. That doesn't mean anything, though; not presenting is adequate evidence of rejection.'

'So what happens next?'

'There'll be a brief period of ritual dancing, and then they'll ask the Sheriff Court to set a date for an interdict hearing. By the end of the week, I'll expect.'

'And the Torrent bid? What's the timetable on that?'

Culshaw shrugged. 'You read the same papers I do. You know as much as me. Torrent's advisers told the Stock Exchange that it would be at the beginning of next week, on either Monday or Tuesday. Fisher's scheduled a board meeting for next Wednesday. Between now and then, I've instructed the investor relations consultants to sound out the minority shareholders . . . excluding you, of course.'

'Did you know that Fisher and Morgan's uncle were pals?'

'Who told you that?'

'Natalie.'

Phil slapped a hand on his forehead. 'Jesus Christ, Oz.' He cut himself off short as the waiter appeared to take our orders.

'You didn't bloody speak to her, did you?' he continued as the young Australian left. (Sometimes, especially when I'm in London, or when I hear an interview with a Scottish rugby international, I find myself thinking that those people are colonising Britain. And why not? What goes around comes around, I suppose.)

173

'Of course I did. No one's rattling her cage, Phil, although they should be. I had to do something to try to put the wind up her.'

'And did you?'

'Not much. She did something funny the day afterwards, though: paid a visit to someone in Glasgow. I don't know what that was about.'

'And I don't want to know any of this. It's one thing for you to set detectives on a business rival, but keep it to yourself, and outside the knowledge of the company. If you're rumbled and I'm called to give evidence at an interdict hearing, I want to be wide-eyed and innocent.'

'Well that's okay, for I didn't tell you that I've been tailing her. Now what about Fisher?'

'What about him?'

'I want his head.'

'You can't do that, Oz. He's too big a fish.'

'He's a fucking shark and he's out to eat my wife. I'm going to harpoon him before that happens. I'm asking you to call an extraordinary board meeting; propose a motion of no confidence. You'll have Susie's proxy.'

'He wouldn't sanction it; I can't call such a meeting without his co-operation.'

'You mean we're stuck with him until the Morgan offer is tabled?'

'I'm afraid so. And you know what'll happen when it is.'

'It's been spelled out to me. That means one thing: we've got seven days to nail Natalie Morgan's olive skin to her office door.'

'And how do we begin to do that?'

'Like you've just said, you don't. I begin with Mr Aidan Keane, just as soon as he surfaces.'

# 33

As it happened, Aidan Keane surfaced at seven o'clock that evening. His return was announced by the screams of a female pedestrian, on the iron footbridge across the Clyde, who happened to be looking over the side when he floated beneath her downstream, staring up at her with a terminally surprised look on his face.

I heard the news on the late-night edition of *Reporting Scotland*: they didn't name the victim at that stage, but I had a terrible suspicion, which was proved right inside half an hour when Arnott Buchan rang me.

'Are you sure?' was all I could say after he told me, although I was certain of it myself.

'I got it from a police source. Identification wasn't a problem. There was a photographic driving licence in his wallet.'

'Did he drown?'

'If he did it was the four bullets in him that weighed him down.'

'What's the betting?' I asked, as innocently as I could.

'My money's on Ravens deciding that he didn't need him on his payroll, or that the other two guys took cold feet and decided to take him off the pitch. If that's right, it could look good for you.'

'How could it? Off the record, our suspicion is that these three guys are colluding to extort money from the company, but Keane was our only real chance of proving it.'

'Hmph.' Buchan gave a muffled grunt. 'Is that all you suspect?' he asked. 'You don't think this is linked to the takeover bid?'

'If I did, I wouldn't fucking tell you. Our counsel won't let us go public with what I just said to you.'

'Sounds to me, then, as if you're as far up the creek as the boy Keane.'

'Maybe that depends on how you guys report his murder.'

'There'll be no mention of the Ravens link I told you about, you can be sure of that. It's no more than pub talk and no lawyer would let an editor run it. The story will be that Keane left the employment of the Gantry Group after Sir Graeme Fisher's investigation into the New Bearsden cock-up, and less than a week later, he's dead. To be brutally honest with you, if the coverage points the finger at anyone it'll be your wife. And, forgive me for saying this, given who her father is, there'll be a few people believe that.'

'I may not forgive you,' I retorted, coldly. 'Any newspaper that does imply that will be sued out of business . . . yours included.'

'Don't worry, Oz, it won't be me that does it. But I will be doing a piece for Sunday, so is there anything else you can tell me about Keane?'

I could have told him that the start of his last journey was witnessed by a detective in my employ, but I decided firmly to keep that to myself for as long as I could. If I spilled that, every one of our surveillance targets would be looking over his, and her, shoulder from that point on.

'I can tell you that it's time something effective was done to stamp out gun crime in this country, but apart from that you're on your own.'

I rang Ricky as soon as Buchan had hung up. Alison Goodchild was with him, so I killed two birds with one call by telling her to call Phil Culshaw and agree a company statement about Keane's death.

Once she had gone to do that on her mobile, I spoke to Ross. He knew, but he hadn't picked up the news from the telly as I had. Avril had called him after a man and a woman she recognised as CID officers turned up at Keane's flat, and took his hysterical wife off shortly afterwards in their car. She had followed them all the way to the city mortuary.

'We may have her,' I told Ricky.

'What the hell do you mean? Have who?'

'Natalie. I threw Keane's name at her on Monday night; I told her that he had been fingered as the inside man in the Three Bears plot. Two days later the guy's fished out of the drink. If that doesn't point in her direction, nothing does.'

176

Ricky growled down the phone. 'Hold your horses there, man. Natalie Morgan is not the sort of person from whom Mark Ravens, or Jock Perry or Kevin Cornwell, takes hit orders. You knew about Keane because that journalist told you. If his source was talking too much and Ravens, or the three of them, decided there was a danger of their being exposed prematurely, they wouldn't need telling to take him out.'

'But she knew, Ricky. She knew and now he's dead. That trip she made to Glasgow yesterday: could it have been one of the Three Bears she saw?'

'I doubt that very much. Her visit was in the city centre, and as far as I know none of them live there. But I'll double check, if you like. Maybe one of them has a fuck pit that his wife doesn't know about.'

'You do that. As for the chat we had earlier, is everything in place?'

'Yup. I just hope you've got the cash to pay for it, after Morgan wipes out the family fortune next week.'

'I thought we agreed this was on a contingency basis. No win, no fee?'

'Hey, wait a minute . . .' he began, then realised that I was pulling his chain.

'Don't worry,' I assured him. 'If the worst does happen, I'm going to make a right few quid on the Gantry shares that I've been buying for the last week or so.'

# 34

Next morning's press stories on the discovery of the latest hazard to navigation in the Clyde were circumspect, to say the least. I guessed that lawyers had poured buckets of cold water down the trousers of each of the tabloid editors, for they reported only the bizarre discovery of Keane's body, interviews with the lady who had been unfortunate enough to spot it, and little else.

There was, of course, the obligatory police quote. Pending the findings of an autopsy, the death was being regarded as 'suspicious'.

Only the *Herald* mentioned the dead man's connection to 'the beleaguered Gantry Group', carrying a quote from 'a company spokesperson' to the effect that 'Aidan was a valued colleague', and that Phil Culshaw, acting Group managing director, had been hoping to persuade him to return to the post that he resigned last week.

To the best of my knowledge that was a complete fabrication; but, like so many other things in this bizarre situation, its truth or otherwise could never be proved. As I read the story, I threw a mental nod in Phil's direction. 'Nice one,' I whispered.

'What?' Susie asked across the breakfast table.

'Nothing.'

She put down her *Scottish Daily Mail*. 'Poor Aidan,' she said. 'This is terrible. It's his poor wife I feel sorry for now. What do you think happened?'

I hadn't filled in all the details when I'd told Susie about Keane's demise that morning, but she'd guessed that he'd been unlikely to have drowned while swimming, fully clothed, in the Clyde in the middle of the day. (Poisoning would have been more of a possibility, actually.)

'I guess he must have bet on the wrong horse, that's all. Aidan was a gambling man by all accounts. The betting shop that he used, the one where he was headed when he disappeared, is part owned by Jock Perry. Maybe he owed a few quid and was pressured into going along with the New Bearsden scam.'

'And maybe the police will be able to prove that,' she exclaimed, brightening up.

'Don't bet on that horse either, love. The police have never proved anything against Perry, or against either of the other two guys, not even when they were young, and answerable to bigger gangsters than *they* were.'

Her fleeting optimism disappeared. 'Do you really think that the whole thing is linked to the takeover bid, Oz? Did Natalie Morgan really set it all up?'

'I think it has to be, Suse, because of the leaks to the media. The Three Bears wouldn't have done that off their own bat, because press coverage is anathema to them. Someone has to have set this up, and the really big winner from the situation will be Torrent, in engineering the acquisition of a supposedly invulnerable company at a realistic price. But I still don't believe that Natalie set it up. She doesn't strike me as having the sort of imagination you'd need to dream up a scheme like this, and she doesn't associate with the sort of people she'd need to carry it out. I come back to this: there's someone behind her.'

'There's another question too,' Susie observed. 'Who's underwriting the takeover?'

'What do you mean?'

'I mean that Torrent as it stands just isn't big enough to buy me. The company doesn't have enough spare cash, and if they write new shares to trade for ours, as people are saying they've done already with the Sapphire holding, it will upset the balance of Torrent itself.'

She sucked her teeth for a second, and then went on. 'I've been doing some sums, love. If I chucked in the towel and we accepted the offer, between us you and I would own at least thirty-five, and maybe forty per cent of the enlarged company. At the moment, Morgan owns ninety per cent of Torrent, but a new share issue would dilute that down to around the fifty mark, if that. She'd be struggling to retain control, and I'd back myself to have her out

179

inside six months. So when this formal offer comes in, you'll find that new shares in Torrent have already been issued and that someone's subscribed for them. When the offer comes in it will be in cash, funded by that new equity, and maybe by some loan and venture capital. That's probably why Marvin de Luca and Nigel Lanark were at that lunch in the Atrium.'

She frowned. 'That's how it's being done, Oz. I'm certain of it. If you're right and the New Bearsden ambush was a planned attack on our share price, then the person who was behind it is almost certainly Natalie's new investor.'

'Need there be one person in the background?' I asked. 'What if I'm wrong and Ravens, Perry and Cornwell have been driving the thing all along?'

Susie shook her head. 'No, not a chance. Guys like those don't think that way. These are Glaswegian heavies, Oz; I was born and bred in the city, and I know the sort. I've even met Jock Perry, years ago in a disco that I think he owned. He tried to pick me up, without any pretence at subtlety either. I invited him to fuck off, which he did eventually, but with an ill grace. Then one of the guys I was with told me who he was. He was shaking in his boots, because he thought we'd all struggle to get home alive. But somebody must have told Perry who I was, because a bottle of champagne in an ice bucket arrived at our table, with a note addressed to me, saying "Sorry".' She paused. 'There's another reason why it couldn't be them. If they underwrote a deal like this, they'd be doing it with bent money. Sure, they all have front businesses, like Ravens' pubs and Perry's betting shops, but none of them are in this league. If the banks had the slightest suspicion that Torrent was funding its expansion by laundering money, they would drop the company like a hot potato. And even if Natalie isn't bright enough to work that one out for herself, her professional advisers certainly are.'

I whistled. 'Magic. So we don't just have a mystery enemy. We have a mystery enemy with serious money, and the ability to persuade Glasgow's three biggest heavies to do his bidding.' I looked across at my wife. 'Do any names suggest themselves to you?'

'If only . . .' she whispered.

'Me neither.' I looked at her. 'Suse, I'm not giving up, but . . .

suppose we don't get lucky before next week? How will you feel if we lose?'

'Richer,' she replied, but bitterly. 'But before that sinks in, I'll feel humiliated, beaten, a failure, all of that stuff.' She smiled at me, softly. 'Oz, love, I'm sorry if I disappoint you. I know you were hoping that when I went on maternity leave I might change, that I might decide to be a full-time mum for a few years, and be content to be non-executive chair, instead of Fisher. That might even have been an attractive proposition, but for all this. There's a lot to be said for spending the next few years travelling the world with you and the kids, from film location to film location. But if it all ends like this, I'll be the most miserable travelling companion you could ever imagine. My mind will always be back in Glasgow, thinking of ways to get back at Morgan and whoever her new partner is.'

She looked away from me, up at the ceiling, and I saw a small tear appear in the corner of her right eye and roll down her cheek. 'I suppose what I'm saying is that if I lose this business, it'll break my heart.'

I reached across and took her hand. 'Then that will not happen, my darling.' I gave it a squeeze. 'You've got my word on that.'

She got up from the table, kissed me on the forehead, ran her fingers through my hair, then, mumbling something about going to see Ethel, hurried out of the room.

I gathered up the newspapers and carried them through to the working conservatory, where I switched on my computer and checked my morning's e-mailbox. I saw one from 'ecap' titled 'Out, out, damned spot' and opened it; it was a brief message from Ewan wishing me well, and advising me that he, on the other hand, had a face, as he put it, 'like a cherry cake' and felt decidedly poorly.

There was also a message from Paul Girone. It was less colourful, but it confirmed Ewan's news and advised me that their insurers . . . to hearty sighs of relief from the investors, no doubt . . . had accepted medical advice and would fund a further week's postponement. He also asked me not to eat too much, since he didn't want me reporting back noticeably fatter than before the break, but I'm professional enough to have worked that out for myself. In any event, obesity is not a Blackstone family trait.

181

My final e-mail brought me my first really good news of the day. It was from Roscoe and it advised me that Miles Grayson was about to achieve a lifelong dream by making a cricket movie. It would be about the notorious Bodyline tour of Australia, in the thirties, in which Douglas Jardine, the captain of England, decided that the best way of combating the threat of Donald Bradman was by trying to kill him with continuously short-pitched bowling.

Miles, a good judge of character, wanted me to play Jardine. He would play Bradman, of course. (A challenge for make-up, I thought, since Miles is around twenty years older than Bradman was then, and looks nothing like the dour little man.) Did I fancy a couple of months next winter touring Australia? Too bloody right I did. I sent Roscoe an instant reply. 'Make a show of being hard to get, then say "yes".'

I signed out of AOL, and swung round in my chair, picking up the *Scotsman*, the only newspaper I hadn't read that morning. I scanned through it until I found the Aidan Keane story. It was there, of course, but buried almost as deep as he would be soon, at the foot of page six. Gangland killings in Glasgow do not figure high on the priority lists of Edinburgh copy-tasters.

It took me less than a minute to read, and then I put it aside and turned my attention to the rest of the paper. Having spent the early part of my adult life in Edinburgh, it was my instinctive paper of choice, even though the issue that was delivered to our home went to bed much earlier than the *Herald*. As I do about once a week, I resolved that I would cancel the lot and read the on-line editions instead, but since that day's issue was there, inking up my hands, I delved into it.

For a few days, I had been keeping an eye out for a certain story. That morning, I found it. It was on page three once again, but, although it commanded more space than a floater in the Clyde, since it emanated from the East of Scotland, it was no longer a front-page lead.

It was headed 'Pig Farm murders: identities confirmed', and it read:

'*Detectives leading the investigation into the deaths of a couple whose bodies were found last week on a remote Fife pig farm confirmed that they are Walter and Andrea Neiporte of Pittenweem, Fife.*

'*Mr Neiporte (37) is an American citizen, although he was officially resident in Scotland, and worked at St Andrews University. His wife (29), an executive with a hotel in North East Fife, is originally from Orpington in Kent.*

'*The identifications were confirmed after the completion of DNA tests on the bodies and on samples from relatives in America and England.*

'*Police last night released further details of what is now officially a double murder hunt. Detective Inspector Tom Reekie, in charge of the investigation, confirmed that police were searching in the vicinity of the farm for the murder weapon, a shotgun.*

'*He revealed also that police suspect that the crime may be drug-related, after a significant quantity of ecstasy tablets were found in an inch-by-inch search of the couple's cottage.*

'*Inspector Reekie said that he believed that the couple were killed on the evening of May 23, the date and time recorded on Mr Neiporte's wristwatch, which had been found on the body, smashed by a shotgun pellet.*'

I blinked when I saw the date. Laying the paper down, I turned back to my computer terminal and opened my electronic diary. It confirmed my first thought; the Neiportes had been killed on the day before I had sent Jay to Fife to deal with them. After all that anxiety, and yes, I confess it now, after all those bad dreams, it turned out to have been just another drug-land execution.

I breathed a single huge sigh of relief. It had barely faded before a question rose up in my mind. 'Why was Jay so secretive?'

But when I thought about it, it took me about three seconds to convince myself that it was simply a sign of his absolute discretion. It was one worry out of the way, but, God knew, there were plenty left. Of these, I realised suddenly, the greatest was that I had made a promise to my wife; but how was I to keep it?

# 35

The problem I faced was a simple one. In the fight against our opposition, I had run out of bullets. Ricky and I were making all the obvious moves to try and find evidence that would tie Natalie Morgan to the Three Bears. The only other things we needed were luck and patience. As I've said, I have more than my fair share of the former, but it's not a weapon that can be called upon at will.

As for patience, I find that the older I get the less I have.

So what could I do, I asked myself, to make things happen? Turning once again to my one-man army, Jay Yuille, was not an option. I was sure he would help, but I could never be sure how, given his 'no questions' policy.

After a day of thought, some of it spent working out in my gym, some spent swimming, and some spent hitting increasingly erratic golf shots, I had decided what to do. It would be chancy, and it might even be risky, given the people involved, but it was all I had, my only weapon. I didn't know how it would work out, but I did know that it would require the performance of my life.

I called Ricky on my mobile, just before six. 'Where's Morgan?' I asked him.

'Homeward bound,' he replied. 'There's nothing on the other three, though, Oz. It's just another day at the offices for all of them.'

'Hang in there,' I said, then hung up.

I found Susie in Janet's playroom; she looked as glum as she had in the morning. 'I have to go out,' I told her.

'Where?'

I pinched a few words from my favourite poem, and recited them in my best Ewan Capperauld accent. 'I have promises to keep, and miles to go before I sleep.'

She sniffed. 'Be mysterious then. Just don't wake me when you come in, that's all.'

I took the Lotus; it's my favourite toy when I'm alone. I didn't burn rubber or anything like that, but I made Edinburgh in an hour and a half, and from where we live, that's reasonable. I was glad that Natalie hadn't moved, for it meant that I knew exactly where I was headed. As I cleared the Barnton roundabout, I called Ricky again. 'Is she still at home?' I asked.

'Yes, and all alone.'

'Good. Tell your operative to be ready for action.'

'When?'

'Soon, I hope.'

Less than five minutes later, I pulled into the private car park attached to Natalie's block. There were several spaces in the visitors' area: I picked one, locked on my steering wheel immobiliser . . . Scotland's capital city hates to admit it, but there are car thieves in Edinburgh too . . . and wandered over to the entrance door. I knew that Ricky's operative would be watching me, but that didn't matter. I was paying his tab, and if things went pear-shaped in any way, and it became necessary, I would have been the Invisible Man. Not that I thought it would. I had rehearsed my performance time and time again. It was going to be good.

The first time I had entered the building, I had done so . . . informally; this time I pressed the button with the name 'Morgan' beside it.

She must have been near the intercom phone for she answered almost straight away. 'Hello?'

'Natalie? It's Oz Blackstone.'

'Oz! What the hell do you want?'

'A chat. We need to talk, you and I. I have news that may interest you.'

'Indeed.' She sounded uncertain. 'You'd better come up then.' The door buzzed: I pushed it and it swung open. Last time I had used the stairs. This time I took the lift, all the way to the top.

She was waiting for me as I stepped out, framed in her doorway, her long legs disappearing into a pair of very brief shorts, her high breasts encased in a matching halter top. 'Sorry to be overdressed,' she murmured, 'but I wasn't expecting you.'

185

The lift door hissed shut behind me as she stood aside, letting me into her sanctum. I looked around. 'You've refurnished,' I said. The place looked a lot more spacious, somehow, than when I'd seen it before.

'Totally,' she replied. 'I had interior decorators give the place a make-over. Then I hired a feng shui consultant. Remember the Fosters ad on the telly? Well, I actually did it.'

I laughed. 'There's one born every minute, Nat, but I never thought you were one of them.'

'Nor I you.' She moved in on me, standing close, gazing up into my eyes. 'So what brings you this way. What do you have to tell me that'll interest me? Got a part for me in your next movie?'

'Sorry. Glenn Close does Cruella De Vil.'

She chuckled. 'Ouch. What can it be then? Is it that you've realised that you fancy me, and that you've decided to trade little Susie in for a winner? If so . . .' She reached up and tugged at the cord securing her top, but I put a hand up and stopped her.

'Sorry, but I've seen a lot better than those at work . . . and at home for that matter. Once upon a time, Natalie, I'd have fucked your brains out before I put the boot in. Not any more, though. That wouldn't be right and proper, so I'll get straight to it.'

Her eyes narrowed. 'How gallant of you to spare my feelings.'

'I don't give a bugger about your feelings. It's my wife I'm thinking about. I wouldn't want to take anything from you back to her.'

'Okay.' She was definitely out of seductress mode. 'Say what you have to say, then go.'

I fixed her with my coldest stare. 'Gladly,' I hissed at her. 'It's this. You will stop this vindictive nonsense towards Susie, and you will announce tomorrow that you are no longer interested in acquiring the Gantry Group.'

'Why should I do that?'

'Because you wouldn't last a week in Cornton Vale Prison. You'd hardly be in there before you'd a brush handle up you. We've got you, Nat, Ricky Ross and I. We know you set up the New Bearsden plot, we know how you did it and why. When I called you a couple of nights ago, I dropped the name Aidan Keane, a little on purpose; let's call it bait. You swallowed it and no mistake; as soon as my call was over . . .

I taped it, by the way . . . you went straight through to Glasgow to see one of your associates, Mr Ravens, we assume, since he was going to be Mr Keane's new boss. Twenty-four hours later, what happens? The poor guy's found in the Clyde, with so many bullets in him it's a fucking miracle he can still float. What that makes you, Nat, is an accessory to murder, and legally as guilty of Keane's death as the guys who pulled the trigger.'

I paused to let that sink in, and to study her face; it was a mixture of anger, uncertainty and fear. 'Offering Keane a job with Mark Ravens if he got found out was a bloody silly thing to do, by the way. But I don't suppose you expected that he would be found out, or that dear old Graeme would provoke him into resigning, or that he would let slip to a mate where his future employment prospects lay.'

'You can't prove any of this,' Natalie shouted, thrusting out her chin and her chest at the same time, in an odd show of hard-nippled defiance.

'Not without corroboration, we couldn't. It's too bad that one of the Three Bears has realised the risk he's been taking, and has given a full statement to Ricky Ross, so that Ricky can cut a deal with the SDEA that'll keep him out of jail while the rest of you go down. I'm not going to tell you which one; but even if I did, I wouldn't recommend that you have a go at him. He'll be expecting you.'

I smiled at her. 'So this is the deal. It's open for twenty-four hours, no more. You either drop the bid, or I will drop you.' I turned on my heel and headed for the door. 'Oh yes, and tell your partners not even to think about coming after Ricky and me either. He's got connections with the police that would make that a very bad idea, and I've got protection that's out of their league. They'd never make it back across the river.'

I was back home in time for the ten o'clock news on telly. Susie was sat on the couch, with an anthology of twentieth-century poetry on her lap. 'So whose woods did you stop by?' she asked.

'With a bit of the luck of the Blackstones, you'll find out soon enough.'

# 36

I had told Ricky to call me any time, but I didn't expect it to be at two in the morning. He doesn't sound excited very often, but this time he did, and no mistake.

'I don't know what the hell you said,' he exclaimed, as I rubbed sleep out of my eyes, and as Susie growled beside me, 'but it worked and no mistake. If you saw a Porsche whistling past you on the M8 it was Natalie Morgan. She went straight to that address she visited before; got there by quarter to ten.'

'She didn't overtake me in that case.'

'Not for the want of trying. My guy had a job keeping her in sight in his poor wee MG. He did, though, trailed her all the way there. This time she stayed longer; till well after midnight, in fact. And while she was there, guess who else turned up?'

'One of the Bears?'

'Better than that. All three of the buggers; by the time the last one arrived my people were tripping over each other at the scene. We've got film and still photos of them arriving, separately, between half ten and eleven, and of them leaving, together and looking rattled.'

'What about Natalie?'

'She left a few minutes after them. She had the makings of a right sore face too: I'd say someone gave her a belting.'

'Shame. She's still walking, though?'

'No thanks to you. How did you kick all that off anyway? What the hell did you tell her?' I gave him a run-down of my pitch to Natalie, in her apartment. Susie was wide awake now, listening to every word. When I finished, he was laughing. 'She is definitely not as bright as she thinks she is. Not only did she not twig she'd been followed to Glasgow the first time, she went straight back again.'

'So who's the guy she went to see?' I asked.

'That we don't know yet. We know the flat he was in, because this time we saw which button she pushed. But we won't be able to find out who he is till tomorrow at least, till the council offices open and we can have a look at the register of electors.'

'Why not just ring his fucking bell? Right now, in fact.'

'I think I'll hold off on that, if you don't mind. Whoever the guy is, he's serious enough to be able to call the Three Bears and have every one of them drop what he was doing and come to see him. Ravens, Perry and Cornwell may not be the Kray brothers, but anyone who can make them jump when he whistles must be a very serious player indeed. Before I go thumping on that door, or have any of my people do it, I want to know who's behind it.'

'So what do we do now?'

'Like I said, we find out who he is.'

'But apart from that. What do we do about Morgan to spike this takeover?'

'Sit on it for a day or so. Let's find out who's behind it.'

'We don't need to. We've got Natalie and the Bears all in the same place at the same time. We could take that to the police.'

'Alleging what, exactly?'

'Conspiracy.'

'There's no such criminal charge in Scotland.'

'Extortion.'

'They never asked you for money. In fact when you offered it, they turned you down. Oz, I'm sure that the Crown Office would come up with a charge, under the Companies Act, maybe, but it would take them a bloody long time to decide what it would be. Let's get the whole picture. Let's find out who the man in the apartment is. Then you can decide what you want to do. But you might be better going to the Sunday papers than the police.'

For once, I could see the sense in everything Ricky said.

'Okay,' I agreed. 'Let's do it that way. But listen, you and your team have done bloody well tonight. Keep a watch on Natalie, and on the mystery man, but give as many of them as you can some time off. I'll do the trace on the owner of the apartment; I've got time, and I can handle that.' I found a pen and a notepad in the drawer of my bedside table. 'Gimme the address,' I said, and began to scribble down what he said.

He hadn't reached the street name before I exploded. 'Jesus Christ, Ricky!' But then I realised that he had never been there before; there was no reason for him to have known.

'What's up?' he demanded.

'That's our old address,' I told him. 'That's where we used to live.'

# 37

There was little likelihood of sleep after that, so Susie and I got up, went down to the kitchen and made ourselves a pot of coffee. 'When you sold, can you remember who the buyer was?' I asked her, when I had my head together.

She shook hers. 'I never knew. I didn't even sign off on the deal. Officially, it was the Gantry Group that bought the place from you: legally I never owned it. So when it was sold, the company secretary handled everything.'

'And of course, in those days Greg McPhillips didn't act for the Group.'

'No. The company secretary then was old Barney Farmer.'

'Okay, I'll talk to him tomorrow.'

'Is Doris Stokes still around?'

'Ah, of course.' I had forgotten that Greg had taken over the company secretary job after his predecessor had fallen down dead in Union Street one day, overcome, it was said, by shock and grief after dropping a two-pound coin down a drain.

'There will be records of the sale, though. Greg took over all Barney's files. I do remember one thing: the old boy told me that the sale was made to another company. That's right, he said they wanted it as a *pied à terre* for their chief executive.'

I almost called Greg there and then and told him to get his ass into his office; however, having met Katrina McPhillips, I decided that a few hours' patience was a better option. I did call Jay, though. Without going into all the details, I told him that the New Bearsden thing had come to the boil and that there was an outside chance of three angry bears looking in my direction.

'I'll talk to Mark Kravitz,' he said, briskly. Mark had been Jay's principal referee when we had employed him. He and I had met on my first film project, when he had been in charge of security. It hadn't taken me long to realise that he was no ordinary security consultant, and that he had contacts in some very dark corners indeed, many of them on the state payroll. He and I had become friends, and he had helped me a couple of times since then, yet I didn't think of him as someone I could call on for this sort of freelance work.

'What will he do?' I asked, a little tentatively.

He laughed. 'Make a couple of phone calls.'

'And?'

'And you won't have a problem.'

'I don't want the police in on this, Jay, not yet, at any rate.'

'They won't be. Mark's contacts have a role in fighting organised crime, but on an international scale. They don't liaise too closely with the locals, but they do know who's who, even relatively small fry like the guys you're talking about. Sometimes they let them run about and play their games, because there's more to be gained by doing that and getting feedback from them.'

'Are you telling me that the Three Bears are MI5 informants?'

'Not necessarily, but MI5 will know about them, and vice versa. Any message that comes from that quarter will not be ignored, I promise you. Okay to do that?'

'Sure,' I told him. 'I wish we'd done it a couple of weeks ago.' A thought struck me. 'Any chance of them knowing the man behind all this?'

'Every chance. I'll ask Mark. Now, boss, you and Mrs Boss turn in. It's the middle of the bloody night.'

We took his advice, feeling a deal more secure than before, and this time slept like logs . . . or in Susie's case like a bag of marbles. When the alarm wakened us again, at seven thirty, I ran the gauntlet of Katrina and called Greg.

Quickly I explained what I was after. 'Is this urgent?' he asked. I've seen bleary eyes often enough, but a truly bleary voice is rarer; our lawyer had one.

'Check the clock, man. Do I make routine calls at this hour? I need to get into those files.'

'You couldn't have picked a worse day. I've got a staff training seminar first thing this morning . . . bloody Law Society requirement . . . and then I'm due in High Court at ten.'

'What are you doing in the criminal court? You're a civil lawyer.'

'Not at this hour of the fucking morning, I'm not,' he shot back. 'Actually it's an old school pal; he's upset the Inland Revenue and I've said I'll prepare his defence.'

'He must have upset them a lot, to be in the High Court.'

'A great deal. Look, I really do have a hellish schedule today, Oz. Is there any chance of you getting to my office by eight thirty?'

'I will if you will. See you there.' I put the phone down and headed for a very quick shower.

Thanks to someone breaking down on the Expressway, it was almost eight forty-five when I walked into Greg's big airy building . . . anything less like Ewan Maltbie's place you could not imagine.

He was in his office, waiting for me, and he hadn't been wasting his time. A pile of documents lay on his desk. Normally he has someone bring things like that to him, as and when they're needed. 'Why the sudden interest in the purchaser?' he asked, when he had stopped looking at his watch.

'I'm not sure yet. I just need to know who he is. It's complicated, but there's a link to the Three Bears business.'

'It's not one of them, I can tell you that. I know all of the lawyers who act for them, and none of them were involved. The legals for the other side were handled by Murphy and Woolfson, a small firm in Largs. But the purchaser wasn't an individual . . .'

'I know that. As far as Susie knew it was another company.'

'Not quite,' said Greg. 'It was a trust: the Glentruish Trust, to be exact, whatever that is.'

'Sounds like an obscure malt whisky. Who signed the documents?'

'Maynard Woolfson, the solicitor, as administrator of the trust.'

'Where did the funds come from?'

'From the solicitor's client account, I assume. There was no record of that on Farmer's files.'

'Was there a mortgage?'

'I can't say for certain,' Greg replied, 'but there's nothing in the correspondence about a survey being carried out. That indicates that

193

it was a cash purchase.' He looked at his watch again. 'And that, Oz, is as much as I can tell you.'

'I'd better go and see Mr Woolfson, in that case.'

'You can try.' He copied a phone number and an address from a document in the file on to the top sheet of a notepad and gave it to me. 'You won't have much trouble finding him. Largs isn't that big a place.'

'Thanks,' I said. 'Good luck in the High Court, by the way.'

'We'll need all we can get. Just make sure you don't wind up there.'

I left with his warning . . . it was, it seemed to me, not wholly in fun . . . ringing in my ears, and retrieved the Lotus from his office car park. Once I was in the open air, I switched on my mobile and called the number Greg had given me. I checked that Woolfson was in, and made an appointment to see him, calling myself Mr More. I thought that it might not be wise to give him advance warning.

There are two roads to Largs; the scenic way and the quick way. I don't believe in combining sightseeing and driving, so I headed for the Kingston Bridge and the Greenock-bound M8.

The traffic was down to a crawl on the bridge, and at one point it stopped altogether. I twisted round in my seat, gazing up at my old home, hoping, I suppose, that I might see that figure again, the one I had spotted when we had crossed in the other direction. There was no chance of that, though; all that hit my eyes was the glare of the sun, reflecting from silvery Venetian blinds. Neither Susie nor I had fitted those; no doubt about it, our successor really valued his privacy.

By the time I was clear of the roadblock that is the Kingston Bridge, the congestion had eased off, and I began to make better time down to Largs. Once I was through Spango Valley and out of Greenock, it didn't take me long at all. I was almost there when my mobile sounded. I was rigged for hands-free, so I took the call: it was Ricky. 'How goes it?' he asked. I explained succinctly how it didn't.

'Surprise me,' he grunted. 'I've just checked the electoral roll. The voter listed there is Miss Susan Gantry: no one's ever changed it. I've checked BT and the cable phone company too. No subscriber listed. But that's not so rare these days.'

I heard myself sigh into my collar mike. I tell you, among the many changes it has wrought in our society, the mobile phone has made things a bloody sight more difficult for private detectives.

194

'He's a cunning bastard,' I muttered. 'I'll let you know if I get anything from my next call.'

I arrived knowing three things about Largs; it's the Millport ferry terminal, the Scottish Sports Council has a centre there, and it has a very famous ice-cream shop. The office of Murphy and Woolfson was as easy to find as Greg had predicted. I parked the Lotus with the hood up . . . it's always windy on the Clyde coast . . . walked across the street, looked for the blue and white Legal Aid logo and spotted it three doors down. A quick look at the brass plate and I knew I had hit the spot.

I had ten minutes to kill before my appointment with the lawyer, so I strolled along to Nardini's and had an ice-cream. That hit the spot too. I resolved that whenever I could, I would bring my family there. Maybe we'd cross to Millport as well; no harm in giving wee Janet and her brother a taste for the high life from the start.

The office of Murphy and Woolfson was on the first floor, above a bank, as so many Scots lawyers' premises seem to be. It was in the Maltbie mode rather than McPhillips, but slightly less dusty. I guessed the sea breezes discouraged cobwebs, even in legal chambers.

There were two desks in the reception area, but one was unattended. There was a girl behind the other; I couldn't describe her as a woman, for she didn't look more than fourteen. 'Work experience?' I asked. She nodded, blushing; the kid couldn't take her eyes off me, so I guessed Mr More's cover was blown.

'I've got an appointment with Mr Woolfson,' I told her. 'Or was it Mr Murphy?'

'There is no Mr Murphy,' she burst out.

I smiled at her candour, and as I did, the driver of the other desk came into the room. She was a woman, and no mistake; tall, busty, dark-haired, and just about old enough to have been the kid's mother, or aunt, for I thought I saw a likeness about the eyes.

'Mr More?' she began, but with not a flash of recognition.

I nodded. 'I called you a while back.'

'Yes, I'm Nancy Macintosh. Mr Woolfson's free now.' She headed back towards the door.

As I made to follow, the youngster let slip an 'Eh?' I turned back, and read her question in her eyes, for I had seen it countless times

195

before. Without a word, I picked up a sheet of headed notepaper from a pile in one of her trays, autographed it and handed it to her. As I did so, I glanced at the heading and saw only one name listed. There never had been a Mr Murphy either, I bet myself.

The whole exchange only took a couple of seconds; Ms Macintosh had been watching, and looked puzzled, but said nothing. I followed her into the hall to a half-glazed door. She opened it and I stepped inside.

Maynard Woolfson was a small man, with a hook nose and black crinkly hair that managed to look younger than the rest of him, which I guessed had to be at least fifty.

'Mr More,' he said, as we shook hands.

'I'm afraid not. He couldn't come. I'm Oz Blackstone.'

He blinked and looked at me again. 'Of course you are,' he exclaimed. If I had a shekel for every time that's been said to me, I'd be richer than all the lawyers in Ayrshire . . . but then again, maybe I am anyway.

'How can I help you?'

'I'm on a detective mission, Mr Woolfson. That used to be my day job, and I just can't get away from it.'

He looked at me with a non-committal expression in his eyes. I'd seen that before too; it's the one lawyers, bankers, and those millions these days who hide, rightly or wrongly, behind the Data Protection Act, give you before the shutters come down.

'A little while ago, you acted in the purchase of an apartment in a block in Glasgow. The vendor was the Gantry Group, and your client was the Glentruish Trust. You signed on its behalf. I need to contact the principal of that trust, but I have no idea who he or she is.'

'Why not just call on them?'

'I want to know on whom I'm calling.'

'Check BT then, or NTL.'

'Have done; it didn't help.'

Woolfson ran his fingers through his hair: I waited for that shutter to fall, but it didn't. 'Then I don't know if I can. The fact is, I have no idea myself who the principal of the Glentruish Trust is.'

'Someone must have instructed you, surely.'

'That's true, someone did, but it was another firm of solicitors. The Glentruish Trust goes back to them, and through them to another vehicle, the Casamayor Trust, this one registered in Douglas, in the Isle of Man. You'll be aware that that is outside UK jurisdiction, like the Channel Islands. I set up and registered Glentruish with funds it provided, then used it as a vehicle to purchase the property in question from the Gantry Group. As trust administrator I pay the council tax on the property, the electricity, service charge and so on. And I concede to you that if there is a BT phone in use at that address, I know nothing of it.'

'So how do I go about cracking the Casamayor Trust? Catch a plane to the Isle of Man?'

'You may have to eventually, but I can help you on the way.' He hesitated, fretting as if he was out of his comfortable depth. 'Your visit isn't a complete bolt from the blue. I had a call this morning from the Casamayor Trust administrator. He said that it was possible someone would visit me with questions about Glentruish. Until now, my instructions have always been to cite client confidence and say nothing at all, but I've been advised that in the light of changed circumstances I can refer you up the chain.'

'Changed circumstances?'

'That was the phrase that was used. It puzzled me, I admit. I wonder if the ultimate beneficiary of this chain of trusts might be deceased.'

That thought had crossed my mind too, but I reckoned that if the Three Bears had offed the mystery man, Natalie Morgan wouldn't have left the place alive either.

'Whatever the circumstances,' Woolfson continued, 'if you wish for further information, you should consult the Casamayor representative. You'll have to go to Edinburgh for that, I'm afraid. His name is Wylie H Smith and he's a partner in the firm of Kendall McGuire.'

'*Well, well,*' I thought. '*Even suppose I was the sort of gullible sod who believes that all life is governed by a chain of coincidences, I still wouldn't buy into that one.*'

# 38

This time I didn't bother to phone ahead to arrange an appointment. I put the pedal down, let the Lotus express itself in the single carriageway road back to the motorway, then creamed it through to Edinburgh. I didn't waste time calling Ricky; anyway, I wanted to do this job myself.

From my days of anonymity as a private enquiry agent, I knew where all the city solicitors were based, including Kendall McGuire, although they were one of the few big players I hadn't worked for.

Edinburgh's a real swine of a place to park, even in something as manoeuvrable as my two-seater, but my destination was in the West End, in one of the big circular places where there were always more private homes than offices, so I found a bay without too much difficulty, even though it was forty minutes after midday.

The Kendall McGuire office had a secure main door, which had to be unlocked by the receptionist pressing a switch beneath her desk. I wasn't sure whether its purpose was to keep the clients in or out, but she didn't ask who I was through the intercom before letting me in, so I guessed that it must be the former.

'Oz Blackstone for the newsagent,' I told the blonde behind the desk; everything about her screamed 'Harvey Nichols!' at me.

She looked at me from under long eyelashes, unimpressed: they were used to having far bigger Hinwies than me walk through their door, I guessed.

'If you mean, Mr Smith, please take a seat, and I'll check whether he's in.'

I pointed to a wooden 'in-out' board on a wall beside the door, an array of slots, each one bearing a lawyer's name. 'That says he is.'

She ignored me and pressed a button on her switchboard console.

'Wylie,' I heard her say, 'there's a man here to see you. He says his name's . . .' Her look said that she expected me to remind her, but I knew that she was putting it on; that pissed me off a little.

'Miles Grayson,' I snapped, 'Rumplefuckingstiltskin, tell him what you like. He's expecting me anyway, I know that.'

Unruffled she looked away, lowering her voice this time. Within a minute, a bulky figure came jogging heavily downstairs. This time, he was wearing a jacket over the blue and white striped shirt. 'Oz,' he exclaimed, 'how good to see you again.' I accepted his handshake, but I squeezed a deal harder than was strictly necessary.

'Time will tell, WHS,' I responded, quietly, 'time will tell.'

'Shall we go for lunch?'

'As long as it's quiet and as long as it's on the Casamayor Trust.'

'Of course,' he exclaimed, but his laugh was a little forced.

It takes the average Edinburgh taxi firm two minutes to answer a call to a lawyer's office; they know where the money is. We had to wait for a minute and a half. The cab took us the short distance to William Street, and dropped us at a small restaurant called Peter's Cellars. (Say it out loud: if you're of a certain age you might laugh, but the Goon's been dead so long that the joke wore off for most people years ago. Still, the name goes on unchanged, and why not, since the punters keep rolling in.) I'd have walked there happily, but it was uphill all the way, and the day was overcast and humid, so I thought of the strain on Wylie's armpits and went along for the ride.

It turned out that he had a table booked, for two, in a discreet corner alcove.

We chose quickly from the interesting lunch menu, then I got straight to business. 'Did you know I was catching the shuttle?' I asked him. 'Or was it an accident? You'd better tell me that it was, because I won't like it if you've been following me.' I held his eyes, trying to make him feel as uncomfortable as I could. I don't mind leaning on guys like him: they invite it, almost.

'Pure chance,' he replied. 'I assure you.'

'But you did ask for the seat next to mine when you saw me check in.'

He tried to smile. 'Yes, I admit that. We're always on the look-out for potential new clients,' he added.

'Do you always go about it as unsubtly as that?' I asked him, hoping that our white wine wouldn't be as acid as my tone. Instinctively I liked the guy, but I had no intention of giving him an easy time.

Smith winced. 'I'm sorry if I appeared overenthusiastic,' he said.

'You did, but apology accepted. Did I let anything slip, incidentally?'

'Pardon?' He looked almost shocked.

'On the plane. Don't kid me; you were on a fishing trip. You told me that you didn't represent Torrent, but I knew all along that you did.'

'How could you have?'

'Because I've had people following Natalie Morgan since I first got wind that she might be having a go at our company. I could give you a list of the visits she's made to your office, and it would start before you and I met on the plane.'

Wylie looked up at me earnestly; I could tell that he was trying to look totally sincere, a difficult skill for a corporate lawyer to master. 'You might never believe this, Oz, but at that time I honestly did not know that we were acting for Torrent. Duncan only let me in on it after I got back to the office. He had said earlier that he'd be grateful for any information that any of us could glean on the Gantry Group, that's all.'

I found that I did believe him. 'So did I let anything slip?'

'No.' He grinned. 'Did I?'

'How could you? You didn't know anything, remember. I can tell you something now, though.'

'What's that?' he asked, but he didn't look as eager as I'd expected.

'Kendall McGuire will never act for the Gantry Group. Not ever.'

'I didn't expect that we would,' he said, almost mournfully. 'Not now; having been caught in the act, as it were.'

I waited as the waiter served our starter. 'That's not important, though,' I told him, when we were alone once more. 'This isn't about Natalie Morgan, it's about the bloke who's been behind her, pulling her strings and orchestrating a concerted, and very clever attack on the Gantry Group share price.'

'That had nothing to do with my firm,' Smith protested.

'You can tell that to the Law Society if we make a complaint. Duncan Kendall's signature won't be on any documents, but if you expect me to believe that he could fail to work out what was going on, you're taking me for an idiot. And you shouldn't do that. As I speak, there's a guy sitting, courtesy of the Glentruish Trust via Mr Woolfson of Largs, in what used to be our apartment, Susie's and mine. The Glentruish Trust goes back to the Casamayor Trust, officially based in the Isle of Man, and that, my friend, is you.'

The solicitor gave a brief nod. 'What do you want to know? I may not be able to answer all your questions, but if I can I will.'

'I want to know who the beneficiary of that trust is. I want to know the name of your client.'

'I'm not allowed to give you that name. Technically, my client is the Casamayor Trust, and that's all. Legally it leads to another trust, in the Cayman Islands this time, and to another firm of lawyers. It's a real spider's web, constructed to preserve the anonymity of the individual behind it.'

'This web,' I asked him, 'what's its total worth?'

'I have no idea,' he answered. 'I am, as a famous boxer once said, just a prawn in the game.'

'How about Duncan? Would he know?'

'Why should he? Casamayor's my client, not his.'

'He might know because we believe that your spider's web is funding the projected takeover of the Gantry Group by Torrent, and because Kendall's involved in that. There has to be outside money, Wylie. Natalie isn't big enough on her own to do what she's doing.'

He gave me the sincere look again. 'Oz,' he began. For a moment I thought that he was going to say, 'Trust me, I'm a lawyer', and that I'd fall off my chair laughing. But he didn't. 'On my children's lives,' he said quietly, 'I know nothing of what went on involving your company, of any of that carry on in New Bearsden, or of any of the detail of the proposed offer by Torrent for Gantry. The Casamayor Trust isn't involved, though, I can tell you that. If you're right, it's happening further up the chain.'

I glared across the small table. 'If you mention that chain once more I'll wrap it round your neck and hang you with it. I don't have time to mess about. I want to know who the guy in the flat is, and unless you and Duncan want to have the heaviest book in the Law Society library thrown at you, you will fucking well tell me.'

'I can't, Oz,' he replied. His smile surprised me, until he continued. 'My specific instruction from the beneficiary is that I must not tell you who he is. Instead, now that you've come asking about him, I am instructed to take you to meet him.'

I threw my napkin on the table and stood up. Seeing me, the waiter rushed over. 'Is everything all right, Mr Blackstone?' he asked.

'The food is perfect,' I told him. 'As good as you'll find in Edinburgh. But I'm afraid that my colleague has just remembered that we're late for an important business meeting in Glasgow. Would you give him the bill, please.'

# 39

With Wylie Henry Smith in the passenger seat, the tiny cockpit of the Lotus seemed distinctly overcrowded. It didn't protest, though, as it whistled us back to Glasgow. Wylie did, though, at one point, as the speedometer neared a hundred. One's arse is quite near the roadway in a vehicle of that type, and if one is not used to it, I suppose it can be a bit scary.

I remembered that I'd said I'd keep Ricky in touch, but I decided to break that promise, in the meantime. Anyway, I guessed that he'd be fully up to date about thirty seconds after I showed up at our destination.

My old apartment, subsequently the property of the Gantry Group, and more recently that of the Glentruish Trust, sits on a hilltop above Sauchiehall Street, not far from Charing Cross. The building was once a big church and my chunk of it was away up at the top of its tower. You will not find a better bolthole in all Glasgow.

As we slipped off the motorway, my companion started to give me directions, until I reminded him that there was no need. As we reached the building, I turned straight in off the street, looking for the two parking spaces that had been mine. Finding them both empty, I parked in the one I'd always used in the past.

It took Smith even longer to extricate himself from the Lotus than it had taken him to climb into it, but just as I thought I'd have to help him, he made it. After a degree of straightening out, and a few awkward smiles, he set off towards the main entrance. I looked over my shoulder and across the street. A woman, sat behind the wheel of a parked Rover, tried to avoid my glance, but I waved to her anyway.

The solicitor took no time at all to work out which door buzzer to press; clearly he had visited his 'beneficiary' before. I tried to catch the voice that crackled from the speaker, but it was too distorted for the owner's mother to have recognised it.

The door swung open and I followed my escort inside. The tower isn't easily found by the casual visitor, but Wylie and I didn't have that problem, and we strode along, silently and purposefully, although I could sense a tension building within him.

When we reached the apartment the front door was ajar, held against its automatic closer by a heavy glass weight. I kicked it aside as we entered, and suddenly the hall was almost dark.

I knew where he would be, but I still motioned Wylie to lead the way along the corridor, until he stopped at the heavy wooden door. He rapped on it; as he turned the handle and began to open it, I looked into his eyes.

In that instant, I'll swear that I knew. It had been unthinkable, totally unimaginable, but when I saw the expression on his face I remembered how he had reacted at the very start of our conversation on the plane. I hadn't appreciated what it was at the time, but his eyes had registered the same look of pure fright that I saw again in that doorway.

I stepped past him and through it.

The room had changed a lot since I had been in it last. All the time I had owned or known it, it had been used at least in part as an office; now it was purely a comfort zone. The floor had been sanded and revarnished until it shone. A huge Bang and Olufsen television stood in one corner and a hi-fi unit by the same maker was on a stand against a side wall, with something by Vivaldi playing quietly through its tall speakers. It was much more spacious, since it was almost minimally furnished, where before it had been almost cluttered. The sofa was white leather, with a matching armchair and a swivel chair. Its back was towards me, as it looked out over the city, through the slanted Venetian blinds.

Slowly, it began to turn.

'Hello Jack,' I said.

'Ha, ha, ha,' the former Lord Provost of Glasgow cackled, a soft laugh that was virtually without humour. 'Well done, son, well done,' he said, pushing himself up to greet me. He knew better than to offer to shake my hand. 'When did you work it out?'

'About a couple of weeks after I should have. About thirty seconds ago, in fact. But what I still don't get is what you're doing here, when you're supposed to be pacing up and down a few yards of carpet in a top-security mental hospital. You're bloody crackers, remember, guilty but insane, so what the everlasting fuck are you doing here?'

'I'd be careful what you say, Mr Blackstone.' Two men stepped through the door from the kitchen. Actually one of them looked more like a trolley-bus than a man, but I knew the speaker well enough, having seen his photo often enough in the *Scotsman*, and other business pages.

'Duncan!' exclaimed W H Smith behind me. 'What are you doing here?'

'Setting you up, pal,' I told him. 'You may not have known what's been going on, but you're going to find out now.'

I glanced at the converted public transport on legs. 'What's this?' I asked Jack Gantry.

'He's my attendant. Call him my nurse, if you like.'

I knew what he was, all right. The guy was about six eight, wearing a white tunic and black slacks. If Florence Nightingale had looked like him, the opposition in the Crimea would have headed for the hills. His hair was sleeked back, and there was a Hispanic look about him. The most remarkable thing about him was his complexion; it was spotless, without a single blemish or mark. I was reminded of the old saying that you shouldn't worry about the thug with the broken nose and the face full of scars half as much as you should worry about the bloke who put them there. That very man stood before me.

'His name's Manolito, by the way,' Jack added. 'Little Manuel; some joke, eh.'

He didn't make me laugh. I looked at Duncan Kendall. 'Who's going to explain this?' I asked.

'Oh I will,' said the Lord Provost. 'Our three companions will step back into the kitchen, please. I just wanted you to see that they were there, Oz. Especially Manolito.' He smiled at me, and I looked into his eyes. The first time I ever met the man, in his gold chain and all his glory in Glasgow City Chambers, that's what struck me about him: those eyes of his and, when you stripped all the rest away, how stone cold they were. He seemed slimmer than in those days, older certainly, but that had stayed with him.

Facially he was much changed, though. He was bald on top now, but he had compensated by growing a reddish beard. His hair, still dark although he was in his early sixties, was combed back, like Manolito's, probably by Manolito, and he wore a pair of designer specs, with blue lenses in light rectangular frames.

My mobile rang as the 'nurse' and the two lawyers left the room; it seemed unnatural in this surreal atmosphere, and for a split second I was startled. When I had gathered myself enough to press the green button, I assumed that Ricky would be on the other end, maybe wondering if he should send in the SAS. But I was wrong.

'Oz?' said Greg McPhillips. 'Can you speak?'

'I can listen,' I replied.

'Then listen to this. Torrent PLC's advisers issued a statement to the Stock Exchange and the business press at two this afternoon, announcing that the company has decided not to proceed with its proposed takeover of the Gantry Group.'

I raised an eyebrow as I glanced across at Jack; he was looking back at me, with half a smile on his face, as if he was making some pretty accurate guesses.

'Why?'

'They said that they no longer regarded the group as a suitable avenue for diversification.'

'Crap.'

'Maybe, but there's more. When I got back from court at lunchtime, I found letters waiting for me from the lawyers acting for Cornwell, Perry and Ravens, offering to accept our terms for withdrawal, if they can do so without publicity.'

'That'll be right. Have you spoken to Culshaw?'

'Yes. He gave me a rather abrupt reply, but he said I should ask you what you thought.'

'Did he now?' I smiled as I looked across at Gantry. 'I think we should remind them, in case they've forgotten, that we cancelled those agreements earlier this week. Have they presented those cheques yet?'

'Yes. All three. This morning.'

'Fine. See they're honoured, then send them another five grand each as a gesture of goodwill, and leak the story to the press. But not through Alison Goodchild: I want you to call Arnott Buchan at the *Sunday Herald* and tell him that it's a present from me. Tell him also that we've made an agreed termination payment to Aidan Keane's estate of one hundred thousand pounds, and that the company will meet his funeral expenses as a gesture to his widow. You should clear all this with Phil first, of course, but he'll agree with me.'

'I'll do as you instruct,' said Greg, but there was doubt in his voice.

'It's the smart thing to do,' I told him. 'The Three Bears won't go away, not all at once anyway. For now they're a fact of Glaswegian life, so there's no point in rubbing their noses in their own mess. As for the payment to Keane's widow, that's good PR, no more, no less. We'd have spent that much defending an interdict hearing, and you know it.'

'I suppose so,' he conceded. 'I'll get it all rolling now.'

'Good, then do something else for me. Call Sir Graeme Fisher and tell him that I will expect his letter of resignation from the board of the Gantry Group to be in the hands of the acting managing director by close of play this afternoon. Statement to the Stock Exchange tomorrow morning, please.'

'What if he refuses to resign?'

'Then he'll face a vote of no confidence at the next board meeting, and will be publicly humiliated. But it won't come to that; he supported Torrent, and he'll know the consequences now they've pulled out.'

'Golden handshake?'

'Not a fucking penny.'

'Who succeeds in the chair?'

'A representative of the minority shareholders. Me.'

'Jesus Christ, you can't appoint yourself chairman.'

'I think you'll find that I have the support of the majority shareholder,' I reminded him. 'And of another significant player in the company.' I looked at Gantry again. 'Isn't that right, Jack?'

He gave that cackling, mirthless laugh of his again, and nodded. 'For now, son, for now. After that, who knows?'

'Oz.' Greg's voice was a whisper in my ear. 'Who are you with?'

'Never mind. Get on with all that.' I pressed the red button. The Lord Provost reached out a hand. I knew what he wanted and gave him the phone so he could be sure it was switched off.

'No tape either,' I said, taking off my antelope hide jacket and throwing it on the couch, then turning so that he could see there were no bulges beneath my tight-fitting tee shirt. He looked at my physique. 'You've been working out, son, and no mistake. Better just drop your kegs, in case you've got a microphone strapped to your cock.' I did as he asked; anything to make him start talking.

'So you called off the Bears,' I said, as I buckled my belt. 'And bloody Goldilocks as well.'

'I had to. When poor silly Natalie panicked last night and came rushing straight here after you'd spun her your story, I knew the game was up. I knew full well that you'd tail her here, indeed that you'd probably done it before, and that you'd be on to me inside twenty-four hours. So I called the boys and told them to get here.'

'You must have been really pleased with Nat, with her falling for the crap I spun her. She took a nice photo when she left. A bit different from when she arrived, though.'

Gantry frowned. 'That was unfortunate. Jock Perry will live to regret doing that. She told them what you had said, you see, that one of the three of them had turned over, and that it was probably either him or Kevin, since she guessed that Ravens had done the boy Keane. Perry was close to her; he gave her a backhander. I have to admit that you had even me wondering for a second.' He tutted, four tuts, in fact. 'Topping Keane was a fucking stupid thing to do, especially straight after Nat had been here.'

'I thought you'd ordered that.'

'As you would, given the sequence of events. But I didn't. That was another example of Mr Perry's impetuosity. He was always a fucking chancer that one, but this time, if I read the situation right, he may find that the other two take the view that he's too risky to have around any longer.'

'He'll be no loss to the city,' I commented. 'Any more than would the other two. But Jack, where do you hang with these guys, to have them running after you?' Then I remembered the story Susie had told me, about Jock Perry in the nightclub, the proposition, and then the champagne apology, 'when he found out who I was'.

'Those three started life as my message boys, Oz,' Jack said, casually. 'They're still my fucking message boys.'

I sat down in the white leather armchair and made myself comfortable. Gantry followed my example and sat back in the swivel chair. He picked up two remotes from the floor beside him: as he pressed one, the Venetian slats levelled and the blinds rose, giving us the uninterrupted view of Glasgow that I knew so well. He pressed the other and Vivaldi segued into Dwight Yoakam. A perfect choice, I thought; we were, after all, in the Nashville of Europe.

'Tell me, Jack,' I said. 'Fill me in on the whole story. But start with my first question, the one I asked earlier. How the fuck do you come to be here? Did you dig a tunnel? Is there a Jack Gantry replica doll in your room in the state funny farm?' As I gazed across at him, I was astonished to discover that for that moment at least, fascination had pushed my anger to one side. The man was hypnotic; whatever emotion you felt as you came into his presence it seemed impossible to sustain it. If you were depressed, he lifted you up; if you were enraged, he calmed you down. Sitting opposite him, I found myself totally intrigued.

He shook his head. 'No need. As Duncan started to say earlier, whatever you may have thought, and with some justification, I admit, I was never convicted of a criminal offence.'

He frowned. 'It's true, as you'd have known if you'd read the right papers at the time, instead of the red-tops. After the unfortunate circumstances that led to my nephew's body being found in my deep freeze, I was examined by half a dozen of the top nutcrackers in the country. They agreed unanimously that I was suffering from schizophrenia, megalomania, delusions of adequacy, inflammation of the willie, and a whole list of other Freudian nonsense that boiled down to one thing. Whether or not I had done the things that the Crown Office suggested I had done, I had been insane at the time and still was. That meant, of course, that I could not stand trial.'

I nodded. It was a lecture, like being back at university. 'Therefore,' he went on, 'under Section 54 of the Criminal Justice Act, an examination of facts was held, at which I was not present, having begun treatment in Gartnavel by that time. This led to my formal acquittal on all charges. However, the Crown did manage to convince the judge that I represented a degree of danger to the public, and so I was committed to the State Hospital for treatment.'

He cackled again. 'I was a good patient, Oz. I responded to the treatment they gave me, and after a year or so it was agreed that I had made sufficient progress to go back to Gartnavel. After a further period of treatment, my consultants expressed the view to Duncan Kendall, my Curator bonis . . . that's a loony's court-appointed manager, if you didn't know . . . that I was fit to return to society.'

Jack nodded. 'And quite right too,' he muttered. I had a feeling that he really believed he shouldn't have been taken away from it in the first place. 'Therefore,' the lecture resumed, 'Duncan, in accordance with the Mental Health Act, instructed a petition to the First Minister for my release. But my counsel also pointed out that all this time I had been a patient and a ward of the state, not its prisoner, and he argued that I was as entitled to have my medical confidentiality preserved as any other individual. This was referred to the Court of Session for a ruling on precedent, and at a hearing held in camera, three senior judges decided that my counsel was dead right. The case went back to the First Minister. As it happens, Seb McTigue, the present chief executive of this country, is a former Glasgow City councillor, and a former colleague of mine. But we go back longer than that; he was another of my message boys, before I spotted something in him and got him into politics. With my file on his desk, he was only too keen to confirm my release, and even keener that it be afforded the privacy I sought.' The Lord Provost smiled at the recollection.

'So I left Gartnavel,' he said, 'and moved across the city, to this place. When I heard it was on the market, I had Duncan buy it for me, not to make any point to you or Susie at all, but because I've always liked it. I built it, remember: this conversion was a Gantry project. More than that, I was actually its first owner.'

'You were?' I exclaimed, taken aback.

'Oh it wasn't in my name. Remember the woman who sold it to you and your poor late wife, son? She was an old girlfriend of mine. I set her up in this place, put it in her name, and then, when I became enamoured of someone else, and we split up, I let her sell it and keep the money.'

210

He held up a hand. 'Incidentally, son, whatever I may have said when the balance of my mind was disturbed, I was not responsible for your wife's death. I admit that at the time I wanted to send the two of you a wee warning, but what my messengers actually did was a breach of my instruction. They've both paid for it since, anyway.'

He had strayed into an area that broke my trance. 'And what about your nephew?' I asked bitterly. 'I don't suppose you killed him, either.'

'Oh aye,' he chuckled. 'I did that all right. But it was genuinely self-defence, and almost accidental. He came to me demanding a ridiculous amount of money, and when I refused he came at me with a blade. It's a blemish on this city, you know, the number of our young people who carry knives. Anyway, the boy picked the wrong place. I had a rack of Kitchen Devils within reach and I used one to fend him off. He ran right on to it.'

I let it pass. He might even have been telling the truth. 'So what's your status now?' I asked him.

'Same as yours. My consultant comes to see me once a month, for a chat, and I'm still on light medication, supervised by Manolito, who really is a nurse, but I'm a free citizen, son, entitled to vote if I chose to register. But I don't. I'm only interested in politics when I'm running the show, and I'll never be seen to be doing that again.'

I waved a hand, abstractly. 'And what about all this? All these trusts, all leading back to you? All these lawyers operating in vacuums? Did your Curator bonis set them up while you were inside?'

'No, no. Duncan set those up for me years ago. Actually when he was appointed Curator, it was really just an extension of what he'd been doing for me all along, and still does. I was his first major client, and I may still be his biggest.'

He leaned forward in the chair, as Mr Yoakam began, appropriately, 'The Home of the Blues'. 'It would be a great mistake to assume that the holding in the Gantry Group, which I put in trust for my daughter, represented all my wealth. It didn't, not by a hell of a long way. The bulk of it remains under my control, in a way devised by Duncan to preserve my anonymity in my business dealings. Would you believe I own two newspapers and a radio station? I'm not telling you where, but I do.'

'And you wanted to own the Gantry Group again as well, didn't you?'

'I have a hankering for it, yes.'

'But why go about it this way, by plotting against your own company?'

He stared at me: no smile, no cackle, only those cold blue eyes behind the fancy specs. 'Since you'll never prove it, son, I'll tell you. I did it for Natalie, in part. Why Natalie?' His voice hardened appreciably. 'Because, Oz, when I was in Carstairs, and then Gartnavel, the only people who ever came to visit me, apart from Duncan, and Kevin Cornwell, who's always been a friend . . . as well as a message boy . . . were James Torrent and his niece. I've been a sleeping partner in Torrent from its early days; I funded its growth with loan capital and I even had Joe Donn sign some photocopier contracts that were no more or less than a means of shovelling money to James by the back door. After he died, Natalie kept on visiting me. I've been a sleeping partner of hers for a while too, in a literal sense.'

'So you're the reason she ditched Ewan Capperauld?'

'He did himself no favours. You actors are all Jessies at heart, you know.'

I laughed. 'I wouldn't say that to Miles Grayson if I were you.'

Gantry cackled again, louder than ever. 'Son, with Manolito behind me I'll say whatever I like to whoever I like, even that big pal of yours, Everett Davis.'

He was overmatching Manolito there, but I let it pass. 'So for Natalie, you set out to break the Group,' I challenged him. 'You had that letter-bomb sent to the office.' He rolled his eyes and looked at the ceiling. 'You recruited your message boys and sent them to buy into New Bearsden, them and their own message boys.'

He shook his bald head. 'No, just the three of them; the others were just a rumour.'

'Big deal. You recruited Aidan Keane, through Jock Perry, his bookie, as your inside fixer.'

'Well done, or was that a guess?'

'A guess, but thanks for confirming it.' I took another shot in the dark. 'And you killed Joe Donn, because he found out that you were out and what you were up to.'

'Wrong there. Joe didn't have a clue that I was released. Anyway, he's the last man I'd have wanted dead.'

'Whatever,' I said. 'The real bottom line is you maybe did some of this for Natalie, but you did it for yourself too, and at the same time to stab Susie in the back.'

'Hardly. The millions she'd have got for her shares would have gone straight into her trust fund. I might even have let her keep it. But not now, though, and it's thanks to you, you clever big bastard.'

I shook my head. 'They let you out too soon, Jack,' I exclaimed, hoping, I suppose, to rile him. 'Susie's trust fund is ring fenced.'

'Ah,' he sighed, 'my poor lad, you're no' as clever as you think. Duncan,' he called out, then leaned back, as the slim, silver-haired solicitor came into the room. 'Tell the boy about Plan B,' he instructed.

'Certainly, Jack.' Kendall smiled at me like a barracuda; I found myself wanting to rip his gills out. 'The terms of the trust under which your wife is the beneficial owner of a majority shareholding in the Gantry Group specify that Mr Gantry has passed this interest irrevocably into the control of his daughter, Susan, and in succession any children she may have.' He paused, knowing that I had caught the emphasis placed on a single word, and letting me guess what was coming.

'Regrettably,' he continued, when he was ready, 'it has been alleged to Mr Gantry that Susan is not in fact his daughter, but is a belated by-product of his late wife's previous marriage to Mr Joe Donn. It is unfortunate that Mr Donn is himself recently deceased and thus unable to confirm this, but I do have evidence that your wife has referred to Mr Donn as her father on a number of occasions.'

He took a breath, for effect, as if he was in court, although I knew that guys like him hardly ever stand up before a judge. They cover their bets by hiring specialist QCs. 'To sum up,' he concluded, 'I have been instructed by Mr Gantry to petition the court to wind up the trust on the basis of this . . .' He gave a light laugh. '. . . misconception. My petition will be heard, Mr Blackstone, and the court will certainly require your wife to provide a DNA sample. My advice to my client is that we will win and that the majority holding in the Group will revert to its rightful owner. The way it's constituted and worded, there can be no other outcome. We will argue that it would be wrong for us to leave it unchallenged.'

I took a long breath and looked at Jack. 'There is another way of making the trust all legal and proper. You could adopt Susie, formally.'

He snorted. 'What? After she returned my letters to her, and eventually had me barred from writing to her at the hospital! I should give her a hug and adopt her? You don't know me at all, boy.'

'She was rather pissed off at you,' I pointed out. 'Apart from killing her cousin, she also found out that you'd been using the Gantry Group nursing home division as a front to obtain prescription drugs for cutting and sale on the street. She also didn't like it that her cousin and his pals had been fencing the gear the poor punters stole to buy your heroin and jellies.'

'I warn you for the last time,' Duncan Kendall exclaimed, dramatically, 'that my client has been formally acquitted of all counts against him.'

'And I warn you for the last time,' I shot back, 'that if you annoy me any more than you have up to now, I will poke your eye out with a sharp stick.' I didn't even bother to look at him. Instead I kept my eyes firmly on the Lord Provost. 'Well?'

'She declared me dead, son. She's burned her boats and the jetty they were tied to.'

I pushed myself out of the white chair and grabbed my jacket. I was well steamed and not even Gantry's hypnotic charm would have cooled me down; Also, I had to get myself out of Mr Kendall's presence before I did something unfortunate. 'You'll lose your anonymity, Jack,' I warned.

'No,' he replied. 'Because when you get out of here you'll take legal advice, and that advice will be to settle. Susie'll decide to become a full-time mother and she'll accept a bid for her holding from the Maplevale Trust. It won't be full value, but it won't be ungenerous.'

'You're not listening. You'll lose your anonymity.'

Finally the real Jack Gantry looked at me; I don't know whether he'd ever really been mad, but I do know he'd always been evil. 'If I do, Susie will lose everything, not just the holding, but all the benefit she's derived from it. If you and she defend in court, you'll lose the bulk of your fortune in costs, plus you'll be so tangled up in hearings,

214

your career will go down the pan . . . unless you decide to sail off in the lifeboat and let poor wee Susie drown.'

The corners of his mouth turned up in something that was not a smile. 'You've got the weekend to decide . . . Mr Chairman. I'd say I'll see you in court, but somehow, I don't think I will.'

# 40

When I got out of there, at first I headed for my car; then, on the spur of the moment, I turned and headed straight for the woman in the Rover. As I neared her she looked at first startled, then confused, but when I motioned her to lower her window she did so.

'It's okay,' I told her. 'I'm the guy you're working for. Call Ricky and tell him that he's bound for Barcelona and that he can pull the operation as of now.' She nodded, and I left her keying a number into her mobile.

Wylie Smith was waiting for me when I got back to the Lotus. 'If you think I'm taking you back to Edinburgh,' I told him, 'you're fucking joking.'

'No,' he said, 'but I'll settle for Queen Street station.'

He didn't say much as we headed through Charing Cross, but he'd had an even harder job getting into the car than before. As it turned out, though, he wasn't breathless, only thinking.

'I can't do this any more, Oz,' he exclaimed, as we drove past the Tron Church and into George Square.

I swung into the station entrance and braked. 'Next time I'll bring the BMW,' I said, icily.

'I'm serious,' he protested. 'I cannot work with Duncan Kendall for one day longer, not after he's kept me deliberately in the dark about matters that affect the firm. I'm a partner being treated like a junior assistant. And I'm not working for that man Gantry either. He's an associate of gangsters . . . and that valet of his scares the shit out of me.'

'Jack's not an associate of anyone,' I countered. 'People associate with him as and when he allows it. He's very rich, very powerful and very ruthless; the nastiest and most dangerous man you're ever likely to meet. All the more so since he's been through the machine and come out the other side. His behaviour and his actions are completely under control, and God help anyone who gets in his way. I think you're dead right to want to quit, but before you do, you should ask yourself: do you know anything that could prove dangerous to him?'

Wylie shuddered.

'But let's suppose you did chuck it,' I went on, 'and you were advising me. Would you agree with Duncan Kendall's assessment of Jack's action to regain control of the Gantry Group? It's true, by the way: Susie isn't his daughter. I believe he knew that when he transferred the business to her control, but I'll never prove it.'

'To be honest,' the lawyer replied, '. . . and don't laugh at that please . . . I would say that such an action would almost certainly succeed.'

I started the car again. 'Come on,' I told him. 'This might not be ethical, but I want you to meet someone.'

I drove straight to Greg McPhillips' office. We arrived unannounced, but he aborted a meeting with another client and saw us when I told his secretary it would not wait. I began to introduce Wylie, but they'd met at university, and on occasions since then, so I went ahead and gave Greg a run-down of my interesting day, and my meeting with the spider at the centre of the web.

'What do we do?' I asked him, when I was finished.

He looked at me dolefully. 'The best deal you can.' I know about the old axiom that fifty per cent of lawyers must be wrong, but I had the feeling that neither of my chums was in this case.

Wylie took a taxi to the station this time, while I headed back to the estate, to break the worst news that Susie had ever had in her life. But when I got there I just couldn't. I thought of her blood pressure, sure, and of the effect that the news might have, but I thought also of the sheer misery it would cause her, and I just couldn't bring myself to make her that unhappy.

So instead I told her to get ready for the road, I told Ethel she could go and visit her sister for the weekend, and not to bother coming back till Monday afternoon, and I told Jay that he was coming with us when we headed for Anstruther in the morning, a day early for the posh frock and black tie dinner in the Old Course Hotel.

Susie, of course, was over the moon. Instead of telling her that the arse was about to fall out of her entire world, I told her that the Torrent bid had collapsed, that the Three Bears had gone away, and that I had taken an executive decision on her behalf to fire Sir Graeme Fisher and replace him, *pro tem*, with her most trusted lieutenant.

She was still elated when we headed off for Fife . . . early next afternoon as it turned out . . . in a small convoy, Jay driving the BMW with the girls in the back, and me in the Lotus. I took it just in case we needed a second car up there, but there was this also; away from Susie's presence I could drop my act and set free all my concerns and anxieties.

I would have to tell her, of course, before the weekend was out. The lawyers' opinions had been firm and convincing. She was going to lose the company, and she would have to be made to face up to it, and to the need to deal with the Devil. I switched on Clyde One, if not to cheer me up, then at least to take my mind off things for a while. At first, Coldplay and Travis did the business, but then came the top of the hour news bulletin.

It began with the latest bickering in the Scottish Executive, went on to a report on the latest bickering in Glasgow City Council, and moved into a story about bickering between a football manager and his star player. After the sport, the usual formula is the latest weather and then a hand-over to the disc-jockey, but the newsreader went on in a glossy, tabloid radio voice, 'And this just in. Strathclyde Police have confirmed that the man found shot dead in a car outside a betting shop in Crow Road was Jock Perry, Glasgow businessman and alleged underworld figure. Detectives refused to speculate on the motive behind Perry's murder, but it is thought it may be linked to the death of Aidan Keane, a Broomhill man found dead in the River Clyde a few days ago.'

I switched the radio off and thought back twenty-four hours, replaying my conversation with Jack Gantry. '*Jock Perry will live to regret that.*' Unless I was very much off target, he had more or less told me that he had ordered an execution. I had dealt with a couple of serious people in my life before, but never anyone nearly as bad as him. I found myself fearing for Wylie Smith, who had gone back to Edinburgh the day before still determined to resign from Kendall

McGuire. If Jack decided that he couldn't afford him outside the tent pissing in . . .

We reached my Dad's just as he finished work for the week: come four o'clock on Friday he's usually seen enough teeth for a while. I had warned him that we were coming, of course, and that we'd want a room for Jay as well. I wasn't sure how I'd find him after our last meeting, but he was fine, seeming to be back to his old self.

'Good to see you all,' he greeted us. 'You canna' have enough family. Your sister's bringing the boys later; it's rare that we all get the chance to eat together, so I thought I'd push the boat out and take us all to the Craw's Nest.'

Enster means just two things to my daughter: the harbour and the ice-cream shop. We were hardly unloaded when she began demanding to be taken to both. My Dad has always been a sucker for a smile, and pretty soon she was heading off in her pushchair, with her grand-parents in charge and Jay going along with them, because Susie wanted to rest up for the evening and I wanted some space to carry on thinking.

We went up to our room and hung in the wardrobe the fancy gear we'd be wearing on the following evening: a voluminous white evening gown, and a white tux and black trousers. Still buoyed by her victory over the hated Natalie, Susie was determined to put on a show at the dinner, so she had brought her best jewellery, which isn't bad at all, and worth more than all our fancy cars put together.

It's so valuable, in fact, that as she undressed and slipped under the duvet, I took it, in its red leather box, downstairs to put it in my Dad's safe. Like most dental or medical practitioners, he keeps one, and always has. It's a big thing, bolted to the floor although it weighs a ton, and it sits in the corner of his surgery, hidden beneath a table which always has a white cloth over it.

I've known the combination since I was a boy, so I threw back the cover and dialled it: at the last click, the door swung open, and I reached in to deposit Susie's valuables.

I actually didn't see it in the shadows, but my hand brushed against it, a flat object with a plastic feel. I fumbled around until I had a grip of it, then drew it out: a Shoei laptop computer, looking top of the range and pretty new. There was a modem port in the rear, and a cable dangled from it.

I stared at it, bewildered. What the hell was my self-confessed computer hater of a father doing with a seriously fast laptop in his safe?

And then I remembered Joe Donn, and his missing top of the range Shoei. Was this it, and if it was, then again, what was it doing in my Dad's safe? Had Joe given it to him as a present? No, any time they'd met I'd been there too. And anyway, why would he? Well if not, had . . .?

'Just hold on there, Blackstone,' I said aloud, and realised that my heart was pounding. 'Get your imagination in check.'

All the same, I picked up the phone, pulled Ewan Maltbie's number from directory enquiries and called him. Happily he was not an early finisher on a Friday. 'Mr Maltbie,' I began, when his secretary connected us. 'Remember Joe's computer?'

'I do indeed,' he replied at once. 'I meant to tell you; sorry I haven't got round to it. A letter arrived yesterday, redirected from the house to my office. It was from the Shoei Computer Company and it said that the laptop which he had returned to the company under warranty had been repaired and would be returned by Parcel Force, within the next few days. It said that the fault had been in the CD rewriter, and that the recordable disks which he had sent with it were perfectly all right. We only checked the supplier and local dealer. It never occurred to us or the police that Joe might have returned it directly to the maker. Oh yes,' he added. 'There was a letter from Laing, the jeweller. The carriage clock and the Piaget watch have been with them being serviced.'

I felt a mixture of relief and guilt. 'Did you tell Fallon?' I asked.

'Yes. He was annoyed at first, but then happy that his people were off the hook.'

'Me too. Cheers.'

I hung up and looked at the Shoei. So it wasn't Joe's. So that meant almost certainly that Joe's death had indeed been an accident, untimely for him, and for Jack Gantry, with Plan B in mind. So was it my Dad's after all?

I flipped it open, took a look at the keyboard layout and pressed what looked like the 'on' key, in the far right corner. It was powerful, all right: it booted up nearly as quickly as my desktop at home.

Before long, the screen displayed an array of icons; some of them were shortcuts to the standard word processing and spreadsheet software that you get with every machine, but others I didn't recognise.

I looked at one. The tag under it was 'Chesty'. I clicked on it, and gasped in astonishment. The screen was filled with the image of a blonde: but this was not your average pin-up. This woman had the biggest breasts I had ever seen.

I closed it and selected another. This had no file name, only an asterisk. I opened it, and saw another blonde, although there was clear evidence that her hair colouring was not natural. There was nothing spectacular about this one's bosom. What made her different was the fact that she was on all fours, side-on to the camera, and was being penetrated from the rear by a large black man. If he had as much inside her as was still showing outside, he was a very large man indeed.

I closed it quickly and flicked through some others. Those with names were not engaged in any field sports, but some of them looked so young that I felt as if ice, not blood, was running through my veins. Those with asterisks were the action shots; some were stills, others were movies, but none were what you called routine porn.

'The old bastard's been downloading,' I whispered to myself.

I opened his programme folders and searched through them. Again, most were standard, but there was one called 'Neptune' that caught my eye. I tried to open it, only to discover that it was not a routine programme, but a link to a website. I took the modem cable, disconnected the surgery phone and plugged it into the jack point, then found an icon marked 'Free internet with Shoei'. I double-clicked; an indicator told me that I was dialling, that my password was being checked, and finally that I was online. Then it vanished, and the Shoei homepage appeared.

I selected 'favourites'. A list of web addresses appeared, and none of them looked like Amazon.com. The Neptune icon was among them, and I hit it. The first web page cleared and another appeared. It showed the old sea-king, trident in hand, only the three prongs on its end looked unsubtly different from the norm. He seemed to be winking too. Below him, there was a line of asterisks, and I knew it was for a

221

password. I thought about it; if this was my naive old Dad, what would he do? I keyed in 'osbert' and got it right first time.

A door opened and Neptune's trident waved me through; a banner appeared across the screen:

'*Welcome to the Sea of Pleasure, member Mac*'

Below it there was an index, a veritable shopping list of kinks, from A for Anal to Z for Zoological. I left that alone and looked at two lines at the foot of the screen. One read 'Interactive', but I left that and clicked on 'Mac's private room'. I was asked for another password. Taking a logical approach, I keyed in 'ellen', and it let me in.

I'm not going to describe in detail the contents of my father's private chamber in King Neptune's Sea of Pleasure. It featured all the usual sexual gymnastics, with a few animal assistants thrown in, and it was without doubt one of the saddest, seediest things I've ever seen in my life. But it all clicked into place when I opened one folder and saw a couple having fairly brutal sex. They were unmasked in this clip, where before they had been wearing various disguises. Like the fake blonde and the fit black man, they were side-on to the camera so that the viewer, sorry, voyeur, could see everything that was going on, and in.

However, they were both looking sideways at the lens, with expressions of a level of rapture that just had to be fake. Beyond any shadow of a doubt, the images were those of the late Andrea and Walter Neiporte.

I looked into 'Interactive' after that, and I will regret doing that to my dying day. All I will tell you is that my father had some-how managed to operate the free digital camera that comes with every Shoei, and had been able to upload head and shoulder images of himself. These had been digitally grafted on to someone else's . . . Walter Neiporte's, I guessed, and when I compared the 'interactive' chest hair, and other, more private features, I saw that I was right . . . so that he appeared to be a participant in a sexual orgy.

'You stupid old man,' I shouted out loud. I killed the image and turned off the laptop without bothering to log off from the Shoei homepage, then walked steadily across to the surgery sink and threw up.

I had rinsed out my mouth and was wiping my face when my father came into the room. He stared at the open computer, still connected to the phone line, and his face contorted with rage in a way that I could never have imagined. It filled me with a horror greater than had anything I'd seen on his computer. 'What have you done?' he hissed, seeming to scream and whisper at the same time.

Try to imagine that you've known someone all your life, and loved them as much as you could ever love anyone in the world, in a special way that was unique unto them. Then imagine that their secret soul, the one that we all possess, is laid open to you, and you see that it is weak and corrupt, that the idol you worshipped has feet not merely of clay, for who hasn't, but of vile slime. Try to imagine how you'd feel.

You can? Well that's how I felt when I saw the other side of my father. He came towards me, looking far crazier at that moment than Jack Gantry ever had. He might have tried to hit me, but I thrust out a hand and seized his collar, holding him at bay.

'No. Not me,' I said, quietly. 'What have *you* done?'

I looked at him, but I couldn't see anyone I knew.

He seemed to break down then; he sagged in my grasp and his face crumpled. 'I've been a fool, son,' said this antithesis of my Dad, in a pathetic, whining voice that filled me with disgust, yet also with a sadness that it pains me to recall.

'You've been a dirty old swine,' I told him, quietly, 'that's what you've been. You have actually fed your face on to that site. You've seen the disgusting things they've done with them, but do you really believe that it was just for your own gratification? Fat chance. How many perverts like you do you think are out there leering at you right now? But forget about you and think about this. If I'm reacting like this, how the hell do you think Mary, and Ellie, and Susie, and even Jonathan will feel if it ever goes public?'

I didn't need to wait for an answer. 'When did you buy the computer?' I asked.

'A few months ago,' he replied, in something like his normal voice. 'Jonny and Colin were on at me so much that I decided I'd better join the twenty-first century. I didn't tell anyone, though; after all the fuss I'd made about it I was too embarrassed. I tried it out, and I used it at night in the surgery, after Mary had gone to bed.'

He looked down at his feet. He was calmer now so I released him from my grasp. 'It all got out of hand,' he whispered, but I wasn't in the mood to take anything that resembled an excuse.

'Did it fuck get out of hand!' I snapped at him. 'This is what happened. You set yourself up an e-mail address, yes?' He nodded. 'But before you even learned to use it, the spam started to arrive.'

'Spam?'

'You must know what that is. It means junk e-mail: Viagra by post, debt management, and most of all, the porn sites. You get e-mails asking, for example, if you'd like to see someone who looks like someone famous sucking someone's cock. Normal e-mail users filter these things out, so that hardly any of them reach them. Not you, though, you stupid old sod; you let them come through, and more than that, when they did, you opened them. Am I on the case?' He nodded again, mute. 'But you did even more than that, didn't you. You clicked on the links, you visited the sites, and . . . you . . . were . . . hooked.' I felt my lip curl with distaste. 'All that indescribable shagging, at your fingertips; I mean how could you resist?'

I felt myself start to shake with anger, but I controlled it. 'You did the really stupid thing next, though.' I felt like a dark side version of Michael Aspel, with the red 'This is Your Life' book. 'You signed up as a member, at a number of sites probably, not just Neptune. And you paid with your credit card.' Nod. 'And the form asked for your address, and you gave that too.' Nod again.

'How many times?'

He shrugged his shoulders; if I'd let him, he'd have turned his back on me. He certainly couldn't look me in the eye. 'I don't know,' he whispered. 'Maybe half a dozen.'

'Maybe. Maybe if I checked your credit card statements I'd find lots more.' I shook my head, struck by an irony. 'You know, in recent times, I've come to think of myself as one of the luckiest guys on the planet. You, on the other hand, must be one of the unluckiest. Most of these sites are run from places like Thailand or Mexico. You just happened to sign up for a do-it-yourself operation run out of Pitten-fucking-weem! And you told them where you lived!'

I tried to catch his eye, but still he looked away. 'There never was a surgery incident, was there?' I asked. 'I'll bet if I look at your list I'll find that Andrea Neiporte wasn't even a patient. Right?' I barked it out.

His shoulders gave a great heave as he sighed. 'Of course you're right. I made that story up, Oz, in the hope . . . Oh, I don't know in what hope.'

'I do. You did it in the hope that I'd take care of it in some way. Pay them off, scare them off; you didn't care as long as I fixed it for you.'

'I suppose so.' Finally, he did look at me. 'Son, I was desperate. It was like living a nightmare. The first thing that happened was that an envelope arrived in the mail, addressed to me, personal and confidential. When I opened it, I found print-outs of some of that stuff you saw in the computer.'

'Let me guess. The personal stuff?'

'Yes, graphic, blown up so you couldn't fail to recognise my face. There was no note with it, but next day Andrea Neiporte phoned me in the surgery. She told me that the next envelope would go to Mary, unless . . .'

He sat on the edge of the table. 'The first time it was five hundred. I agreed, and I posted it to her, in cash. I thought that would be it, but a week or so later, she called again. She said that they'd spent the five hundred, so would I give her a thousand, please. I did, of course. It was the third phone call that asked for the fifty grand. I said that I didn't have that sort of ready cash. She laughed and said that you did. She said she'd call me in a couple of weeks, and that when she did, they'd be expecting the money. It was a couple of days after that that you came up.'

'What would you have done if I hadn't?'

'I don't know. Paid her, I suppose.'

'But instead you turned me loose on them.' He nodded.

'When did you know that hadn't worked?'

'I had that first nasty, spitting phone call from her, the one I told you about. She said she'd show me how scared they were, then she'd be back in touch.'

'The can of paint at the premiere; that was a message for you, not me?'

225

'That's right. When she called me again, the day after, she said that the timescale had shortened. They wanted the money in three days, or Mary got the photos.'

'So,' I said, 'finally, you plucked up the courage and you killed them. And that show of outrage on the golf course afterwards, that was all a sham.'

'No!' he shouted, violently, vehemently. 'No, I did not kill them! I wasn't kidding that day. I really thought you killed them, or you had your man Jay do it. If you want to know the truth, I still do.'

'Well you're wrong,' I told him, 'although you might have been on the mark. I sent Jay up to Fife to put them off for good, and I gave him an open ticket. Our deal was that we wouldn't talk about it when he got back, and when the bodies were found, I will admit that I thought the same as you. But then the police published the date and time of death, and I knew it couldn't have been him.'

'And that's how I can prove it wasn't me,' my father exclaimed, with a sudden exultation that struck me as shameless, given the circumstances. 'When it happened, Mary and I were in Kirkcaldy, at a Fife Rotary and Inner Wheel joint fundraiser. I have a couple of hundred witnesses to say I didn't do it.'

I looked at him for a while. I knew that my life wasn't the same any more, and that it never would be. My Dad . . . I always thought of him with a capital letter, like God . . . didn't exist any more, not as such. I could never think of him in that light again, in the special way I always had until then. I realised that I had suffered a bereavement as real as I had when Jack Gantry's overenthusiastic messengers had killed Jan.

Is there no forgiveness in me, do I hear you ask? Truly I wish that there could be. I wish that I could excuse him by rationalising that every one of us has a weakness, something that's beyond our control. But I can't, not completely: for there were people on that computer, victims, who were no more than kids, and I'm a father myself.

'What would you have done?' I asked him.

'I don't know,' he replied. 'I sat at home waiting for a phone call but it never came. If it had, I might have called you again, or I might just have paid them.'

'And hoped that it was over?'

'Yes,' he whispered.

'Just as you think it's over now?' He frowned up at me, puzzled. 'The website's still open,' I pointed out. 'I just logged on to it, using your woefully insecure passwords. It'll stay open until the unscrupulous service provider who maintains it stops getting paid and shuts it down. Then there's the police investigation. You're not fucking special you know, other than having a rich son; the Neiportes were probably blackmailing other people, one of whom had them done. Fife CID will be looking through their database right now for suspects, and sooner or later they'll come to you. When they do, coppers being as they are, some detective constable or uniformed PC in the know will phone the *Sun* or the *Record* and tell them that Oz Blackstone's father's a suspect in a porn ring murder, and you'll be all over the fucking papers anyway. And when that happens, and they come to me for a quote, you know what? I may well disown you. I'll have trouble finding anything sympathetic to say, that's for sure.'

'Son,' he began. I knew that a plea was on the way, but I wasn't in the mood to listen.

'I'm not sure that I am,' I retorted, 'not any more. I don't know if I have a father any more. I'll need to work that out over time. But for now, let me show you something.'

I picked up his two grand laptop, the sturdily built top of the range Shoei, and I broke it to pieces with my bare hands. I ripped the screen off, easily, and threw it away, then I took the base and twisted it as hard as I could. It buckled, and character pads started to fly from the keyboard, until finally it cracked and split open. I wrenched at it, furiously, until the inner workings were exposed and I could see the hard disk, where all that filth was stored. I pulled it out, slipped it into my pocket and threw the debris into the surgery waste bin.

'There. You'll feel better for that, once you think about it. I won't, though.'

I walked towards the door. 'A couple more things,' I said, before I left. 'That ice-cream's made you sick. You're not going to be able to face the Craw's Nest tonight. I just can't sit at the same table as you and pretend this didn't happen, so I'll take everyone out and you'll stay home. And there's this too. I'm not going to shop you; if the police come to you, that's your tough luck. But when you think about

227

it, you may decide that you'll never be a man again until you've told Mary about this, and Ellen. Apart from that, they might appreciate hearing of your sins directly from you, rather than from a string of tabloid reporters.'

As far as I know, he's still thinking about that.

# 41

I found Jay in the kitchen, making himself coffee. 'Change of plan,' I told him. 'We're going to stay at Ellie's tomorrow night, after the dinner, and Sunday. We'll put you up in Rusack's Hotel, so you can enjoy the exciting nightlife of St Andrews. Who knows, maybe you'll find a nice American co-ed. The place is dripping with them, especially since Thingummy went there.'

'I should be closer to you, boss.'

'No need. There's only two Bears left now, and they'll be too busy dividing up Jock Perry's bit of the empire to bother with the likes of us.' He looked at me, surprised. Clearly, Jay hadn't been listening to the radio on the drive through.

'Make an extra coffee and come with me for a minute, though.' When he was finished we picked up our mugs and I led him out of the kitchen and into the long garden of my father's house. There's a bench seat at the foot, looking out over the Firth of Forth, and we sat there. I laid down my coffee, took out my mobile and called Mark Kravitz, on a number he gave me once. He filters all his calls, so I left a message and he called me back a minute later.

'Hi Oz,' he said, cheerily. 'What is it this time? Another favour or a job?'

'The latter, if you can do it.' I gave him the web address of King Neptune's Sea of Pleasure. 'I want the ISP traced and I want the site shut down, whatever the cost.'

'The proprietors might want a lot.'

'The proprietors have become part of cyberspace itself.'

'Should be easy, then.'

'Today if you can. Send the bill to Jay, not directly to me.'

'Sure. Take care up there.' He hung up. That last part was a big speech for Mark.

I turned to my minder. 'Jay, I need to know,' I told him. 'My whole fucking world's gone pear-shaped here. When you came back from your trip to Pittenweem, you said I wouldn't want to know what you'd done. I went along with that because I put the wrong interpretation on it. But now I really do have to know what happened.'

He nodded. 'If you've had a face-to-face with your old man, and I heard some of it, I guess you do.' He took a sip from his mug. 'I did as you asked; went to the Neiportes' cottage. I had a game plan all worked out; you don't need to know the details but I have certain calling cards that imply I'm officially connected, if you understand me. I intended to put on a small show for them and to convince them that by messing with your family they had stepped on some very sensitive toes, and that if they didn't desist, Walter would find himself deported and back in the States faster than you could say "Elvis". This could have been awkward for him, since there are a couple of small cases of internet fraud that the FBI wanted to discuss with him.'

Jay looked at me. 'I didn't anticipate any problems. That sort of approach never fails with small-timers like these were. But the big difficulty was, they weren't home. It was seven thirty in the evening, and the house was empty. So I went in, through a back window, easy as you like. I could tell they hadn't been home for a while, a day at least. The breakfast dishes in the sink were not from that morning, and the mail, and the newspaper, were still in the hall.'

He drank some more coffee. 'So I had a really good look around. There was nothing downstairs that told me anything, but upstairs, in a couple of attic rooms . . .' he whistled '. . . that was different. They told me the whole story. One was like a photographic studio, with a bed and various cameras, masks, costumes, props . . . it reminded me of a street in Amsterdam. The other room was full of computer equipment; a couple of desktops, one newer and a lot faster than the other, scanners and the like. I switched them on . . . no security at all. Probably figured they didn't need passwords. They were running a porn website, Oz; bloody hardcore too.'

Jay seemed to wince at the memory. 'Anyway, I wasn't interested in that. I wanted their diary, and it didn't take me long to find it, on the newer computer. There was an entry for the day before and it said "19:00. M. Blackstone. Lesser Saltgate Farm, Arncroach". So I let myself out . . . I took a key with me, so I could get back in through the door if necessary . . . and headed for that farm.'

He looked at me, sadly. 'People should not be allowed to keep animals that way, Oz. The place was deserted and it didn't look like anyone goes there very often. The poor bastards were filthy. They were penned in, and they were fed in troughs from these bloody great hoppers that were filled with this horrible stinking swill. There were dead piglets lying about too, and some of them . . .' He broke off.

'I found the bodies easy enough. They were in one of the troughs, but they hadn't been covered up properly. They'd been shot, him in the chest, her in the chest and head, close range, with a shotgun, not sawn-off, though, or the spread would have been wider and the wounds would have been worse.'

'What did you do?' I asked him quietly. I was struck by the fact that he had been a lot more distressed by the state of the pigs than that of the Neiportes. Me too, I'm sure, had I seen them.

'I covered them up properly, that's all, then I got out of there before the farmer or one of his hands turned up.' He held his mug close, in both hands. 'Let's just say, boss, that I reached certain conclusions, and I acted accordingly. I went back to the cottage and I stripped it as best I could. I found a couple of suitcases and I packed all the stuff from the studio into them, then I made it up with clean sheets and covers to make it look like an ordinary bedroom. Then I had another look at the computers. I wiped them clean of all the porn stuff, all the databases, all the addresses, all the client information: and when I say clean I mean really clean. There's nothing in any wastebaskets or anything like that. I spent half the night deleting and removing all traces of what had been there, and then, just to make sure, I reinstalled the system software in each of them. There's nothing left there to connect that place with what had been happening there. I sold the cameras to a bloke with a stall at Barrowlands in Glasgow; they'll be untraceable by now.'

'What about the money?' I asked. 'The Neiportes were collecting through credit cards.'

'That all went into a bank account in Jersey, with a false name. The police won't find that, not by accident at any rate. I found the records in a filing cabinet, and a lot of other stuff too. When I was done, there was nothing left in the house other than purely domestic papers. Everything else is ashes.'

'And the tabs? The ecstasy? What about that?'

'I got them through Mark,' he replied. 'I figured that I needed to send the CID off on a false trail, so I called him and asked him if he could get me a supply of something or other to plant on a bad guy. He sent me somewhere up in the Highlands. I picked up the gear, went back to the house again and hid it for the police to find when the bodies were discovered. Then I headed home.'

He looked into his mug intently, as if something was swimming in it. 'You don't have to worry, Oz. Your old man's safe.'

'I know he is. He didn't do it. He was up to his elbows in Rotarians when the Neiportes got it; as alibi-ed as you could get.'

'Eh?' Jay had been as convinced as me of my father's guilt. 'But that only leaves . . .'

I nodded. 'Exactly; me. I sound just like my father on the phone.'

'You mean you sent me up there to clear up the mess?'

I winked at him. 'Sorry. I didn't know there would be so much work. I didn't know about the porn site until today.'

'What happens to me, now I know?' he asked, quietly.

'Nothing. You're as guilty as me in the eyes of the law. Accessory after the fact. All that happens to you is that you live long and prosper, like Mr Spock.'

He laughed. 'You doing a Star Trek movie next?'

'Some day, mate, some day.'

I glanced at him again. 'How am I paying you for all that stuff? The gear must have cost more than you got for the cameras.'

'I've been looking for a way your accountants won't spot,' he said. 'You'll be paying me extra for the installation work on Janet's playground.'

I smiled. 'As much as you like. See you later.'

He stood and walked back towards the house. The smile left my face as soon as he had gone. As I've said, I've been in some personal danger in my life, but I've never felt scared; it's all happened too fast for that, I suppose. Yet as Jay's footsteps crunched on the gravel behind me, I sat there feeling more frightened than at any moment in my life.

# 42

When I went back to the house myself, Ellie and the boys had just arrived. She greeted me like a long-lost brother . . . which I was to an extent, as it had been weeks since I'd seen her, and she and I have always been very close.

'Hey,' I asked her, 'would you fancy putting up the junior branch of the family for a couple of nights? I've been thinking, it's daft to come all the way back to Enster after the dinner. And I thought that Sunday will give you a chance to get to know your niece better.'

'That'll be great, Oz; as long as I can cook for you on Sunday night.'

I grinned. 'I can live with that.' I turned to Jonathan, who was standing quietly behind her, Colin having gone crashing off to the garden. 'Young man,' I began. He looked up at me, but not far up. I still wasn't used to his eye level being so close to mine. 'Do you fancy a ride in a genuine Lotus sports car?'

'Right now?' he exclaimed, a child's reaction in a man's tone.

'Sure, we've got time.'

My nephew and I headed outside. As he slid easily into the passenger seat, I thought of Wylie Smith and smiled. As I started the engine he looked around the cockpit. 'When you're finished with this, Uncle Oz,' he asked, cheekily, 'can I have it?'

'I'll tell you what,' I told him, as we slipped out on to the main road and turned westwards. 'When I'm done with it, I'll put it away for you. But you won't drive it until you can afford to insure it yourself. If that isn't an incentive to get your head into the books I don't know what is.'

'Who said I need an incentive? Has my Mum been talking about me?'

'Actually, she's been singing your praises. She says you're just like me when I was your age. What bigger compliment could there be? It's not quite true, though. When I was your age I wasn't your height and I still spoke with a bit of a squeak.'

'Do you think I'm too young to have a girlfriend, Uncle Oz?' he asked me, seriously. I guessed that he and Ellie had been in a confrontation, and I knew automatically that he'd lost.

This was the chat I'd been meaning to have with him. 'I think you're too young to have sex with a girlfriend,' I told him, slowly, 'especially if she's under sixteen too, however arbitrary you may think the law is in this matter. I don't think you're too young to have a special friend who is a girl, as long as you keep the physical side of it under control. The danger is, when your manhood is pointing skywards most of the time, that can be very difficult. I remember that all too well.'

'Did you manage?' he asked boldly. 'You and Aunt Jan?'

'That is none of your damn business, boy,' I told him. 'But as a matter of fact we did, although I admit it was more down to her self-control than mine. I'll tell you something else too. It was all the more worth it in the end. Self-control is the second most difficult art for a man to master, but when we do we find that we're in control of more than ourselves.'

'What's the most difficult?'

'Sincerity. As Bob Monkhouse said, master that and you've cracked it.'

As I spoke we passed out of Pittenweem and I took a right turn. 'Where are we going?' Jonny asked. I said nothing, but drove. Not far along the road, a sign pointed right again, to Arncroach; I swung the Lotus into the narrow road.

'Uncle Oz.' I could feel the panic rising in him. 'Where are we going?' he repeated.

'You know where we're going, Jonny, don't you?' I had to raise my voice above the sound of the engine and the rush of the air. He simply nodded, and then the tears began. His wide, but still bony shoulders started to shake, and he buried his face in his hands. There was an opening ahead, a recessed farm gate that served as a makeshift lay-by. I slowed and pulled in there.

'Do you love your Granddad that much, son, that you did that for him?'

'I didn't mean to,' he whispered.

'You were listening to us, weren't you?' I asked him. 'That day in Elie when we were in the pub, talking, and you were outside; you were listening.' I could picture it in my mind; our table, an open window.

'I didn't mean to do that either,' he sniffed, 'but I thought it was strange you not asking me inside when there was hardly anyone there. And I could tell there was something wrong with Granddad too; he wasn't acting like himself at all. I thought he must have cancer or something, and I was frightened. I heard it all, Uncle Oz; all that he said about those terrible people threatening him. And I heard how afraid he sounded.'

He wiped his eyes. 'I hoped you would go and beat them up, make them stop.'

'I did, son, I did . . . only they didn't stop.'

'I know. After that I started going to see him as often as I could. I would get on my bike after school and cycle over to Anstruther. We'd talk like we've always done, but I could tell he wasn't right. He was bad-tempered, and once he even hit Colin. I couldn't tell him that I knew, of course. I just had to look at him, sitting there worrying, but having to keep it hidden from everybody. I felt so sorry for him and so angry with them.'

'So you called them. You phoned them up, didn't you?'

'Uh-huh.' He nodded. 'I found their number in the book and I phoned them. He answered. I tried to make myself sound older and I said "It's Mac Blackstone. Okay, I'll pay you, but I don't want to be seen." And I told them both to meet me . . . to meet Granddad . . . at the farm. I didn't know whether they believed me or not.'

'Obviously they did. How did you know about the farm, son?'

'The farmer's the uncle of a boy I'm at school with. He and I went there one day, on our bikes. I knew there wouldn't be anyone there, not in the evening at least.'

'And the gun? Where did you get the shotgun, Jonny?'

'It's my dad's. He bought it and got a permit and everything when he joined that shooting club, and then when we moved to France he took it. Everyone's got a shotgun there. When we came back, it was packed with our stuff by mistake, in its wrapper, and the shells in their box. I took it in my light golf bag, over my shoulder, on my bike.'

I threw my head back, banging it against the seat's restraint. My daft sister. Keeping an unregistered firearm in the house. 'Mum was going to give it back to him the first time he came to St Andrews; but he never has.'

No, he hadn't, had he. Allan Sinclair, would-be country sportsman and father of the year.

'I only took it to frighten them, Uncle Oz, honest.' Jonathan was wide-eyed; he is also incapable of lying. 'They turned up all right, when I said. I was hiding in the sheds, and when they got near I stepped out and I pointed the gun at them. I remember shouting, "You leave my Granddad alone, do you understand, or else." The man just laughed at me. She wasn't so sure, but he just laughed and he came to take the gun away from me. He grabbed the barrel and tried to pull it out of my hand . . . and it went off!'

As he spoke, his voice had risen, and risen. I put a hand on his shoulder, to calm his hysteria.

'It was awful, Uncle Oz.' Jonny was crying again. 'There was a huge bang, and he fell down. He rolled about for a bit, but then he was still. Honest, Uncle Oz, I didn't even know the gun was loaded.'

'Fuck me,' I whispered. Allan Sinclair, would-be country sportsman who was so incredibly stupid as to leave a loaded shotgun in a house with kids in it.

'She started screaming then,' Allan's son, my nephew, continued, 'and so did I. The gun had a sort of a pump thing on it; I was frightened so I pulled it, and then the gun just went off again. She was further away and it hit her in the chest and face. Ahh!' The boy screamed again, at the memory. 'It was awful. And then she was dead, they were both dead.'

I waited for his sobs to subside; it took a while. 'So you hid them in the pig troughs?' I asked him, quietly, once I thought he was ready.

He nodded a silent 'yes'. 'It was hard, but I did. I was scared stiff, Uncle Oz. I still am. I'll go to prison, won't I?' he asked, his child's eyes big in his young man's face. It appalled me that in a few minutes our conversation had come from the sexual confusion of the average adolescent, to this dark place.

I reached out an arm and hugged him, awkwardly in the confines of the car. 'No, son,' I told him. 'You won't go anywhere. If you'd only spoken to me, though.'

He looked at me, sideways. 'I was afraid that if I did you might have killed them, and then you'd have got into trouble.'

I felt tears well in my own eyes. 'Aw, Jonny, love. So you wound up killing them yourself instead.' It was a while before I could speak again.

When I could, I told him that I had sent Jay up to get rid of them. I told him that he had found a note in the cottage about the meeting, and I told him that he had made everything all right. I even told him that Jay thought I had done it, and that I wasn't about to advise him otherwise.

'You don't have to worry, son,' I promised him. 'Ever. That doesn't mean that you forget, though. You will never speak of what happened at that farm again, as long as you live. But you'll remember it always. It's your own private burden to carry for ever. You've got the strength for it; you may doubt it now, but believe me, you have. Never forget this either, though. Those people were as bad as you could ever imagine, but they were not worth risking your life over.'

'But I did it for Granddad,' he protested.

'He's not worth it either, nor am I. You are more precious than the two of us put together, and don't you ever forget it. Remember this too. Don't you ever go tackling trouble alone, not as long as I'm alive.'

I let him think about that for a while as I looked at him. Be it by accident, terror-stricken panic or whatever, he'd killed two people, this lad, this gawky boy. And yet he'd been brought to it by the purest motivator of all: love.

I don't care how anybody else might look at him. As far as I'm concerned he's a bloody hero.

'Now,' I demanded, forcing myself into action and starting the car once more, 'about this gun. Where is it?'

'Back at St Andrews. I didn't want my Mum to know it was missing, so I put it back.'

I drove there as fast as I could, and I made him give it to me. 'What about Mum?' he asked. 'She'll notice it's gone, eventually.'

'When she does, you'll tell her that you told me by accident that she had it, and that I went bananas and made you give it to me. That's the truth, more or less.'

I took it and the ammo, put it in what passes for the trunk of the Lotus and drove the two of us back to Anstruther, for the weirdest family dinner I ever had. I couldn't take my eyes off Jonathan as we sat across the table from each other in the Craw's Nest dining room. He was paler than usual, and he didn't say much, but there was a quiet dignity about him.

And as I studied him, I thought of my own big problem, and I knew there was only one way for me to deal with it. I'd have come to that conclusion eventually anyway, but the example of the boy's unshakeable courage in defence of what he had thought was his grandfather's honour, left me, as I see it to this day, without any choice.

# 43

I swung the BMW into the empty parking space. Saturday had come and gone, a day of golf in the morning, lazing in the afternoon and dinner in swank and splendour in the evening. Susie was still in St Andrews, happily; she and Ellie have become almost as close as my sister was to my first, dead, wife, and that pleases me very much. I had told her I had left something at home that I needed, and she hadn't questioned me at all.

I was pleased that the parking spaces were empty. Almost certainly, it meant that he was alone, apart from the man mountain that is, if he counted as company.

Manolito answered my pressing of the buzzer. 'Yesss?' he hissed. It was the first time I'd heard him speak, I realised.

'You know who this is,' I said. 'Put him on.'

I didn't have to wait more than a second or two. 'Yes, son,' said Jack, metallically. 'What can you do for me?'

'Deal,' I told him.

'Sensible boy. Come on up.'

'No bloody way am I stupid enough to come up there and be alone with you two. You come down and we go for a drive. Besides, I want it on my turf; I've got a reason.'

I caught a moment's hesitation. 'You realise Manolito will be coming with us?'

'Fine, as long as he doesn't overpower us with the intellectual purity of his discourse.'

Jack cackled at that. 'Don't worry, he won't say a word. Pull your car as close to the door as you can.'

I did as he asked. There was nobody around when they emerged; that made me happy. Jack climbed in beside me and Manolito got in the back, blocking out most of the view in the mirror. I put the complex machine in Drive, and moved off.

Jack said nothing for a while. Instead he just looked out of the window, first to one side of the motorway, then to the other, gazing at the city, some of which he had helped to build, and over which he had presided, officially or unofficially, for years.

'Glasgow,' I heard him whisper, as we passed under the sign for the airport turn-off.

'You're wise, boy,' he said, finally, as we crossed the Erskine Bridge, deserted as always. 'We both know you'd have been gubbed in court.'

'That's my legal advice too,' I admitted, seeing no reason to bullshit.

'How's Natalie?' I asked him. 'Seen her since Mr Perry met his end?'

'No. She called me when she heard about it. She was a bit upset, and more than a bit scared; she seemed to think I had something to do with it. Not that I had, of course.' Hint then denial, I had learned that that was his way. It struck me also that he might suspect that the car was bugged.

'How about Kendall? He'll be working on your petition, I suppose.'

'No. He'll be on his boat as usual, I suppose. I told him not to go any further at this stage. I was pretty certain I'd be hearing from you.'

He didn't say any more; nor did I until we reached the estate. I didn't need to.

The gate opened automatically at the press of my remote control, and closed again after us. 'Very nice,' said Jack as we cruised up the drive and parked in front of the big house.

'It is,' I agreed. 'Let me show you around,' I offered as the three of us stepped out into the late afternoon sunshine.

I gave him the complete guided tour of the house, including both conservatory wings, the office and the pool. He clucked and nodded all the way round.

'Very chic,' he said as we finished.

'There's more,' I told him. 'The fun bits are outside.' The buggy was parked at the back, not far from the area that Jay and I had chosen for the playground. One of the structures was in place, and the foundations were dug for another and part-filled with concrete. The cement mixer lay idle nearby.

With Manolito crouched on the golf bag platform, I drove us out and across the estate, until we came to the three-hole golf course. A bucket of balls lay on the ground and a set of clubs that I'd carelessly left out there. I took out a four iron and began hitting shots, aiming at the furthest green, and striking long and hard and straight. I noticed, though, that when I'd picked up the club, Manolito had positioned himself between me and his boss; sorry, his patient.

'What's the deal?' I asked quietly as I watched another Titleist arrowing towards the flag.

'Twenty pence a share, and that's pretty generous,' said Jack.

'Have you any idea of current market value?'

'Of course I have. And are you familiar with the term "fuck all"? I'm sure you are. Well, that's the alternative.'

'Elegantly put.' I laid down the club and began to stroll across the grounds. 'Now here's what I'd like.' We were near the estate's high boundary wall and the trees that grew around it, planted to protect the owners' privacy still further. I threw out a hand in a sweeping gesture. 'I'd like this place, and that's all. It belongs to the Gantry Group officially, but it's our home, and Susie and I love it.'

The back gate lay open. I wandered towards and through it, Manolito a few paces behind, but Jack beside me, seeming to be considering what I'd said. 'I can accommodate that,' he announced, at last, 'if the value lies within the parameters of my offer. If it doesn't, you'll have to find some cash.'

'Yeah, Jack?' I said, and I laughed. 'Well, fuck you.'

He stopped. 'You think you can hard-ball me, son?' he exclaimed, sounding truly incredulous.

We had walked thirty yards or so down the path. 'I think you're at it, old man,' I told him.

He looked around. 'You do, do you.' He pointed to the marshy ground on either side of the track. 'I may be a townie, but I know about these places, the bogs around Loch Lomondside. Have you any idea how deep they are?'

I shook my head.

'No,' he said, almost greedily, 'and neither does anyone else. There's a right few of Glasgow's grimier citizens gone into these things, I'll tell you. Christ, you were feared to come up into the flat with us . . .'

A look of sheer mirth crossed his face '. . . and yet you were stupid enough to take us here.'

He glanced over his shoulder, nodded towards me, and then towards the bog on our right. 'Big fella,' he called out. 'Time to do some nursing.'

I still hadn't seen Manolito smile, but there was a hint of one on his face as he started steadily towards me. I backed away from him, but then my foot seemed to catch on something. I fell backwards and rolled over.

The shotgun was there, where I'd planted it, hidden behind a log, partly wrapped in towels, to muffle the noise as best I could. It was in my hands as I spun and sprang to my feet.

I'd doctored the cartridges, putting extra pellets into each, but it wasn't until the third shot that Manolito stopped coming for me. That one went off with the barrel jammed into his throat, and it separated his head cleanly from his shoulders. He didn't drop right away, though; instead he stood for a few seconds, twitching, until the message, or rather the lack of a message, got through and he crumpled up.

Before he'd hit the ground, I'd hit Jack; in the belly with the butt of the gun, winding him and sending him back in a heap on the track.

'Stay there,' I warned him. I laid the weapon on the ground, clean lifted the thing at my feet and tossed it into the bog. Actually, it wasn't as impressive a feat as it looked, since the foreshortened Manolito was about thirty pounds lighter than before. He landed with a soft 'splodge' and disappeared beneath the black, gluey surface almost at once.

I turned back to Jack. He had recovered some of his composure, but not much of his breath, as he stared up at me. 'Where do we go from here?' he gasped at last.

'You don't,' I told him. 'You stay here.' I nodded sideways, at his grave.

'You're crazy,' he whispered.

'That's a laugh coming from you.'

'You'll never get away with it,' he protested. 'I'll be missed.'

'By whom?' I asked him. 'Natalie? I think not; she knows what you are now. Duncan Kendall? He'll be so busy fighting off Law Society complaints that he won't have time to think about you. Wylie Smith?

I've got news for you. Wylie had a chat with my friend Greg the other day. It could lead to him joining McPhillips and Company as a partner, but even if that doesn't happen, he wants no more to do with you and Duncan, and that is for sure. How about your old message boy, the First Minister? No, Jack; I reckon if he was here right now, he'd be holding my jacket.'

A desperate, crafty look crept on to Gantry's face. 'Aye, but what about Kevin and Mark? They'll be looking out for me.'

I laughed at that. 'I've just bunged Kevin and Mark ten grand for nothing. And what have they got with you gone? Glasgow between them, that's what.' I took a step to the side, leaned over and picked up Manolito's head by the ears; even in death, his face was unblemished. I held it for Jack to see, and watched as he cringed away from it. Then I heaved it into the bog. 'Anyway,' I said to him, as it vanished, 'do you seriously think that I'm afraid of those two guys?'

As he sat there, staring up at me, I knew that finally he was convinced. 'Okay,' he croaked. 'I'll do it. I'll adopt Susie, legally and everything. She can keep the company. She'll inherit all the rest too.'

'If she lived long enough,' I retorted. 'No, Jack,' I told him. 'That's not going to happen, because if it did, that would make you my father-in-law. The model that Susie's got is bad enough, but there's no way that I'd have you.'

I leaned over, picked him up by the lapels of his blue blazer, and hauled him upright. 'But above all that, there's something else. Whatever you say about your boys exceeding their brief, the ones you sent into our home, you did send them, and you were responsible for the death of my Jan, and the kid she had in her. You, My Lord Provost, first and foremost.'

I looked into his eyes. They weren't scary any more, just scared.

'You were their murderer, and in doing that you turned me into what I am now. I may not have realised it until a couple of days ago, but I've always been waiting to kill you for it, Jack, ever since then.'

I turned half round and I lifted him up, clear off his feet. 'So all actors are Jessies, are they?' I whispered, as I pitched him, up and out. He hit the bog feet first, and was chest deep in a second. He squealed, and I smiled. 'Some of Glasgow's grimier citizens, you said? They'll look spotless beside you.'

I waved him goodbye as his head went under. A few seconds later, a last loud bubble burst on the surface. 'Like a fart in the bath,' I said, then walked away.

I took the shotgun back to the house and dropped it into the half-filled foundation of the tree-house, 'for gardens that don't have trees'. I turned on the cement mixer, went looking for the hose, and half an hour later, it was buried for ever.

# 44

I was back in St Andrews for seven thirty, keeping my promise to my sister that I'd be there for dinner. Jonathan was still quiet, but once or twice during the meal our eyes met, and I knew that he'd be all right. He will too: I've promised him that.

Ellen knew that something had happened between my father and me. We had been a trio for so long that it couldn't be otherwise. But she chose not to ask me and she never has since. I have seen my father since then, of course, even if at first it was only because I care for Mary. We speak cordially again, and once or twice we've even laughed together, yet there will always be a certain distance between us. The police never did come calling on him, but I am fairly certain that he has never plucked up the courage to tell Mary, or Ellen, of his surrender to his weakness. No, I am completely certain, because my sister still speaks fondly of him.

I know also that he has said nothing to Jonathan. I know that because I've made him swear he never will. The one thing that worries me about my nephew is his reaction were he ever to find out the truth about his grandfather, and the real reason for his blackmail. By the same token I've kept the truth about the Neiportes' deaths from him, for I know that he would be unable to live with it, and although I rebelled against the fact at first, he's still my father. However much we'd like to on occasion, we can't change the genes that built us.

Jay joined us for dinner at Ellie's that night. If, when we returned to the estate, he was surprised to find that work on the tree-house 'for gardens that don't have trees' had progressed in his absence, he said nothing about it. However, as it turned out he had indeed found himself a nice co-ed on that Saturday night in St Andrews, the daughter of a US senator. He left me to join her in the States a few months later, and has since found a job with the American Secret Service, which is, of course, not secret at all.

Life for me has gone on as what passes for normal ever since. *Mathew's Tale* was completed, and I'm told will win me a BAFTA. I may have to come back from Australia to get it, though, for that's where I'm heading now, with Susie, Ethel, Janet and her new brother, wee Jonathan. The Gantry Group is in the capable hands of Phil Culshaw, still acting chief executive, and Wylie Smith is taking the chair in my absence. Natalie Morgan has renewed her relationship with Ewan Capperauld, who's always been a sucker for olive-skinned women with big eyes. Duncan Kendall? He's in jail. I'm not sure why.

I still remember that time at Ellie's. When the evening was over, and Susie and I had retired to our room, I was undressing when she said to me, 'You know, Oz, one of the things I love about you?'

I grinned at her, over my shoulder, as I do. 'Whassat?'

'You get things done. I have to say, in that respect, there's a bit of the Jack Gantry in you.'

I looked into the mirror, smiling that all-gathering smile of mine, into bright eyes that deep down, I saw, were as hard as the stone that builds a city, and I said to her, 'Nobody's perfect. Still, I've always thought of myself as a nice guy at heart.'

I have come to believe that we are all governed by the spirits that live within us. Some, like my nephew Jonathan's, my wife Susie's, and, I hope, my children's, are pure and good. Some, like my poor old father's, are fundamentally weak, and have within them the inevitable downfall of their bearer. Some, like Jack Gantry's, are wholly and irredeemably evil from the start.

Mine? The jury's still out on that.